Readers love
TA MOORE

Liar, Liar

"*Liar, Liar* is a great suspense with some twisty moments and really fun characters. I can definitely recommend this one, particularly if you are a fan of romantic suspense and like your heroes a little bit outside the box."

—Joyfully Jay

"TA Moore didn't disappoint with this suspense, espionage thriller. *Liar, Liar* is a fast-paced page turner."

—The Novel Approach

Dog Days

"Wow. *Dog Days* turned out to be even more than I expected… Trust me when I say you won't regret reading this… not if you love twists, turns, and horror."

—Rainbow Book Reviews

"…I highly recommend this to all the shifter lovers out there."

—Diverse Reader

By TA MOORE

Bone to Pick
Dog Days
Liar, Liar

Published by DREAMSPINNER PRESS
www.dreamspinnerpress.com

TA Moore (signature)

BONE TO PICK

TA MOORE

DREAMSPINNER
PRESS

Published by

DREAMSPINNER PRESS

5032 Capital Circle SW, Suite 2, PMB# 279, Tallahassee, FL 32305-7886 USA
www.dreamspinnerpress.com

Bone to Pick
© 2017 TA Moore.

Cover Art
© 2017 Anne Cain.
annecain.art@gmail.com
Cover content is for illustrative purposes only and any person depicted on the cover is a model.

ISBN: 978-1-63533-838-6
Digital ISBN: 978-1-63533-839-3
Library of Congress Control Number: 2017904537
Published August 2017
v. 1.0

Printed in the United States of America
∞
This paper meets the requirements of
ANSI/NISO Z39.48-1992 (Permanence of Paper).

With thanks to my mum, who remains my biggest cheerleader,
and The Five, who put up with my weirdness.
Also to Lady—my first dog, my best dog,
and the inspiration for Bourneville.

CHAPTER ONE

EVERY COP had their own bible of superstitions.

Down in vice, cockeyed Jimmy Daley swore that every time he pulled in one particular red-haired hooker, the week went to hell. Lieutenant Frome would never admit it out loud, but whenever he hit red at the Mendes and Third intersection, he brought a black mood to work with him. When Deputy Kelly Tancredi was pregnant last year, her biggest complaint was that her lucky bra was uncomfortable.

Cloister knew it was going to be a bad night when the devil winds came rolling in from the desert. It was a given that Southern California was always hot, but the winds parched it dry as well. You couldn't even *sweat* without it turning to salt, and where it wasn't salty, it was sandy.

It was more than just batterers and brawlers pushed over the edges of their own worse natures, though. The winds blew in the sort of bad shit that stuck in your nightmares—little corpses, bruised thighs, questions that never got answered.

Worst thing was, there was no calling in superstitious in the Plenty Sheriff's Department. You knew everything was going to go to hell, but all you could do was turn up for work and wait for the shit to hit the fan.

Three hours into the midnight shift, and Cloister was still waiting. Maybe he was wrong, but the drunk-and-disorderly collar of a barefoot meth head didn't weigh on his conscience that much.

Ignoring the yelled orders to "Get down!" and "Put your hands where I can see them!" the weathered, desert-dried-out man had scrambled out of a broken window and run across the parking lot. He ran like an Olympic athlete in the weeds, with his arms pumping and his head thrown back so the tendons in his neck strained under his faded blue tats. It wasn't going to do him any good, but he put his all into it.

"Why do they always run when it's hot as hell?" Cloister asked. Nothing ran like a guilty conscience, whatever the weather. Besides, his partner wasn't one for much chat. Cloister stooped and unclipped her collar in one smooth, practiced motion. She perked up, and her shoulders tensed under her thick ruff of tan-and-black hair, but she held herself back. Cloister put the command snap in his voice. "*Fuss!*"

She went.

Cloister had worked with a lot of dogs over the years, from his stepdad's hunting pack to an idiot-savant spaniel in Iraq—it ate rocks but could find explosive residue after five days—but none of them had a prey drive like Bourneville. The black shepherd went off the blocks like a greyhound and cleared the window in a long, clean leap— low enough to make Cloister wince as the shards of broken glass in the frame brushed through her fawn stomach fur. She hit the ground running.

He flicked the leash, wrapped the heavy nylon around his wrist, and took his turn through the window. He felt the constriction of the bulletproof vest as he ducked, and the glass caught in the heavy canvas fabric of his trousers as he folded his six-foot-two length through the dry-rotted wooden square.

Across the parking lot, the meth head scrambled up and over the chain link fence. The barbed wire at the top caught his shirt and ripped it off, leaving a flapping, bloodied rag dangling. He kept running and dodged behind a row of houses.

Bourneville didn't lose a step as she jumped onto the hood of a parked truck, not even stopping to measure the distance. She stumbled over her paws on landing, nearly cracked her chin, and then was up and off again.

The fence rattled as Cloister hit it, and it swayed as he scrambled up and over. He caught his hand on the wire, and a spur dug into the meat under his thumb. The jab of pain made him grimace, but he didn't slow down.

He dropped onto the other side and followed the wolf brush of Bourneville's tail down the back of the houses. The shout and scuffle of the raid at the drug house faded behind him. The habit of risk assessment made him drop his hand to his gun, and his fingers found their familiar spots in the molded plastic grip.

The Heights wasn't a bad area of town. It was just poor. Unlike some of the other deputies, Cloister had grown up in a place where it was important to know the difference. Poor still meant closed curtains and minding your own business because the sheriff's gratitude didn't have the half-life of the local gangs' resentment.

Couldn't really blame them. They had to live there, raise their kids there. The last thing they wanted was trouble.

So Cloister kept his hand on his gun, but the gun stayed on his hip.

At the end of the alley, the meth head grabbed a recycling bin and spun it around to shove behind him. It tipped over and spilled bundles of cans and crumpled plastic bottles onto the ground. The obstacle gave him a second's head start on Bourneville as the dog scrabbled briefly to dodge the skidding box. He gained a few more when Cloister had to kick it out of the way.

It was enough for Cloister to lose sight of Bourneville for a second as she skidded around the corner while he skidded on a piece of greasy plastic wrap. He swore under his breath, put on a burst of speed, and nearly tripped over Bourneville as he raced around the corner to find her just standing still.

Her head was cocked to the side, and she watched the meth head with a confused look. Cloister couldn't blame her. The scrawny man—all bone and muscle under shrink-wrapped skin—had grabbed a little girl's bike from the garden. It was pink and still had training wheels on, but the guy was trying to ride it to freedom. His bare feet balanced on the narrow pedals, his skinny ass was in the air, and his knees pumped furiously. All that effort didn't do him much good. There was more side-to-side motion than forward, but he seemed committed.

"Jesus," Cloister muttered.

He glanced down at Bourneville, and she looked up at him with the "what now?" tilt to her head that meant her training had briefly been derailed. Her head went to one side and then the other, and her fuzzy black ears flopped.

"Yeah, I'm with you, girl. This is going to be fun to write up."

He gave her an ear rub and a "Good girl." She'd done her job. Then he stalked after the slow-motion getaway, grabbed the meth head's clammy shoulder, and dragged him off the bike.

"You made me run for this?" he asked as he put the man back on his feet and glowered at him. It usually worked. The Wittes ran to big, blond, and mean-looking, and Cloister had come into the world ready for a fight, with his fists up and his nose already broken. Little kids liked him—God knew why—but everyone else kept their distance. Although apparently enough meth diluted the impact.

"Did y'see that bear?" the meth head asked. "Fucking bear chased me. Minding my own business."

"In a crack house?" Cloister asked. Meth head shrugged and tried to look insolent. He mostly looked stupid. Under the bad ink and the drug years, the guy and the bicycle might almost be age appropriate— early twenties, maybe even late teens if he shot a needle into his vein as young as some did. Physically he might be young enough to recoup what the drugs had taken—if he ever got clean—but there was nothing much left behind his murky blue eyes. Cloister sighed. "Right. Turn out your pockets."

He didn't expect to find anything. Any junkie worth his salt knew to ditch whatever was on them when they ran. Sure enough, he pulled lint, sand, and a half-licked mint out of his baggy jeans.

"Right, Bozo, you're under arrest," Cloister said as he fixed the plastic zip-tie cuffs snugly around scrawny, scabby wrists. "You have the right to—"

His radio crackled.

"Deputy Witte," Mel said. "What's your situation?"

There was something tight in Mel's voice that made Cloister's stomach tighten nervously. Thin, tin-sharp Mel had been at the job longer than any of them, grandfathered in from when Plenty had its own Police Department instead of a sheriff's station, and she knew the town. When she sounded unhappy, it was time to pay attention.

"I was in pursuit on a 390," he said. "Just reading him his rights now."

"We've got a request from the Feds for a K-9," Mel said.

Cloister grimaced. "Is there no one else available?" he asked. "Last time I was seconded to them, I ended up on a disciplinary after I nearly decked the Special Agent in Charge."

"Sorry," Mel said without sounding it. "All the other teams are fully committed or not in the area." Then she dropped the shoe he knew was coming since he heard the wind that morning. "It's a 920C out at the Retreat."

Shit.

Cloister "copy'd" her and got the location. He shoved Bozo back down onto the bike, and the cheap pink leather seat cut into his bony ass.

"Your lucky night, Bozo," he said. "I've got somewhere to be."

Bozo grinned sloppily. "That's me," he said. One eye wandered, briefly detached from whatever fired in Bozo's skull. "Lucky boy."

He held up his hands. The plastic tag stuck up between his thumbs like a handle. He looked expectant.

"Not that lucky," Cloister told him. He stepped back and radioed in to the other deputy on the raid. "Witte here. Got a 390 in custody, but I've been called to a 920. You send someone out to pick him up? Round the back."

Confirmation came quickly and without the usual complaints. Cloister closed the line and glanced at Bozo. "Stay where you are. If you make them look for you, they'll get the bears out again."

He snapped his fingers to call Bourneville to heel and left Bozo on his little pink bike. If he did manage to get loose or pedal away before someone picked him up, he'd just get picked up again the next week. Cloister's boots hit the ground as he pushed himself into a hard, distance-eating jog. Bourneville stuck to his heels like a shadow, panting happily because it was just a run and not a chase. He passed Jim on the way to collect the wayward dealer.

920C. Missing child *and* the Feds. Just once he'd like to be wrong about a shift going to hell.

CHAPTER TWO

THE RETREAT was what happened when gentrification bumped up against hippies. It used to be a dried-up commune in the mountains. It produced badly carved tchotchkes to sell at markets and a hybridized strain of Oaxacan cannabis they sold in bulk and in baggies. Then, ten years back, Plenty became an overflow community for San Diego. The struggling rural community sprouted suburbs like it used to sprout lettuce, and the Retreat's last hippy heard opportunity knocking. He bought up the neighboring plots of land, stripped the grow lights out of the barn, and repackaged the counterculture, off-grid lifestyle as glamping.

That was all before Cloister's time. In the years since he'd been there, the Retreat always had five-star yurts, moon baths, and the occasional sexual assault complaint.

Lights flashing, Cloister sped past the old feed store on the outskirts of town with its sale banners flapping viciously in the wind and took the next left. In the back of the car, Bourneville lay like a Sphinx, her paws crossed and her head up and interested. She knew the lights meant they were going to work. All she had to do was wait until they stopped.

The road narrowed as he headed into the foothills. The windblown pines cast spindly, moonlit shadows over the tarmac, but the surface was like a ribbon. There were roads in the bad part of town that had potholes older than Bourneville, but the Retreat's road was repaved every spring. No one wanted to risk some wealthy townie breaking an axle on their BMW on the way up.

It was forty minutes from Plenty to the Retreat. Cloister made it to the cut-out, fancy-worked copper sign in twenty. He flicked the lights off as he took the last turn and blinked as his eyes adjusted to the sudden shift to monotone. He lifted his foot off the gas. It was an attempt at discretion that was wasted on the Retreat.

Every tent and cabin was lit up, lights blazed from the main office, and people milled about in nervous clusters. Lots of hands clutched children's shoulders. Pajamas and nighties flapped in the wind.

Cloister pulled in behind the black SUV parked in front of the rocking-chair-decked porch. It looked like the Feds were still there.

He flicked the engine off, got out, and opened the back door so he could unclip Bourneville. She scrambled out, shook herself, and then stood impatiently and waited for him to check her harness. A girl came out of the office while he was doing that. She was slim and tanned and wore the jeans and teal T-shirt uniform of the Retreat.

"Umm, they asked me to show you to Morocco when you got here," she said. The "what" blink Cloister gave her made her flush into her hairline. "It's the cabin. They all have names. The Hartleys always stay in Morocco."

Apparently he must have looked like he was ready because she bolted off through the camp. There were a couple of other deputies taking statements from fretful families. Somewhere in the camp, a dog barked with a small-dog yap.

"Morocco" was a low cabin built of silky amber wood and raw tree branches. The door was open and leaked fan-cooled air into the hot night. Cloister stopped the girl before she walked in.

People under stress were like dogs under stress. It made them more likely to snap at small offences. If a kid really was missing—not just sulking at a friend's house to scare his parents or off with her dad as part of a custody dispute—then Cloister didn't need to ruffle feelings right off the bat.

He rapped his knuckles against door.

The soft murmur of voices inside faltered, and then a tall, dark man with a good haircut and a better suit stepped into the hall. The tension lines that bracketed his mouth deepened when he saw Cloister. Apparently Agent Javier Merlo hadn't forgotten their last meeting either.

"Deputy."

Asshole.

"Special Agent."

Merlo glanced at the girl. "You can go. Let me know if anyone else arrives."

She hesitated for a second and then nodded and hurried into the dark. Merlo swung his attention back to Cloister. The shame of it was that he was the best-looking dickhead in town, with the sharp, chiseled features you usually only saw in fashion magazines and on Greek statues.

"I asked for three K-9 teams."

"I'm the only one available right now," Cloister said. "The others are occupied. They'll be here as soon as they can. What happened?"

The corner of Merlo's mouth curled, and he adjusted the cuffs of his shirt. It was the first sign of emotion other than impatience and smugness that Cloister could remember seeing from their resident special agent.

"Ten-year-old boy," Merlo told him in a tight voice, pitched low so the wind couldn't carry it away. "Drew Hartley. He went missing sometime today. Parents were at a workshop. His brother, William, was with him until three and then went to see a friend. His parents were due back, but they were delayed. They all assumed Drew was with someone else."

Cloister checked his watch. It was closer to 1:00 a.m. than midnight. Drew had potentially been missing for over nine hours. Not impossible to catch a scent after that long, but it wasn't ideal—especially not on a hot dry day in an area that had a lot of bodies moving through it.

Not impossible, though.

He nodded at the cabin. "This is the last place he was seen?"

Merlo nodded. "Deputy Witte, I've sent in a request for a helicopter with thermal imaging capability, but until that arrives, I have to depend on you. So whatever issues we might have had last time we worked together—"

"No issues," Cloister said.

Not exactly true. He didn't like Merlo, mostly because Merlo made it clear he thought K-9 officers were a fond anachronism who should put their faith in technology instead of good dogs and sharp noises, but a little because he looked at Cloister like he'd found something nasty in his shoe. And that was a bad way for a crush to die.

None of that mattered right now. They both had a job to do.

"Introduce us to the family?" Cloister asked.

Merlo looked like he wasn't happy about something but inclined his head and led the way back inside. There was an old chip on Cloister's shoulder that wanted him to sneer at the family inside—absentee yuppie parents who hadn't even known their child was missing—but the Hartleys didn't look that different from any other parents in the same situation. Nicer clothes on their backs and better furniture to sit on, maybe, but the same sour-salt smell of fear and the hollow slump of pretrained grief. Deputy Tancredi was sitting with them, giving her best line of reassuring, noncommittal platitudes.

"Ken, Lara." Merlo dropped his voice to an awkwardly gentle tone. It was obviously not something he was good at.

The parents looked up with eyes desperate to believe that Cloister was going to help. The father was short and dark—the undiluted Slavic lines of his face not quite matched with the unexceptional Hartley surname. His wife was thin and angular, with deep-set, bruised-looking eyes and a puff of dark curls that defied her fear. Perched behind them in the window seat like he wasn't entirely sure of his place in the room, their son was an unfinished sketch of them both.

William. Probably Bill or Billy to anyone without a stick up their ass. Cloister didn't have any urge to poke at the miserable kid.

Merlo reached up to tap Cloister's shoulder. "This is Deputy Witte, one of the sheriff's department's dog handlers." He left it at that.

Cloister freed his hand from the collar and reached down to slap Bourneville's side. "And this is my partner, Bourneville," he said. "She's one of our best trackers."

She panted at them with her ears up and her jaw open in a dog smile. Cloister could feel Merlo's irritated impatience with him, but he didn't get it. The Hartleys didn't need to have faith in Cloister. They needed to believe the dog was a lot more capable than the pets they saw in everyday life.

The wife—Lara—twisted her hands together in bony, knuckly knots. "He's a good boy," she said. Her voice was thin and taut. She was barely holding on over the panic. "Drew wouldn't just go off with his friends or something without leaving us a note. He'd know we'd worry."

"They know that, Mom," Billy said.

Something ugly hit Lara's face. She grimaced it away and rubbed her hand over her mouth. She took a deep breath, and lifted her narrow shoulders toward her ears before she could speak again.

"No, they don't," she said. Billy winced and squeezed himself back into the window. "They come up here, and they look at us, and they think Drew's just another neglected little rich boy. Well, he's not. He's a good boy."

Cloister tilted his head to catch her gaze and hold it. "He's a little boy," he said. "Good or bad, a little boy needs to be found."

Her face crumpled for a second, and tears welled to tremble on her thick lashes. Then she lifted her chin, visibly pulled herself together, and pressed her lips into an uncompromising line.

"You'll, umm, need something that belongs to Drew? A toy or some of his clothes?"

Cloister nodded. "Something he's worn recently, unwashed," he said.

She nodded and stood up. Her husband reached for her hand, but her fingers slid out of his as she walked away. Once she'd left the room, he turned to Cloister.

"We were late," he said. "There was an accident at the workshop. Someone cut themselves quite badly, and we're doctors. It didn't seem urgent to get back. This place is like home, really. We know everyone."

What he wanted to hear was "It's not your fault." Even the families where it *was* their fault still wanted to hear that.

"It's not your fault, Ken," Merlo said. "I'm sure Drew's fine."

Cloister noticed he said "Ken" like an acquaintance, not a cop. It was just a name, not a power play.

"The last time you saw Drew, it was here?" he checked.

Ken nodded and then hesitated. He turned to look at his son. "Bill? You stayed here, right? Like we told you?"

Billy hunched his shoulders, bony with a growth spurt under his *Star Trek* T-shirt. "'Course."

So that was up in the air. If the boys had left the cabin, no way Bill would admit it in answer to that loaded question.

Lara came back in, absently folding a crumpled Captain America T-shirt into a neat square. She hesitated but then handed it over. "It's his favorite."

"I'll bring it back," Cloister promised.

Merlo followed him outside and caught him before he could get started. He caught his hand in the sweaty bend of Cloister's elbow. The touch prickled down his arm like electricity and made the fine hair on his arms stand on end and his muscles tighten. He cursed himself for being easily led. Right then he didn't need the distraction.

"Something happened here," Merlo said. His eyes squinted against the thrown-up dust as he frowned at Cloister. "I know the family. Lara Hartley's father was an FBI agent and a friend of mine. They're happy. They're careful. There's no risk factors. I want to find this boy."

"I always want to find them," Cloister told him. "It's my job to bring them home, not care how they got lost."

He pulled his arm free, dropped into a crouch, and offered the handful of T-shirt to Bourneville. She sniffed and snorted and burrowed her nose into the folds to get to the sweat-soaked seams. Once she was sure she had the scent, she looked up at Cloister expectantly.

"*Such.*" He snapped out the track command.

She dropped her nose to the dirt as she cast around. She sneezed when the dry earth went up her nose, and then she made a beeline down into a gully. In better, wetter weather, it might have been a stream. In the middle of a drought, it was just damp. Bourneville pulled against the lead as she headed east, away from the Retreat, and Cloister broke into a jog.

The lackluster moonlight was enough for the dog to see, but as the lit-up glow of the Retreat faded behind them, Cloister unclipped the flashlight from his vest. He flicked it on with his thumb and played the beam of light over the ground in front of Bourneville.

A startled lizard mad-legged out of the unexpected light and scuttled over the rocks. Its loose-limbed run made it look as though the wind were going to pick it up and send it tumbling.

The gully petered out as its high sides collapsed into rattling scrub and thorns. Worked into the sand and roots, a suggestion of a foot-worn path wound between the mesquite. Bourneville followed it faithfully for yards and then suddenly veered off to the side. She trotted forward, stopped, and tried again. Eventually she found what she was sniffing for. She stopped, growled quietly, and pawed at the dirt.

Cloister whistled her off. She backed up reluctantly, paw over paw, so he could get in and see what it was. Caught in the roots of the tree, a crumpled bottle lay in a sticky, muddle puddle. He put the flashlight in his mouth, his teeth digging into their usual spots in the rubber coating, and poked the bottle curiously. There was a dribble of liquid left inside, and it looked gritty.

Could just be more sand.

Unwilling to leave the bottle to the elements, he snapped a picture and quickly bagged it up. He stuffed it into his vest pocket as he stood up, but the crinkle of it against his ribs as he breathed was distracting.

Bourneville waited until he stood up and then pulled again. There was no path this time, just roots and stones and the wire-strung boundary of the Retreat's property line. Between two trees there was a body-sized depression in the dirt that probably marked the escape route of a few dozen kids over the years. Bourneville made it under easily, but whatever teen had made the gap was a lot narrower through the chest than Cloister was. It caught at his hair and shirt as he squirmed through, and it hooked into the straps of his vest.

On the other side, there was an old dirt road. The ruts were worn ankle deep and rock hard. It didn't look like they'd been disturbed for a while. Probably one of the old farm access roads, he guessed, although he couldn't swear to what one. After five years he knew Plenty pretty well, but not as well as someone who grew up there.

Bourneville scratched the dirt again and whined anxiously for Cloister to see what she'd found.

"Hold on," Cloister told her. He scratched the back of his neck where a scrape stung with sweat, and he knelt down next to her. The grass on the side of the road was flattened and creased, and there was an indentation in the dirt where something had recently been pried up.

The stains on the grass weren't soda this time.

Cloister rocked back onto his heels and felt the pull in his thighs. It could just have been a tumble, but Bourneville had stopped sniffing around. The trail was cold, and there was blood on the ground.

He quickly praised Bourneville, scrubbed his hand down her back, told her she was a good dog, and radioed in. There was a cold weight in the pit of his stomach.

No one would say "snatched." Not yet. It wouldn't do to cause panic, and for an ex-hippie, the owner of the Retreat was very good at greasing palms to make bad press go away. But maybe it wasn't that. Drew might turn up in an hour, next to a gopher hole with a swollen ankle or in a hospital after some Good Samaritan picked up an injured kid on the road.

Except that wasn't going to happen. The kid wasn't lost. He'd been taken.

Cloister was still going to find him. That was what he *did*, but… that was as far as he'd let himself get. After the *but* was where hope started to fade, and Cloister wouldn't go there. Until he knew better, there was going to be a happy ending.

Eventually one of the endings had to be happy.

CHAPTER THREE

THE COFFEE was road-stop shit, bought from a gas station that also sold deep-fried chicken gizzards and wilted, wrinkled french fries. It tasted like grease and gas. Javi drank it anyhow. The sun had just risen on the second day of Drew Hartley's disappearance, and Javi needed all the fuzzy-edged clarity he could pull together.

"Learn to nap. In this job forty winks is better than nothing." It was Drew's grandfather, Saul Lee, who gave Javi that advice. Not that Javi had ever seen the man heed his own counsel. It had been three in the morning when Saul died, and he was still at the office—facedown in that day's caseload, a cup of coffee going cold on the desk.

Javi still owed him. It was Saul's intervention after Phoenix that got Javi posted here instead of moldering away somewhere quiet and unobtrusive. Plenty wasn't much of a tourist destination, but it was a solid, professional stepping stone. Even though half the reason his supervisors approved him was for the good optics of having a Mexican-American agent in San Diego.

Probably not so much, though, if the case that made your name was the unsolved mystery around a decorated FBI officer's missing grandson.

The vinegary cynicism made Javi flinch with guilt, mostly because it wasn't the first time it had happened, although he'd never let it get as far as a full thought before.

"Results, not intentions, are all that matter in the write-up." That was Saul too.

KEEPING ONE hand on the steering wheel, Javi drained the coffee to the unappetizing dregs as he drove down Plenty's Main Street. It was quaint in a way that towns rarely evolved naturally, with leaded glass in the storefronts and no trash on the sidewalks. The shops sold yogurt-and-kale smoothies, designer shoes, and Native jewelry at three times the price they paid the artists. Antique shops sold upcycled furniture and relics retrieved from abandoned farms and houses.

The uglier side of Plenty—the drug cartels and trafficking that were the reason the FBI had a resident agency there—was kept out of sight. Out of mind, for those who could afford it.

He turned left at the bus station and then pulled into the police station's horseshoe-shaped parking lot. The building was a factory once—iron machinery, scarred wood floors, and red brick walls. These days it was home to the police station, the Plenty Records Office, the town morgue, and on the top floor, where the executive offices used to be, the FBI's resident agency—their version of a regional office. Thankfully they didn't all have to share an entrance.

Patrol cars were lined up in neat rows, waiting for the morning shift to roll out. A tired-looking woman in jogging pants and a *Batman needs naps too* T-shirt leaned against the wall, smoking with the intensity of someone who needed more than just a nicotine fix. Her hair, a flat shade of home-bleached brass, was dragged back into a tight ponytail, and her eyes were puffy and dark ringed.

As Javi got out of the car, she ground the cigarette out against the wall. It left an ashy comma smudged into the brick.

"Fucker," she said flatly.

Her lack of affect made it hard to tell if she was talking to Javi about her situation or condemning the world at large. She went back inside and left the shredded butt on the ground.

The woman on duty at the front desk glanced up when he came in.

"Special Agent Merlo," she said. She covered the mouthpiece of the phone with her hand to muffle it. "The lieutenant is waiting for you."

POLICE STATION coffee didn't taste any better than gas station coffee, but it was served hot enough that, after the first mouthful, your taste buds were too stunned to register it. Javi nursed a mug as he stood and stared at the search parameters scratched out on the wall-mounted map. Red pins marked the locations of nearby sex and violent offenders. There was a constellation of them.

Up in the foothills, it seemed like the fear and panic over the lost little boy was an intrusion into an idyll. The sort of thing that didn't happen in a place like that. Except it did, apparently.

"I've got deputies checking in with all registered pervs," Lieutenant Frome said from behind his desk. He licked his thumb and scrubbed at a blotch of coffee stain on his cuff. "That only covers the ones we've caught and who do keep up with signing in."

He shrugged off the last statement tiredly. Javi already knew the issues.

"I want to pull in Mr. Reed for a chat," Javi said, naming the affable, ethical-clothing-wearing reptile who owned the Retreat.

Frome frowned. "You think he's involved?" He shook his head dubiously. "We've never had much problem with him. Even when he was dealing pot, he kept it quiet and polite. Threw a few 'pigs' and 'filths' at us when we went up, but that was for show as much as anything."

"Since the Retreat opened, there've been twelve complaints of sexual misconduct and harassment."

Frome shrugged. "A couple of girls from town who thought they'd get a settlement from a wealthy guest. Or teenagers who got a bit out of hand. It was nothing serious, and no one's ever made any suggestion that Reed was involved."

It was an effort for Javi to keep the grimace off his mouth. Frome wasn't a bad cop, but he was a political one. Sometimes that made for ugly things coming out of his mouth, but calling him on it wasn't going to help.

"Still," he said. "He's king of the castle up there. I'd like to talk to him where he's less comfortable."

Frome gave in with a nod, and his pen scratched over the pad as he made a note. "I'll ask him to come down, tell him we just want to discuss the area?"

"And make sure that we have an officer up there to stay with the family," Javi added. "Two if you can manage it. Use my authorization. I want to know everything they do when they're together and when they aren't."

"You sure?" Frome asked doubtfully. "We all know them. They're good people. Lara's worked in the ER for years. She's saved people's lives. Deputies' lives."

"Until we have something, I'd rather maintain a nonconfrontational relationship with the family," he said. "But the parents and the brother are the ones who saw the boy last. If we don't look at them, you know that would be negligence."

It wasn't nice, but the truth behind all those asshole detectives harassing desperate parents in crime dramas was that, more often than not—say seven times out of ten—it wasn't the creepy neighbor or the predatory store clerk. It was someone in the family—one of the people who had unquestioned access to and control over the child.

"I can't imagine Lara doing something like that. Not to her own son." Frome shook his head.

The image of the beaten-down woman who was smoking outside a police station like it was a work break flicked through Javi's mind.

"Every deviant and pervert in jail had people in their life who just couldn't believe it of them," he said. "I don't think they've done anything to their son. I hope they haven't. But if they have, I don't want them to get away with it."

Frome sat back, and the chair creaked under him. His uniform shirt strained gently over the gut that made itself known in that position. He tapped his pen against the pad hard enough to leave dents in the paper.

"You should talk to Witte."

Even from inside it, the expression on Javi's face felt supercilious. He couldn't help it. Deputy Witte rubbed him the wrong way.

"About what?" he asked. "Dogs or country music."

Frome gave him a smile that was amused but not entirely approving. "Don't underestimate him," he said. "He's good at what he does."

"Chase dogs?"

"Find people," Frome said. "He volunteers with San Diego's mountain rescue. He's trained for Structural Collapse Urban Search and Rescue, and the only reason he's not up on that mountain right now is that I pulled him off so his dog could get some sleep. He's dealt with more missing and lost people than either of us have, or probably ever will, and he was the first deputy up there that night. Maybe he noticed something. If anyone was in a position to, it was him. Talk to Witte."

He ripped the top page off the pad and held it out. Javi took it from him and glanced at the scrawled writing. It was a phone number and address. Javi raised an eyebrow. Not how he usually got a man's number, but....

"I'll talk to him," he said and tucked the page into his pocket. "You can let me know when you're bringing Reed down for an interview."

When he left, the woman in the Batman sleep shirt was outside again. This time she was crying in her car, a beat-up old Ford with bags of clothes and a sleeping bag shoved into the backseat. Homeless. Part of the growing population in Plenty, where there was a lot of work to be had but nowhere to live unless you had enough for a two-story house with a pool and solar panels.

Javi knew that if *she'd* called in a missing child, there would have been no kid gloves for her. Life wasn't fair, but he supposed she already knew that.

CHAPTER FOUR

JAVI HEADED out of town. The candy store had closed, he noticed on his way by, and a Starbucks had moved into the space like a hermit crab. Javi ran his tongue over the back of his teeth and tasted burned coffee and the fuzz of cheap creamer. About time they got a good coffee shop in town.

Maybe he'd grab a cup later. For the moment, he followed the signs that pointed the way out to Plenty's unprepossessing shoreline—more shale than sand—and the trailer park where Deputy Witte was living the stereotype.

To think Javi believed he was being insulting when he called the big blond deputy trailer trash after their last argument.

The Sunnyside Trailer Park played host to tourists during the summer. There wasn't a whole lot to see in Plenty—the quaint Main Street, a winery that did tours up in the foothills near the Retreat, and a cave system on the beach that was mostly underwater and never had seals in it—but it was close enough to actual tourist destinations to serve as a stopover.

At this time of year, rows of lots stood empty. The rest of the lots were filled with the longtimers' trailers, complete with low fences and summer-bleached garden furniture. Most of them were construction workers or field hands, seasonal labor at the farms and building sites that surrounded the town. There were a few drifters too—people who rolled aimlessly into town and hung around doing odd jobs and petty crime until they had a reason to leave.

Javi pulled in under the peeling wooden sign and parked in the half-moon lot next to a pickup that stank of old fruit pulp. A couple of kids chased each other around the trailers, stripped to swimwear and with the dark, year-round tans of beach dwellers. Skinny, shaved-down dogs barked at their heels and twisted between their legs.

Javi got out of the car, and the kids stopped what they were doing. They side-eyed him in his suit and then ran away before he could ask them anything.

Helpful as always. He tipped his shades down his nose and checked the address Frome had given him.

Lot 275. Old silver Airstream. Can't miss it.

That was true enough. Javi looked up, and his eyes fell on the big silver pill parked at the far corner of the park, right next to the drop down to the beach. It was dented with pockmarks along the front and had a white plastic fence that marked off a patchy square of garden. Javi tucked his phone in his pocket, headed across the rutted lot, and tried to ignore the sweat as it ran down the back of his neck and the wind as it scraped his skin.

Up close, the trailer was spotlessly clean and echoed oddly when Javi climbed the dimpled steel steps and rapped on the door. No answer. Not even from the dog. Javi went to step back and caught himself before he tripped down the narrow stairs as his heel caught on the edge of the step. He probably should have called first. It just seemed easier not to.

And maybe he wanted to see Witte again, a sly little voice in the back of his head jabbed. Just to remind himself how irritating Witte was, of course. The voice sounded an awful lot like him when he was being clever in interrogations. Javi could see why it bugged people.

He fished his phone and the square of notepaper out of his pocket and pulled up the messages app to text Cloister. Halfway through *call the office*, a rough voice, pitched to carry, interrupted him.

"Slumming it, Special Agent?"

Javi turned around and saw Witte making his way up the stairs from the beach.

A pair of faded jersey shorts hung low around his hips, and he'd slung a wrung-out T-shirt around his neck. He was tanned the color of whiskey, and his hair was wet and honey streaked, dripping onto his shoulders. Ink scrawled up over his ribs, but the pattern was shattered by a burst of pale white scar tissue.

Javi's mouth went dry. *So that's what a bad decision looks like in the flesh.* "Any news about the kid?" Witte asked as he stopped at the top of the steps. He pulled the T-shirt from over his shoulder and wiped his face on it. The dog shoved between his knees and sat down on his feet, tongue lolling out over sharp white teeth as it panted.

"Not yet," Javi said. He lifted his hand to block the sun and squinted. "Can we talk inside?"

Witte stared at him for a second with his eyes narrowed. Then he shrugged and waved his hand at the trailer. "Sure. Let yourself in. Door's not locked."

Javi nudged the door open, stepped over the threshold, and ducked his head to avoid the frame. The trailer smelled better than he expected, and every surface was scrupulously clean and uncluttered. Not his idea of a living space, but he supposed it could be worse.

"We were the first two at the scene last night," Javi said. He glanced around as he moved out of the way of the door. There was a scuffed-up MacBook on the kitchen table and a stack of books lined up along the window. An empty pot was shoved into the corner of the counter next to the microwave—the smoking gun of plant ownership for cops. He turned around to face the door as Witte hunched through it. "We're coming up empty-handed at the moment, so I thought reviewing the initial search might help."

"Sure," Witte said. He scratched his shoulder absently as he shrugged. "Just let me clean up a bit. Bon Bon, stay."

The crack of command curled under Javi's balls and squeezed, making him bite the inside of his cheek in irritation. Witte wasn't his *type*. Javi liked smart, well-read, academic types—elegant hands and easily led. Not six feet of brooding, blond, aggressively straight California redneck who looked like he cut his own hair.

Witte wasn't pretty. He wasn't even *handsome*. With that jacked nose and the harsh Dust-Bowl Germanic lines of his face, he was barely holding on to rugged with his fingertips.

So whatever it was about Witte that got under Javi's skin, it *wasn't* attraction.

Which was good, since Witte had ducked into the trailer's cubicle bathroom and apparently didn't believe in closing doors all the way. There was just enough space to catch movement, bare lines of hip, and the wet slap of a washcloth. But that wasn't the point. Voyeurs didn't peep because they wanted to see a naked person. It was the illusion of intimacy....

And, Javi reminded himself as he looked away, the only thing he wanted *less* than a trailer-park deputy was actual intimacy. He sat down at the booth-style kitchen table and realized that, while he had *not* been watching Witte, the dog had been watching him. It sat with its tail tucked around its feet and stared.

Javi looked away—he was sure he'd read somewhere that you shouldn't make eye contact with dogs—and found his attention back on that distracting gap of door.

"Was there anything you saw up at the Retreat the other night that seemed out of place?" he asked. The reminder of why he was *actually* there made guilt pinch. There was a child missing, his friend's family was under suspicion, and he was distracted by muscles and a tight ass. Irritation sharpened his voice. "Something you missed or left out of your report?"

Witte jabbed the bathroom door open with his elbow and stepped out, absently clutching a hand towel at his hip. He'd washed off most of the sweat, but sand still clung to his shoulders and knees. A scowl hinted around the corners of his mouth, making his eyes narrow.

"Are we trading notes, or am I defending my work?" he asked.

"Do you have something to hide?" Javi asked.

He regretted the words the minute they were out, but that was always too late. Witte had made him uncomfortable, and there was an unhappy little gremlin at the controls in his brain that wouldn't settle until he returned the favor.

They missed the mark this time. Witte just shrugged.

"Course I do," he said. "That's why we have union reps. Do I need mine?"

"No," Javi said. "You need pants but not a rep. Sorry. I'm tired. No one to send me home."

For a second he thought the apology wasn't going to be enough. Then Witte shrugged and disappeared into another room. Still didn't close the door behind him.

"I do dogs, not detection," Witte said. "I'm not sure what you want."

To fuck. The answer popped into Javi's head with such clarity that for a second he wasn't sure if he'd said it out loud. It was only the lack of reaction from Witte that convinced him he hadn't. The thought still lurked in his head, though less of a word and more a cluster of sensations—heat, hands, the clench of an ass around his cock.

Witte still wasn't his type, but apparently that didn't matter. He wanted to fuck him anyhow, and he was never going to. Even if Witte didn't look like the poster child for straight jocks, Javi didn't fuck where he lived. It made his life messier. So he gathered up the whole tangle of lust and shoved it into the back of his brain, out of sight and out of the way.

He cleared his throat and focused on more appropriate answers. "Was there anything about the family that struck you as off? That didn't seem… genuine?"

Witte came back into the main area of the trailer, tugging an old Disney T-shirt down over his chest. His jeans were worn white along the seams and pulled tight across his thighs.

"I thought you said they were good people," he said.

"I did," Javi said. "I think they are. What if I'm wrong?"

The tic of Witte's mouth betrayed that he'd been there himself. He glanced down, absently buried his fingers in the dog's thick ruff, and finally shrugged one shoulder.

"I'm off today, anyhow," he said. "Do you want to go up to the Retreat, and we can walk through it?"

It was a generous offer. Javi was grateful, but at the same time, the easy grace of the gesture rubbed him the wrong way. He wasn't sure why. It could just be the unflattering fact that it made it harder to feel superior to Witte.

Sometimes Javi was such a prick it was hard to share his head with himself.

"I'd appreciate it," he said.

He might be a prick, but he did have manners.

CHAPTER FIVE

CLOISTER PULLED off the road at the feedlot. It had just opened, and workers in khaki T-shirts were loading up pallets and wrestling wire buckets of produce to flank the doors. He stopped at the back of the lot, next to a Buick with a spray-can paint job. Bourneville barked enthusiastically at birds. She clearly enjoyed the novelty of being in the car when she wasn't working.

"I figure this is where Drew was going, or thought he was going," he said as he nodded at the vending machines lined up against the wall. Bright plastic curves advertised M&Ms and Arizona Iced Teas, although they didn't glow as seductively as they did at night. "A lot of the kids sneak down here to get snacks or soda... or pay someone to go and get them booze, but ten's probably a bit young for that."

"You'd be surprised."

"Probably not," Cloister admitted. "Either way it's a popular spot. Deputies get called out all the time to ferry the kids back up the road, but they cut across."

He pointed toward the Retreat. Javi looked that way, visibly spinning a compass in his head. "The same way that Drew went when he left the cabin."

"Morocco," Cloister corrected him and quirked his mouth around the mockery. "But yeah, I think so."

"Think?"

"Not my beat," Cloister said. "I get called out for missing people and raids, not kids loitering at the vending machines. There was a path, though, and it went around the obstacles and bushes, not over. Adults go over, Special Agent Merlo."

That got him a withering look. "Javier. Or Javi. You make the 'Special' sound like it has air quotes."

"That's what I was going for," Cloister said. He swung the car around and headed back to the road.

"So I'm just to keep calling you deputy?"

Fair enough. "Cloister."

"Really?" Javi asked. "I thought that was a nickname because you were religious. I didn't know your mother hated you."

Cloister did a rolling stop at the exit. There weren't enough people on the road to merit a full stop. Sometimes being a cop made you worryingly blasé about traffic laws.

"It was her maiden name," he said. "She didn't hate me till later."

There was a pause for a second. Cloister could feel Javi studying his profile. He rolled the name over his mental tongue to try it out. It was shorter than "Special Agent," anyhow. Eventually Javi went, "Huh," as though he'd worked something out, and changed the subject.

"That's not something the parents would know," he said. "At home, maybe. But a camp where they're spending a week or weekend a couple of times a year? They're too busy making the most of their free time and the yoga workshops to map out the children's time. The whole point of going somewhere like the Retreat is that it's a safe environment to let the kids run around in nature."

"Maybe Drew was on his own when he left the cabin?" Cloister suggested. He had to struggle to resist the urge to bring his mother up again. The whole point of being disconcertingly frank with people was to make them uncomfortable, not to make them think they knew something about him.

"Then who gave him the soda?" Javi asked.

Cloister hung his arm out the window. The metal was hot against his arms, the wind hotter as it sanded dust against his forearm. The radio that morning warned about forest fires.

"You said the lab results weren't back," he said. "He could have just taken a drink with him."

Out of the corner of his eye, he saw Javi turn to look at him. "Then why did you lose his trail at the road?"

Maybe there was a good reason for that. But if there was, Cloister couldn't think of it. He grunted and shifted gear.

"You ask a lot of questions."

"It's like fishing," Javi said. "You have to throw out a lot of lines before you get a bite."

Cloister took his eyes off the road for a second and gave Javi a dubious look.

"You fish?" he mocked.

"Not much these days. My uncle used to take us out on the boat when we were kids, fishing for marlin." Javi paused. "You?"

The question hung in the air like one of those lines Javi had been talking about. Baited and waiting for Cloister to fall for the hook with a story. Or it was, he reminded himself, just someone making conversation by talking about family. That wasn't a sore spot for everyone.

"We got our food in the store."

Javi went, "Huh," again. It made Cloister shift, and tension pulled tightly across his shoulders, but he tried to ignore it. It wasn't as though there were any secrets. He might avoid talking about his family, but if Javi was that interested, the whole mucky story was recorded in black and white in his various records. His juvenile records should have been sealed, but he knew better than to believe that mattered to the Feds.

"Did you have a lot of friends when you were a child?" Javi asked.

Change of topic or more prying? Cloister took a deep breath of dry, hot air and tried to react like a sane person.

"No," Cloister said.

"Me neither. I wonder if Drew did."

IT WAS in the eye of the beholder. What was a fuck-off scary, big black dog to Bozo the Meth-head was a cute puppy to a bunch of kids. Given permission to be friendly, Bourneville was in her element. Her ears had been petted, her tail tugged, and she had chased balls. She flopped down over Cloister's feet and gnawed on an old tennis ball while he talked to one of her new friends.

Children liked him. He'd never been sure why, but it was the same effect his stepdad had on them. Kids and dogs loved Vincent Witte. Everyone else had more sense.

"Did you know Drew?" he asked.

Millie wrinkled her nose and glanced at her worried-looking mom and got an encouraging nod in answer. All the parents looked worried. At the trailer park, kids ran around all day with no supervision. Up here none of them were allowed out of the reach of a parent's arm. Millie heaved a sigh and pushed her glasses up her nose.

"We were friends last year," she said, "but not this year."

"Oh?"

She rolled her eyes. "He said he doesn't play with girls or little kids anymore," she said. "He called me specky."

"You didn't tell me that, Millie," her mother said.

"I didn't care," Millie said sagely. "He was just stupid. He said he had a *girlfriend* now, but he was *ten*."

Older-than-her-years Millie had no more stories. Three kids later Bourneville delicately accepted a bacon chip from the sticky hand of a toddler named Sean. His brother petted her the way kids did, like he was playing drums on her shoulder. His dad kept saying "gently" and giving Cloister apologetic grimaces. It didn't bother Bourneville, but she was clearly contemplating sticky toddler fingers, and Cloister tapped her hip to remind her to behave.

"He wanted to go, but his brother wouldn't take him," Sean said. He scratched the end of his nose and picked off scorched skin to reveal newborn freckles underneath. "You're going to find him, aren't you? Like on TV."

"I'll do my best," Cloister said.

At the same time, Sean's dad said, "Of course he will. I told you he won't be far."

He grabbed Sean by the shoulder, twisted his fingers in his son's *Ben 10* T-shirt, and shrugged at Cloister. "He had nightmares," he said. "I think that's enough."

Cloister nodded his understanding and asked, "Just a minute more? One more question."

Sean's dad looked reluctant, probably torn between concern for a missing boy he could put a face to and the idea that he could protect his own kid from anything like that—as though bad things couldn't happen to Sean if he didn't know about them. Instead of giving him the chance to make up his mind, Cloister asked his question.

"Is there anything that Drew did this year that was weird?" he asked. "Did he have any new friends or somewhere he played?"

Sean pulled a thoughtful face and twisted his mouth to the side.

"I 'unno." He shrugged. After a squirming second, he blurted out, "He was really mad this was his last year? He said it was all Billy's fault. He was really mad, I guess. Is that good?"

Cloister nodded. "That's great," he said and held out his hand. Sean put his sticky little mitt into it and grinned gappily at the solemn handshake. "You've been a big help."

Sean got to shake Bourneville's paw too as she gave her best lolling dog grin. Then his dad pulled him and his sister away. Cloister watched them go and then unfolded himself from the rock he'd been perched on. He brushed off the seat of his jeans and turned to look around, although he wasn't sure whose benefit that bit of pantomime was for. Bourneville didn't care, and Cloister already knew he'd keep track of where Javi was. Awareness of the dark, intense Javi was an itch at the base of Cloister's neck.

Or maybe balls would be more accurate.

It was distracting, and that was disconcerting. He never got sidetracked at work, certainly not by nice shoulders in custom tailoring. Especially not when it was a missing-person case. Those were always bad ones. He didn't sleep much anyway, but hardly at all when someone was lost. All of a sudden, though, his brain had decided to dedicate processing power to mooning over a hopeless crush.

Maybe he should get some sleep later.

Javi was standing in front of the Retreat's office, dark head inclined toward a scruffy man in worn overalls. Groundsman, Cloister assumed from the dirt on the knees and the heavy-duty pruning shears he held as he talked.

Muttered, really. He kept his head down and shoulders up—awkward with either social interaction, authority, or sharply handsome men with elegant hands.

Cloister could sympathize. He wasn't comfortable around any of those things either. His instincts made him bristle instead of cower. But then he had a gun and maybe a foot in height on the dark, scruffy gardener.

"Come on, girl," he said as he clipped Bourneville's leash onto her collar. "Fuss."

Back to work. She shook her head, shedding chip crumbs, and took up her usual position at this side. Her shoulder bumped companionably against Cloister's knee as they walked to the office.

According to the girl he spoke to, Reed was away. He had an "important appointment." Cloister assumed it was with his lawyer, insurance company, or both.

Up close the groundsman had the well-worn face of someone who worked outside. It made it difficult to tell how old he was. The stubble on his dusty jaw was patchy, but the skin was rough and full of dark pores. Somewhere between twenty-five and thirty, Cloister guessed.

"I never saw a boy out on his own," the man muttered, wrinkling his nose and blinking nervously. "Told the other cops that."

"I'm just making sure you didn't forget anything, Matthew," Javi said. "Sometimes you say something in the heat of the moment and then realize you left details out. So you didn't see any boys that night?"

Matthew hunched his bony shoulders, scratched at a welt on his neck, and fidgeted. "Saw lots of boys. Always lots of kids around. I don't watch them, but I see 'em."

"Did you see the Hartley boys?" Javi asked. "William and Andrew?"

The corner of Matthew's mouth jerked, and he shifted in place. "Might have seen them." He drew the words out like he was using pliers. "Weren't alone, though. If they'd been alone, I'd have said something."

"Who were they with?" Javi asked.

He snipped the air nervously with the pruning shears, and the rusted hinge creaked. "Each other," the man said. "The older boy was going somewhere, and the kid wanted to tag along."

"When?"

"I don't know. Late. I was going home."

"Were they arguing?" Cloister asked as he leaned against the low fence. It creaked under his weight, but it held.

"I guess," the man shrugged out the answer. "Bickering. Brothers do. Can I go?"

Javi finished writing in his notebook and snapped it shut. "Sure," he said.

Matthew snapped the shears closed again, thumbed the lock into place as he stashed them in his pocket, and scurried away. They both watched him go. His neck was pimpled and red from a fresh shave.

"Why did you ask if they were fighting?" Javi broke the brief silence.

"Apparently Drew had been telling the other kids that it was his last summer at the Retreat. He said it was his brother's fault. Also he told Millie that he had a girlfriend, but I think he was trying to impress her."

"Did it work?"

"Don't think so." That sent a flicker of humor through Javi's hazel eyes, but it faded quickly. Cloister waited as Javi tucked his notebook back into his pocket and then cleared his throat. "It doesn't mean anything. Brothers fight. Kids get the wrong end of the stick."

"Or it means something," Javi said. "Bill said he left his brother at the cabin, not that he followed him through the park."

Fair enough. Cloister pushed himself off the fence, and the wood creaked as his weight shifted. He twisted the lead absently around his hand and felt the sweat on it.

"Do you want to head down to where we lost the scent?" he asked.

The corners of Javi's mouth were tight as he stared over the Retreat toward the Hartleys' cabin. After a second he nodded. "Go there first," he said.

It was an easier hike in the daylight, with Bourneville padding at his heel instead of ranging ahead, but it was hotter. The wind rattled the trees and slashed ribbons of sand around their legs and up into their faces.

Cloister squinted and spat. Javi pulled a pair of aviator sunglasses out of his pocket—as though he weren't hard enough to read without hiding his eyes behind dark glass.

A single yellow evidence tag was jabbed into the ground where Cloister had found the bottle of soda. The tag had been canary yellow to start with, but between the sun and the sandblasting, it had already faded down to old egg.

"Did he just drop it?" Javi speculated. He turned to look back at the distance they'd covered from the Retreat. "He walked a fair distance, he was tired, and there was no one to see him littering."

Cloister squatted down, balanced on the balls of his feet.

"It was hot that night," he said. "Dry. I was parched. I wouldn't have thrown away a drink, and the bottle had a third left in it when it dropped."

Javi turned to frown at him. In the polarized curve of the glasses, Cloister could see his reflection with one eye squinted shut against the glare.

"That wasn't in the report."

Cloister switched the eye he was squinting and cupped his hand over his nose. "It was in mine," he said. "I took a picture."

A muscle clenched in Javi's jaw. "There were just dregs in the bottle when it got to the lab. What did you do? Drink it?"

Cloister braced his hand, fingers steepled against the ground, and pushed himself to his feet. He walked to the tree and scuffed his foot over the hard crust of dried dirt. Ants scuttled around, disturbed and irritated. "The bottle leaked," he said. "He threw it away for some reason."

"What?"

Cloister shrugged. "He's ten. I'm not. Maybe he was angry about something? Or the soda tasted funny. Or...." He hesitated and then turned around and glanced toward where he knew the boundary was. In his mind a boy ran across the hard-packed dirt, sweating and swerving around obstacles an adult would have lumbered through. But it wasn't dark, curly-haired Drew, who looked like his mother and brother but not at all like his father. "Maybe I was wrong? If Drew left the Retreat with someone, got to here, and realized something was wrong—"

"He throws away the bottle"—Javi took up the story and mimed the toss—"and runs. He gets as far as the road and then either trips, or whoever was chasing him caught up with him."

The scenario sounded viable to Cloister, but it didn't make Javi look any happier. Cloister supposed it didn't sound good for Drew—or Billy, if Matthew was right about seeing them out together.

"The search parties are still out," he said.

"Two days," Javi reminded him.

They walked the rest of the way to the road. The ruts had been flattened by traffic, and a police van was parked on the shoulder to serve as a mobile HQ for the search. Tancredi was sitting on the bumper when they got there, her sleeves rolled up and sweat rolling down her face as she filled in a report. Across the road, yellow vests flashing as they went through the trees, the search party made their way down toward the main road.

At least Cloister didn't have to crawl under the fence. It had been cut and peeled back to give them access.

"Tancredi," Cloister said. "Anything?"

She wiped her hand over her face to flick the sweat away. "Nothing." Looking up she caught sight of Javi and scrambled to her feet. "Sorry," she said as she waved a fly away impatiently. "I didn't realize you were down here, sir."

Last year Tancredi had applied to join the FBI, Cloister remembered. She'd withdrawn after she got pregnant, but from the way she was trying to impress Javi, it looked like she was thinking about it again.

"No need to call me sir," Javi said. "Agent Merlo will do."

Tancredi sucked her lower lip between her teeth and bit down. A dull flush slapped her throat. "Yes, Agent Merlo."

Turning his back, shoulder bumping against Javi's arm, Cloister muttered, "Dick."

Javi probably heard it. If he did, he ignored it.

"How far has the search perimeter expanded?" he asked Tancredi. She showed him around the side of the van and pointed to the maps inside.

The leash tugged at Cloister's hand. He looked down and along the length of woven nylon. Bourneville pulled against her collar, her tail twitching as though she'd caught a scent of something. Probably a baggie of pot one of the volunteers had dropped. It was California, and the sheriff's department always had a suspicion that the Retreat hadn't gotten rid of all their pot plants.

Not what they were looking for, but it was an easy find for Bourneville, and she needed a win. She probably didn't understand the details of a missing child or the deathwatch countdown of how long they'd been gone, but she knew she was meant to find what he told her to. Failing made her mope.

Besides, Cloister was soft enough to believe she understood *some* of what was going on—at least that some cases bothered Cloister more than others.

He let her have her head and doled out the leash as she trotted back and forth along the shoulder. The wind blew dust up her nose, making her stop and sneeze. Then she caught whatever scent molecules had been teasing her, and her nose stayed down as she scrambled up to the fence. She tried to squeeze into the roll of peeled-back wire and yelped in frustration.

"Bourneville, *Platz*," Cloister barked. She grumbled in her chest but flopped down and lay trembling in place until he reached her. "Good girl."

Cloister reeled the leash in as he climbed up to her side and looped the length of it around his wrist. There was blood on her paw, bright against the rusty fur. Cloister went down on his knee and lifted her foot to check it quickly. She'd caught her pad on the sharp-clipped wire, and a fat drop of blood oozed out between her toes when he manipulated it. It wasn't dripping on its own, though, so it wasn't too serious. Bourneville whined at having her hurt foot fiddled with, but her attention was still on the wire.

Easier to let her make her find than drag her away. Cloister leaned forward and hooked his fingers through the diamond-shaped gaps. A yank pulled it back, although he could feel the springy pressure of it cutting into his fingers. "*Bring!*"

Bourneville darted forward, pawed at the dirt, and turned up a battered white oblong that she carefully pinched between her front teeth and brought out with her. She sat up, dropped the phone on the dirt, and looked at Cloister expectantly.

"Good girl," he told her absently and patted her head as he let the fence go. It snapped back into the curl, the sharp ends of it scraping rake lines into the dirt. He shook the blood back into his red-welted fingers as he yelled, "Tancredi. You got any gloves?"

She did. It was Javi who snapped them on, though, and reached for the phone without waiting for Cloister to okay it. Bourneville growled at him—a low noise that rattled up her throat and down her nose. Javi froze, and tension trembled in his shoulders.

"Easy," Cloister said. He put his hand on Bourneville's shoulder and dug his fingers into her ruff. "Let it go."

She grumbled a bit but let her lips fold back down over her teeth, and she stepped back. Javi scooped up the phone. His mouth twisted in distaste at the slobber on it, and he wiped it on his leg. Once it was clean, he jabbed his thumb on the home button, and the thin latex stuck to the sticky white surface. The screen lit up at the pressure, and Javi flicked his thumb up and down.

"Unlocked?"

"Notifications," Javi said flatly. His mouth was tight, and behind his sunglasses, the skin was pulled taut over his cheekbones. "Billy's girlfriend wants to know why he's been ignoring her."

Javi stood up in one smooth motion and snapped at Tancredi, "Get me an evidence bag and a car to take me back up to the Retreat."

She nodded enthusiastically, hair bouncing, and ran back to the van.

"It doesn't mean the family was involved," Cloister pointed out. "He might have dropped it when he was down here. The parents wanted to come down yesterday, help with the search."

Even through the tinted glasses, Cloister could feel the glare.

"You do dogs, not detection," Javi reminded him. He held the phone up with the corners pinched between his fingers. "Now it looks like you don't even do dogs that well. So why not leave this to people who know what they're doing?"

He gave a hard, brief twist of his mouth and stalked back down the shoulder. Cloister glared after him, his jaw set so tightly it ached, and tried to decide whether he wanted to kiss or punch the smug look off Javier Merlo's pretty, damn mouth. Or his damn-pretty mouth.

What the hell, he decided as he clicked his tongue for Bourneville and headed back to the road. He could imagine both.

CHAPTER SIX

KEN FOLDED like a man who'd lost his breath and deflated onto the huge creamy sofa. Grief and worry had worn the luxe off the glossy cabin. Dust and dirty footprints covered the polished wood floors, and torn-open boxes of freshly printed *MISSING* posters were stacked against the walls. The smell of hot paper and ink nearly hid the sourness of food that no one had the appetite to eat.

"We just need to talk to Bill," Javi said. It was always a lie, but it felt like more of one than usual right then. "There's some things about what happened that night, when Drew went missing, that we want to clarify."

Lara's face was taut, and dark circles bruised under her eyes, but the look of contempt she gave him was robust. She was hugging Billy, one arm wrapped around his shoulders to block the deputy who was trying to take custody of the boy.

"Who do you think you're talking to?" she asked. "You can talk to him here or you can get out of my house."

"Lara...."

Her lips trembled for a second, and then she grimly pressed them into a firm line and blinked the tears from her eyes. She shook her head, curls flying. "You don't get to call me that. We aren't friends right now. If you take my son away, we won't be friends again."

That caught in Javi's throat like a pebble. It surprised him. He had friends—if you defined *friend* as someone you could ask for a favor in a pinch. Lara had invited him to Thanksgiving. He hadn't gone, but it had still been kind.

"It's my job," he said. "If you want to get Drew back, I have to follow every lead. Even if you don't like it."

"No. No." Lara said. "You *do not* get my baby back by taking my son. That is not how this works. No."

"I'm afraid it is," Javi said. He nodded to the deputy and gave a grim little dip of his chin to give permission to a grim little task. The man pried Billy out of Lara's grip and walked him outside, one hand firmly around his elbow. Ken finally dragged himself up, caught her, and tried to embrace her while she shoved his comfort away.

"It'll be alright, Lara," Ken said. "We need to trust the police. They want to find Drew too."

Lara clenched her hands so tightly that it had to hurt. Tendons stood out in her bony wrists, stark under her skin. She closed her eyes, swallowed hard, and wobbled in place for a second. Javi thought she was going to faint, but then she breathed in, and her spine went rigid.

"My son is missing. Someone took him. You should be looking for him, not trying to blame Billy. He loves his brother."

"And I'm not saying he doesn't, or that he's done anything," Javi said. "Right now I just need to talk to him, and for everyone's sake, it's best if it's official."

Lara sniffed stickily and pulled away from Ken. She twisted her arms up to yank her hair back from her face and snapped a band around the heavy mass of it. "You know what my dad would tell me if he were here?" she said. "Trust the police but get an expensive lawyer."

She grabbed a set of keys and a handful of posters from the table. Then she gave Ken a sharp look. Even standing up he still looked somehow deflated, like something he needed to buoy him up had leaked.

"Don't be useless," Lara told him. It wasn't an insult. She didn't sound angry. It was just a flat directive. Then she gave Javi a hard look. "I will meet you at the station. If you talk to my son before I get there, I will ruin you. And fuck you for doing this."

She stalked out of the cabin.

Ken swallowed, wiped his hand over his face, and rubbed his puffy lids with his thumb and forefinger.

"This is just protocol, right?" he asked. Ken was an orthopedic surgeon. This wasn't the sort of tension he could deal with. "You know Billy didn't do this? He wouldn't do this?"

He probably didn't mean to sound that doubtful. Javi gripped his shoulder for a second.

"You should go with Lara," he said. There should have been a rider, a "she needs you." It was disingenuous enough to catch in his throat. The only person Ken would help by being there was Javi. Ken had a good middle-class boy's respect for the authorities.

Ken hesitated for a second, as though he were expecting something, and then he nodded and went after Lara. Neither of them bothered locking the doors. Javi supposed there wasn't anything else they were worried about losing.

On the way out, he saw Matthew, the groundskeeper, loitering around a withered patch of grass as he watched Billy getting escorted to the patrol car. He was the first rubbernecker, but he wouldn't be the last. By the next day, Billy would be famous in his own right.

JAVI RODE the bronze-and-glass elevator up from the garage and frowned over his phone as he checked his emails. Authorization to fund the sheriff's task force against the new meth dealers in town, requests for "clarifications" on three of his reports, five letters from Saul's old friends in the bureau asking him for updates on the case.

"Fuck," he muttered as he shoved them into a Deal With Later folder.

At this rate, next time he needed a favor, he'd have to take Cloister Witte to dinner. He side-eyed that thought as the elevator jolted to a halt at his floor, but he decided it was harmless enough. So he wouldn't mind taking Cloister to dinner—and all the things they could do afterward in a nice rented hotel bed. That didn't mean he had any intention of breaking his "never fuck where you live" rule.

Even if it would probably be a cheap date. Cloister looked like the type who'd prefer McDonald's Filet-O-Fish to Truluck's sesame-seared ahi.

He let the brief notion fade away as the doors slid open to let him step out. At the end of the short hall, the office admin glanced up from her computer and nodded briefly as she recognized him. She pulled her desk together and filled her hands with information in order of importance for when he actually entered the office. He walked briskly over and pushed the door open to let her get started.

"Agent Merlo." She stood up from behind the desk and tucked her stack of paperwork into the crook of her arm. Under her neat bob of fashionably graying hair, there was a disapproving cant to her jaw. "The sheriff called. The Hartleys are at the station. He's waiting for you to arrive before he interrogates their son."

Ah. Javi stopped, let the doors swing shut behind him, and tucked his phone in his pocket. "Is that a problem, Sue?" he asked.

She blinked and nudged her glasses up her nose. "Personally or professionally?"

"Professionally," he said.

"Then no," she said. "My job is to keep this office running, Agent Merlo. My personal feelings aren't relevant to that."

Saul would have asked her what her personal feelings were anyhow. That was probably why she liked Saul better. Lara had almost definitely invited Ms. Daly to one of her barbeques.

"Good," Javi said. "I won't keep them waiting, then. Is there anything I need to deal with now? Or can it wait until this evening?"

She shuffled her folders. "I need your signature for these acquisitions." She dealt the red folder to him. He flipped it open and leaned over her desk as he scanned, ticked, and signed the forms.

"The lab still doesn't have anything on the residue in the bottle," she said. Javi paused midsignature and glanced up, irritation pinching at his forehead. She shrugged. "It got bumped by a case in Los Angeles. I called in one of Saul's favors to expedite it, but that still takes time."

He nodded. There were advantages to working in a resident agency—he wouldn't be there otherwise—but there were also advantages to being near enough to the lab to pitch your case to the techs in person. He signed the last form, tapped them together neatly, and handed them back. "What about the files I requested?"

She returned the folder to her stack and shifted it closer to her body.

"I've uploaded Saul's—Agent Lee's—case files to your server. Anything where there was no custodial jail time or where the suspects have been released. Also all the old death threats that he used to get. Most of them are... performative, but that doesn't mean there's no feeling there. It's quite a substantial package. Do you still think it's relevant?"

"The investigation is ongoing," he said. "I'm not shutting down any avenues of investigation yet."

Her eyebrows ticked up one precisely measured space. "Not my area of expertise." She turned, set the folders neatly back on her desk, and checked her wristwatch. "I'm going to take an early lunch today, and since this is my own personal time? That boy didn't do this, Agent. You should keep that in mind."

Piece said, she left. The heavy glass doors swung shut behind her. Irritation bubbled in the back of Javi's throat. He could taste it as he stalked into his office, logged in to his computer, and accessed the server. He jerked his fingers over the keys as he input his password and sent the files to his tablet to read later. Why did everyone act like he wanted William Hartley to have done something horrible to his brother? He *wanted* to believe Billy was innocent. His gut said there had to be another explanation.

The evidence said otherwise, and following the evidence was his job. Saul was the one who taught him that.

Flying stop at the office done, he logged off and headed back downstairs. He texted the Sheriff that he'd be there in fifteen minutes, but he made it in twenty. When he got to the station, the press was already there, squinting against the wind with the sheriff's department shield as their backdrop.

"Special Agent Merlo, do you have any comment on why the Hartleys were brought in?"

"FBI Agent Javier Merlo has arrived at the police station just minutes after the missing boy's family were escorted inside."

"Drew Hartley has been missing now for three days. Should the police have been looking closer to home?"

Javi "no commented" his way past them. A camera flashed as he went through the door, and a distracted part of his brain wondered how the image would be framed the next day. Hero or dupe?

There was a different person behind the desk than there had been that morning. Javi had to check his watch to be sure enough time had passed that there had been a shift change.

"Agent," the young man said as he stuck a pen behind his ear, "the Hartleys are in the interrogation room, and the sheriff is waiting for you."

"Thanks," Javi said. "Could you check in with them, get them water and coffee if they want it?"

The man—if Javi cared to squint, he could have read his name tag—looked briefly surprised but nodded his agreement.

There was no point trying to discomfit Billy by leaving him thirsty. It would just alienate the family more, and one way or another, they were still victims. With the press outside, it was important to remember that.

Javi headed down to Frome's office and let himself in, announcing himself with a perfunctory rap of his knuckles against the door. He registered the growl of voices through the glass and wood, but it was only as he stepped inside that he realized that it was Frome disciplining Cloister.

His brain tripped over that word, all dark heat and slap-pink skin, but it wasn't in the sexy way.

Frome was so angry the veins stood out in his temples and bubbled as his blood pressure went up, and Cloister was… flat… slouched down in the office chair, arms crossed, and his lean, still not-pretty face completely expressionless.

"…you get a lot of leeway because you're one of the sheriff's department's best dog handlers, so don't start failing at that, Witte. Not if you want to keep your job and your dog."

Cloister blinked and waited.

It was the face of someone who'd had a lot of practice at taking abuse and not reacting to it. Javi didn't know what it said about him that he filed that away for later. Good or bad, he did it anyhow.

"Anything to say?" Frome asked.

Cloister shifted for the first time and lifted his chin slightly. It was his first reaction to escape the controlled reserve that kept his face still and his hands relaxed on his bicep.

"No," he said. "Sir."

Irritation dragged Frome's cheeks into flat planes. "Insolence doesn't cover up your mistakes, Witte. Thanks to you we've wasted time looking for that boy in the wrong place."

That jab caught something raw, although Javi wasn't clear if Frome noticed. Cloister narrowed his eyes for a second and then relaxed again.

"Sir." It was inflectionless.

"On the other hand," Javi interrupted, "it's thanks to him that now we know we were looking in the wrong place."

He didn't know why he suddenly felt the urge to defend Cloister. It couldn't be the slow simmer of lust. It hadn't stopped him from writing Cloister up that time he told Javi to go fuck himself. And the effort didn't get him any thanks either, just a grunt from Frome and a brief, closed-off glance from Cloister.

"Should I send the phone you found on to the lab?" Frome sat down behind his desk. He wiped his forehead and blotted the sweat into his hairline.

"Not yet," Javi said. "I think it will be more use here for now. Do you want to sit in on the interview, Lieutenant?"

"I don't think that's necessary," Frome said. "They already have a relationship with you. Introducing me will only muddy the waters."

What he *meant* was that the fallout might come back on him, and he'd rather aim it at the FBI. Javi didn't mind—he preferred to remain in control of the investigation—but he wasn't fooled either.

"Can I borrow Deputy Witte?" he asked.

"You can keep him," Frome said. He pointed across the table at Cloister. "Be what Agent Merlo wants. Say what he wants. Do what he wants. If you go off script, I'll put you on administrative leave for the rest of the case and assign the dog to Kent."

Javi had to clear his throat and try not to be distracted by a variety of enjoyable scenarios he could set up with those orders. There were more pressing issues, but it wasn't every day a professional acquaintance hit your personal kinks quite that sharply on the head.

"He just needs to present the evidence," Javi said. "They know him. Lara knows that he's been out looking for her son and, right now, she's going to have a more positive reaction to him than she will to me. So I want to take advantage of that."

Cloister frowned and shifted in his chair for the first time. The cheap plastic creaked under him and caught on the seams of his jeans. "I don't do interrogations," he said.

"What did I *just* tell you?" Frome asked him sharply. "You want to clear your ticket, find this boy? Do what the agent tells you."

It would be counterproductive to smirk, but it was hard not to. Javi nodded to Frome. "I'll go and speak to them now. Until we know more, though, I still want to bring Reed in for a formal interview. Any luck with that?"

There was something in Frome's scowl. Javi supposed it could have been frustration at not being able to produce the Retreat's owner, but he thought it was more disappointment that Javi still wanted to pursue that line of the investigation. The parents or brother taking the fall was a lot more politically convenient.

"Not yet," Frome said. "I'll let you know when we do."

Javi left him to follow up with that and stepped out to the hall with Cloister on his heels. He glanced down. The leg of Cloister's uniform was fuzzed with dog hair but missing the dog.

"Put your better half in her kennel?"

"She's in her run," Cloister confirmed. Or corrected. He frowned and screwed bar-straight brows together over his crooked nose. "I'm not comfortable doing this interview."

"Good," Javi said. "It'll make you more sympathetic. Just remember what your boss told you and do what you're told."

He probably enjoyed saying that more than he really should have, but the feeling faded quickly as he turned his attention to the unpleasant task at hand. It was never easy to interrogate a minor in front of their parent—even less so when you knew them.

"Just stay quiet until I ask you to say something," he told Cloister. Giving him a dubious up and down, Javi twisted his mouth wryly. "Just try and look less like you want to punch someone."

Cloister sighed. "You ain't playing to my strengths here."

The dust-dry flash of humor was brief, but it caught Javi off guard the same way the scar-splattered tattoo on Cloister's ribs did. It was the hint that there was more to him than the aggressively simple presentation. Javi resented having to know that.

"Are we on the same page, Deputy Witte?" he asked, using the formality to put a bit of distance between them. "If you undercut me in there, Lieutenant Frome will be the least of your worries."

"Don't fret yourself, Special Agent Merlo," Cloister said as he hitched a shoulder in a lazy shrug. "I don't worry about either of you."

Javi smiled to stretch the tension out of his jaw, felt the hinge click, and said, "Then I guess it's time to tell Lara that her son probably killed his brother."

CHAPTER SEVEN

THE INTERROGATION room was a relic of the past. The walls were institutional green plaster, paint slowly leeching down into old cracks and a suspiciously head-sized dent roughly spackled in. Fifty years of nicotine stained the plastic cover of the florescent light on the ceiling. A metal ring was sunk into the center of the battered old table, scraped and dented from years of cuffs being snapped to it.

Billy couldn't take his eyes off the grim semicircle of metal. He sat hunched over in his chair and picked at his nails with nervous fingers with his lawyer on one side of him and his mother on the other. Lara looked like there was a steel rod in place of her spine—so straight you could feel the tension of it in your own muscles—and her arm was tucked around Billy's shoulder.

J. J. Diggs was the sort of lawyer who made sharks object to the comparison—rich, fastidiously dressed, and completely amoral. Saul had hated him, but Javi supposed it made sense for Lara to call him. If you were keeping count, Diggs had fucked the FBI over on four major cases, lost hard twice, and on a personal note, been thoroughly fucked by Javi once.

That didn't count as breaking Javi's "not where he lived" rule, although it did bend it a bit. Diggs was based in LA.

"Just happened to be in the area when Lara called?" Javi asked, raising his eyebrows.

Diggs smiled back at him, all perfect teeth and practice. "Isn't that lucky?" He adjusted his tie and settled the blue silk knot over his Adam's apple. "I assume this isn't going to take long. My clients are obviously eager to get back to the Retreat and look for their son."

"We all want to find Drew," Cloister said. The rough drawl of his voice made Diggs glance his way with a quick, measuring look that took in the rough edges and wide shoulders. "If we didn't think Billy could help, we wouldn't be in here. We'd still be out looking."

The simple sincerity in Cloister's voice caught Lara and drained some of the steel out of her spine. Cloister looked like a terrible liar. It was written all over that not-exactly handsome face of his, but honesty could get you what you wanted as well. If you knew how to apply it.

Javi could hate himself for that later.

"Which is exactly what you should be doing," Diggs cut in. "Not harassing the family on some trumped-up suspicions so Special Agent Merlo can improve his close rates."

Billy shifted and unfolded himself from his slouch to sit as straight as a teenager could manage. He twisted his hands together on the table and squeezed his knuckles until they folded.

"I wanna help," he said. "If you have any questions, I'll answer them."

"Billy," Diggs held up his hand. "Let me—"

"No." Billy shook his head. "I want to help find my brother. I didn't hurt him. He's my *brother*."

Javi leaned forward. "That's not what we're saying, Billy," he said. Not yet, anyhow. "You've been telling us the truth, but not all the truth."

"That's not true," Lara said. She tightened her fingers on Billy's arm and wrinkled the fabric between her knuckles. "Billy already told you everything. He left Drew alone in the cabin, and something terrible happened. If he was going to lie, it would have been about that."

Billy swallowed hard. His Adam's apple bobbed in his throat, knobby against razor-rash flushed skin, and he blinked twice.

"Because Drew didn't stay in the cabin, did he, Billy?" Javi asked.

"I don't—"

Javi ignored him and pushed. "We have a witness who saw you arguing with Drew that night," he said. "He wanted to go with you, didn't he? Hang out with his big brother?"

"No."

"Had to get on your nerves," Javi said. "When I was a teenager, I wouldn't have wanted a ten-year-old hanging out with me. Not when I was trying to impress girls."

Across the table, Diggs looked up long enough to give him an amused glance at that claim. His pen scratched across the pad.

"You aren't my client," he said. "Billy was a devoted brother."

"Is," Lara said.

"He *is* a devoted brother," Diggs corrected smoothly. He reached up and touched Lara's hand briefly. "And we know Billy was taken from the cabin. So I'm not sure what you're getting at, Agent."

Javi watched Billy chew on the inside of his lip. "Did Drew threaten to tell your parents you'd left him alone?" he asked. "You were already in trouble, weren't you, Billy?"

"How did you know—"

"He's a teenager," Diggs said. "He's always in trouble."

"And he was at a party," Lara broke in again and leaned forward. "You know that. There were people there, other kids who saw him. His friends. His girlfriend."

"Allison, right?" Javi asked. "Unfortunately she didn't see Billy that night, did she, Billy? You didn't answer her texts either."

Billy shrugged uncomfortably, still twisting his hands together on the table. "I... I lost my phone," he said. "That's all."

"I know," Javi said. He put his fingers on the evidence bag sitting on the table and tipped it up. The phone slid out. "We found it. Or rather Deputy Witte did."

Cloister's reluctance was obvious as he shifted his weight in the chair, but he did his part. "It was down by the road," he said. "Where we lost Drew's trail."

The phone lay on the table, scratched and battered. Lara relaxed her hand, slid it off Billy's shoulder, and visibly shifted her body away from him. Billy reached for the phone, but Javi blocked him.

"Is there anything you want to tell us?"

"I *lost* it," Billy said. He looked to Javi first and then swung his eyes to Lara, and his voice cracked. "Mom, I lost it. I swear."

This time it was Diggs's hand on Billy's shoulder. It looked manicured and elegant against the scruffy, gray, too-well-loved band shirt. "I think that's enough questions," he said. "Unless you want to make this official, Agent Merlo, we'll be leaving."

"Is that your phone?" Lara asked. Her voice cracked, and tension pulled the cords in her neck into taut lines under her skin. "Billy. Is that your phone?"

"I... I don't know," Billy stammered. The need to answer her outweighed the pressure of Diggs's hand on his shoulder. "I don't know where it went, Mom. I lost it."

Lara cupped her trembling hands over her mouth and pressed her knuckles so hard against her lips that they left white divots in the skin. "What did you do?" she breathed.

"Nothing!"

Billy reached for her, and she cringed back from him and slapped his hand away. "If you did something, you tell them now," she said. Her voice shuddered up in pitch. "You tell them where my baby is."

Diggs talked over both of them. "You say nothing, William," he said. He swung his attention to Javi and narrowed his blue eyes as he stated firmly, "This interview is suspended, Agent Merlo. My client isn't saying anything more."

"Yes he is," Lara said. "He's going to tell them why his phone was there. He's going to tell them what happened. I want to know."

"I don't work for you, Doctor Hartley," he said. "I work for Billy, and until I have a chance to discuss this with him, it isn't in his best interests to talk to you. So, are we free to leave or not?"

Javi inclined his head. "For now."

Diggs shushed Billy before he could spill anything else and hurried him out of the room. "Mom?" Billy protested over his shoulder. His voice got more panicked and rose over Diggs's quiet instructions. "Mom, I didn't do anything."

Across the table Lara turned her whole body away from him. Her shoulders looked sharp enough to scrape as she hunched in on herself.

"Lara," Javi said gently, and she didn't correct him. "Do you think Billy could have done something to his brother?"

She sniffed. The corners of her mouth turned down, and she wiped her finger over her upper lip. "I don't know," she said. "He never used to be…. He's just gotten so *angry*."

Cloister leaned over the table but hunched down to look smaller. "Apparently Drew was saying that it might be the last year you went to the Retreat, and it was because of Billy?"

"No. Not just Billy," she said. "I want to move to San Diego this summer, get Billy into a new environment, but Ken wanted to wait until Christmas. He didn't want to upset his father."

The bitterness in her words had taken a long time to get there—more than the few months between summer and now. Before they could ask any other questions, Ken burst into the room.

"Our lawyer says we shouldn't be talking to you," he said. He grabbed Lara's arm and pulled, but she didn't move. "Lara. It's time to go."

"It's his phone," she said. "He wasn't at the party, and it's his phone, Ken. My baby is out there somewhere, and Billy—"

"No," Ken said flatly. "You will not finish that sentence. Our son did not do this."

"Doctor Hartley," Javi said as he stood up. "You need to calm down."

"No I don't," Ken said. "My lawyer says we should leave. That's what we're going to do."

He bullied Lara to her feet and out of the room, muttering in her ear with every step. Javi grimaced. Five more minutes and he might have gotten some answers.

"I did not expect him to find his balls," he muttered.

Cloister rocked onto the back legs of the chair and braced his long legs against the floor. His face was closed off again with a layer of sullenness that masked whatever else he was feeling.

"What?" Javi asked.

"Nothin'," Cloister said. He hesitated and then added slowly, "Just something feels off."

"A boy might have murdered his little brother," Javi said. Frustration bled into his voice and turned into sarcasm somewhere along the way. "We have to prove it for his parents. Is there anything there, Deputy Witte, that *isn't* off?"

Cloister scratched his jaw, and his nails scraped in the fuzz of almost-invisible gold stubble. He changed the subject. "Ken has a new script, but Lara's still the one with the spine. If she hadn't budged."

"I know," Javi said, and annoyance pleated his lips. "Five more minutes and we could have gotten something useful from her. It doesn't matter. We'll get another chance. The seed's planted now. Every time she looks at Billy, she'll wonder if maybe we're right."

"Yeah." Cloister pushed himself up from the chair. He hooked his thumbs in the pockets of his jeans and stared out the door for a second. "And if we aren't right?"

"Then we've wasted time on the wrong avenue of investigation," Javi said, "and helped keep a family therapist in business. Our job is finding out who took Drew Hartley, not worrying about his family."

The muscles in Cloister's jaw flexed. "Your job," he said. "My job's finding Drew. I should get back to that, if there's nothing else?"

There wasn't. Nothing appropriate for the workplace, anyhow. Javi let him go, and if he lingered at the door to watch his long, rangy body cross the floor, it was only partly for the view. It was mostly because he wondered if Cloister had seen something he hadn't or because he didn't want another kid to grow up thinking his mother hated him.

Maybe it was both.

CHAPTER EIGHT

IT WAS a nightmare. Cloister knew that. The fear of it was familiar as an old pair of sweats, but it didn't help. He was still afraid.

It was dry and hot. Cloister was thirsty—that wringing thirst that almost choked you—and the sand scratched his legs as he ran. He didn't know what he was running from or where he was going. Just that he didn't want to be there. There was something bad ahead and worse behind.

So he ran, mouth dry and eyes stinging as the wind flicked dust under his lashes.

It was only as he stumbled and hit a rock that he wondered why he was so small. He didn't have time to make sense of it. First he heard the whistling, and then he heard the dogs. That was always the order. Whistle, then dogs.

A wet nose in the heart of Cloister's hand jolted him awake. For a second he wasn't sure he actually was awake. His mouth was still dry, and sweat itched in the folds of his body. But when he swung his legs out of the cot, they were longer than his entire body had been in the dream. The scar on his knee—where a fall and a bottle had left him looking at his kneecap in more detail than he ever wanted—was there too, and he never dreamed about that.

Maybe because the memory of dirty bone and the wrinkled flap of degloved knee skin was too gross for his subconscious to touch.

Bourneville shoved her way between his legs and demanded attention. Cloister wasn't sure if it was the fear stink of his nightmare that annoyed her or the fruitless afternoon they'd spent quartering the ground between oak trees in search of something belonging to Drew Hartley.

Something else they'd missed.

He let the thought sit for a second and tried it out for size, but it still didn't feel right. Everyone made mistakes, but he couldn't see how this one had happened. There was enough of Drew's scent on the phone that Bon picked it up two hot days after the boy disappeared, but not when it was fresh? And it might have been dark that night, but Cloister had crawled under that fence on his belly. The phone would have been right under his elbow.

Except what then? If someone planted it, how had they gotten hold of it if Billy wasn't out there that night? And what was Billy doing that night that he was lying about?

Bourneville butted his chin with her head and clicked his teeth together with enough force to make his eyes water. Apparently he'd gotten distracted enough to stop paying attention to her. He scratched her ears, shoved her away, and checked his watch.

Two hours' sleep. He scrubbed the heel of his hand over his eyes and felt the grit of sand. It was probably more like an hour and a half. He was still tired—his brain felt the way your mouth did after the dentist stuffed it with cotton—but if he went back to sleep, he'd just tip back into the nightmare. He always did, and it was never better the second time around. So he got up instead, swung his leg over Bourneville, and grabbed some clothes.

"Want to go for a run?" he asked. She thumped the ground with her tail in answer and cocked her head to the side. He grinned at her. "C'mon, then."

He shoved the door open and let Bourneville jump down first. Then he sat down on the steps as he pulled on a battered, sandy pair of sneakers. The wind was still up, bowling discarded soda cans and torn paper bags across the trailer park. It was dark but not quiet. A child was squalling somewhere—that dull whine that was in for the long haul—and the dull thump of bass from the stoners' trailer was like a heartbeat.

Some of the other deputies gave him shit for living there, and he'd seen the sneer on Javi's mouth earlier, but it suited him. When you were a lifelong insomniac, the last thing you wanted at night was peace and quiet. Silence just felt like the world taunting you with how well it was sleeping.

Besides, the only roots he ever had turned out to be poisoned. So he paid rent on a battered old Airstream, and his old kitbag did double duty as a wardrobe.

He stood up and whistled for Bourneville. She came wriggling out from under the trailer, spiderwebs decorating her ears and a scabby old tennis ball in her mouth.

"I buy you shit, Bon," he told her. "Good shit, but you'd rather run around with some thrift-store reject ball? People talk."

She grinned at him, her tongue hanging out behind the ball until he laughed. A wave of his hand sent her loping down to the shore. He rolled his shoulders back hard to loosen the muscles and raced her there.

The dog won.

CLOISTER HAD spent his life running—into trouble, after dogs, away from whatever was in his nightmares. The mistake people like Bozo the Meth-head made was to think you could outrun your problems. That never worked. The problems always beat you to the finish line. All you could do was run until the biggest problem was whether you were going to puke or come.

It was puke this time.

Cloister limped into the tide, his muscles aching from running on the shifting footing of the coarse sand. He scooped up a handful of seawater and swilled it around his mouth. Salt and grit cut the taste of grease and acid, and he spat.

Behind him Bon rolled enthusiastically, adding elflocks of sand to the salt that matted her fluffy coat. She was going to need a bath.

Cloister ran for that one minute of exhausted clarity when his brain was empty. Bon ran because she was a dog. But why had Drew Hartley run? Ten-year-old boys didn't run away from their big brothers, not unless something had already established itself as very wrong in that household.

The tremble of Lara's voice replayed in his ear. "He's been so *angry*." But was that how she'd have phrased it before Drew went missing? Once you started to think your child could have done something horrible, everything else they did was warped by association. No one said that Drew was scared of Billy. Annoyed with him, pestering him, but not scared.

Ten-year-olds drank what their brothers gave them, even if it tasted weird. Ten-year-olds ran after they knew someone wanted to hurt them—not because they thought someone might. The fear of looking stupid had kicked in by then.

The dread that usually confined itself to his nightmares stretched in the back of Cloister's brain, making the skin at the nape of his neck prickle clammily. He could guess *why*, but he didn't see how a fractured memory made years ago and miles away could help.

Cloister stood for a second more and stared over the stretch of choppy black water as the tide washed waves in around his knees. He still didn't think Billy was guilty, but he couldn't pin that feeling down to a reason.

The case against Billy had evidence, witness testimony, and a mother's doubt. He had nightmares and a blurry scene in his head that could be a theory or could be wishful thinking. If it wasn't *his* gut, even he'd admit the merits of the case damned Billy.

"What do you think?" he asked Bourneville as he waded out of the sea. His sneakers were wet. The rough seams rubbed his ankles while the sodden laces trailed in the dirt. "Am I just being soft on the kid, or what?"

Bourneville scrambled to her feet and shook violently, shedding half a beach of sand and shell. The other half stayed tangled in her fluffy black coat. Her tongue dangled out of her mouth behind what was left of the ball.

"You're right." He walked up the beach to her. There was seaweed in her muttonchops. He picked it out and gave her a scratch under the chin. "We should stick to what we're good at—finding people and staying up late. Leave the detective work to the guys who have to wear suits."

She wagged her tail in agreement and stirred up the sand.

"C'mon, then," he said as he hooked his hand in her collar. "Let's get home and get you rinsed off. Maybe I can grab another hour's shut eye before I gotta get up."

Instead of going back along the beach, following the long jut of headland, Cloister took the narrow path up to the scenic overlook at the road. The narrow dirt path crawled up the steep hill, and dry dirt and shells slid under foot. By the time he reached the potholed oval of tarmac, his sodden sneakers were dry and salt-stiff against his toes as they bent.

They walked back along the road, and Bourneville stuck obediently to Cloister's side on the shoulder. Two cars passed them, music blaring and men wearing sunglasses driving. Back at the trailer park, Khaled Hirmiz—a construction worker and neighbor—was swearing quietly at his truck.

"Problems?" Cloister paused on his way across the plot.

Khaled looked up, his mouth open to rant, but caught himself as he registered who was talking to him. He shut his mouth and pursed his lips under a week-old moustache. He'd always been uneasy around Cloister since he learned he was a cop, not that Cloister had ever seen him or his small, well-behaved family even litter.

"No," Khaled said. He shuffled away from Bourneville as she sniffed around the tires. "Just the kids. They untied all the ropes again. I can do it."

Usually that would have been the end of their interaction. Cloister only played mascot when the lieutenant sent him and Bourneville out to schools to be the approachable, fuzzy face of the department. Tonight he lingered and stared at the new plastic sign zip-tied to the pickup.

Andres and Son Construction

His brain felt like a car stuck in neutral, revving until it smoked but stuck in one place. The "off" that he needed to pinpoint, to pin down, was right there. He just couldn't bring it into focus. It hadn't been Andres, it had been....

"Deputy?"

Cloister glanced at Khaled. "Is there a builder in town called Atkins?"

Khaled frowned and shook his head. "I don't think so." He shrugged and hazarded uncertainly, "There's Utkin, the property developer?"

That was it. Birdie Utkin.

Cloister clapped his hand on Khaled's shoulder. "Thanks," he said. "That's been bothering me all day."

Cloister left a confused Khaled to finish tying down the equipment in the back of the pickup and loped back to his trailer. Any thought of sleep was gone. Now that he'd worked out what had been bothering him about the case, he needed to work out what it meant.

That's *if* it meant anything. It had been ten years since Birdie Utkin disappeared.

CHAPTER NINE

THERE WAS a half-empty bottle of whiskey sitting on the desk, doing double duty as a paperweight for a stack of photocopied driver's licenses. The one on top belonged to the Retreat's owner, Tranquil Reed. Either the removal of his granny-framed glasses or the smudgy ink had taken the genteel sheen off him. He looked ratty and pinched in the photo.

"What do you want?" Javi asked impatiently as he shoved the office doors shut behind Cloister. "I don't have the time to coddle you through this investigation. If the evidence is so hard for you to stomach, get taken off the case. You can't be the only dog cop in town."

He stalked back to the desk and sat down in the heavy leather chair. Whoever had downed the shots of whiskey, it wasn't him. He looked tired, not drunk. His collar was undone, the tie pulled loose, and the crisp sleeves of his fancy shirt were rolled back over his lean, hard forearms. An expensive watch—gears and crystal face expensive, not chips and scratch-resistant expensive—hung heavily around one wrist. Faint white scars ran up the insides of his forearms in neat, parallel lines, but if he wasn't going to bring that up, neither was Cloister.

It really didn't seem fair that assholes were allowed to be that hot.

"The clerk downstairs said you were still working," Cloister said. "Have you got anything?"

Javi leaned back in his chair. The leather sighed under his weight, and he waved his hand irritably at the desk. "I've got fire alerts for the hills tomorrow, excuses from the lab techs, and a *very* carefully worded memo from San Diego regarding the thin ice my career is on. And now I've got the smell of dog in my office."

"She had a bath," Cloister said. He glanced down at Bourneville, who'd made herself at home on the floor. "The smell lingers for a bit. Look, remember I said something was off?"

"And I said you should leave investigations to people who knew what they were doing," Javi said. He pointed to the room's other chair at the same time, though. "Sit. What is it?"

Cloister took a seat and immediately regretted it. Sitting on the other side of the desk from Javi made him feel as though it were a job interview or as though he were asking his boss for a raise. He could feel his hackles trying to rise, all raw edges and resentment over the expectation that someone would say something. Because they always did.

He dropped his hand over the arm of the chair and brushed his fingers over the coarse ruff on Bourneville's shoulders.

"Ten years ago a girl went missing," Cloister said. "Her name was Birdie Utkin. She was fifteen years old."

Javi rolled his sleeves down over his arms and buttoned the cuffs without looking. "Different gender, different age group, large time gap," he said. "I'm not seeing the connection."

The "fuck it" felt like a lump in Cloister's throat. He had to clench his jaw to keep it in, and he shifted uncomfortably. Across the desk Javi waited with his head tilted back against the headrest of the chair.

He wanted to get up, storm out, and slam the door so hard he could imagine glass shattering. The muscles in his thighs were tight with it, ready to move. It would be a stupid, childish thing to do it, but satisfying.

"What you're supposed to do now," Javi said, "is explain your theory. Did she disappear from the Retreat?"

Cloister stood up. He talked better on his feet. Bourneville lifted her head from the floor, her ears pricked as she watched him. He gave her the hand signal to stay, and she dropped her chin back to her paws.

"No. The Retreat was still a group of hippies then." He shoved his hands into his pockets. "It wasn't even Reed in charge. There was someone before him. Real old anarchist type, by all accounts. Birdie Utkin was a good girl—rich family, good grades, boyfriend that her dad liked."

A frown line creased the skin between Javi's eyebrows. "Still in the dark," he said. "And how do you know so much about the case? It would have been before your time."

"I looked into some old case files when I was assigned here," Cloister said. There was a stack of them at his trailer, next to his bed, to fill the hours when he couldn't sleep and Bourneville was too tired to run. Missing kids, lost mothers, dads who never came home—it really didn't take a shrink to work out his issues. "This one stuck with me. Thing is, there was a Hartley mentioned in the original investigation. The boyfriend."

Javi looked skeptical. "Ken Hartley is thirty-four. Unless the Utkins were very open-minded, they wouldn't have approved of him dating their daughter ten years ago."

"Not him. The boyfriend was John Hartley. Still, the name turning up in two missing-child cases?"

Javi looked dubious. "It's not that uncommon a name, Cloister."

The lack of enthusiasm was deflating. When Cloister retrieved the memory that had been itching at him, he was sure it meant something. Maybe he'd been wrong. Except in his gut, he didn't believe that. It had been years since he read Birdie Utkin's file, but there was a reason the Hartley case reminded him of it.

"They never found Birdie," he said.

"That's sad," Javi said. "It doesn't mean it's anything to do with this case."

He paused expectantly, as though he were waiting for Cloister to say something else. There was probably an argument to be made that would at least get Javi to look at the cold case. Cloister couldn't put it into words, though. He just knew there was something linking Birdie Utkin and Drew Hartley beyond the fact that they were both gone.

"Fine," he rasped. A snap of his fingers brought Bourneville to her feet. She yawned to show off sharp white teeth and left a smudge of black fluff on the coarse carpet. "I shouldn't have wasted your time, Agent Merlo."

He took a step toward the door.

"Wait," Javi said. He sounded irritated... or frustrated. "You're jumping to conclusions, Deputy Witte. I'm not saying there's no connection between the cases, but you're the one with the hunch. Convince me."

Cloister didn't want to. His hunches were usually to do with whether to take upstream or down during a manhunt, and he never had to justify them. Then he heard the distinctive sound of a metal cap being screwed off a glass bottle.

"Have a drink," Javi offered as Cloister turned around. He pulled two cloudy glass tumblers from a drawer, tilted the bottle over them, and filled each two-thirds up. "Convince me."

It wasn't the whiskey that convinced him to stay. For once it wasn't even the thought of that poor lost kid. Cloister stayed for the dark look in Javi's eyes and the smug smile on his mouth when Cloister took the glass. He stayed because he was a glutton for punishment.

"To Saul," Javi said as he tapped the base of his glass against Cloister's. Whiskey sloshed against the curved sides of the tumblers, and they gave the flat clink of cheap glass. When Cloister looked askance at the toast, Javi shrugged and lifted the drink to his lips. "His bottle."

They both tossed the whiskey back.

It burned like straight white spirits and had an aftertaste that mixed pine car freshener and sour honey. Cloister held it in his mouth for a second, desperately not wanting to give offense, but then he spat it back into the glass. The taste of it lingered in his mouth and throat like a film of grease.

"That's—"

"Rank." Javi grimaced around the taste. He scrubbed his hand over his mouth. "New plan. Go somewhere with good whiskey, and you can convince me."

IT TURNED out that "somewhere with good whiskey" was the red-brick and plate-glass loft Javi was renting nearby. One wall had been completely replaced with glass, giving a ridiculously good view over the derelict factories and freshly renovated boutiques that filled the neighborhood.

Cloister sat in one of the elegant leather chairs, his long legs sprawled out in front of him, and sipped his glass of whiskey. It was smooth, with a hard, smoky bite, and definitely better than the paint stripper Agent Saul Lee kept hidden in his desk drawer.

Under the blurry comfort of whiskey, guilt gnawed persistently at the pit of Cloister's stomach. A little boy was lost, and what was he doing? Drinking whiskey and, he kinda suspected, being seduced. His conscience would make him pay later, but for the moment, he dulled it with another drink of whiskey. Sometimes you just had to find a way to live with living.

"So you're drinking the whiskey," Javi said as he walked out of the bedroom. He glanced to where Bourneville was snoozing on a tossed-down towel, curled up in a fuzzy black comma. "And your dog has made itself at home. Are you ever going to get around to trying to convince me, or not?"

The suit was gone. Javi had changed into loose black sweatpants and a long-sleeved T-shirt. His feet were bare, and his hair was damp and starting to curl around his ears. It should have looked like he'd loosened up, but he still managed to look intimidatingly severe.

And fucking hot.

Cloister shifted in the chair, and his balls tightened with the reminder that it had been a while since he'd... anything. An insomniac with issues could burn a lot of bridges in a short space of time. The slow-building interest of *thought* sharpened to *hoped* he was getting seduced.

It would probably help if he answered the question instead of sitting there like an idiot. He shifted in the chair to ease the tug of denim across his cock.

"I've got a name and a gut feeling," Cloister said. "Not sure how to sell that to you."

Javi walked over and leaned against the window, long, lean, and silhouetted against the night sky. He lifted the tumbler to his mouth and took a slow sip.

"You make it relevant to my interests," he said. "You explain how doing what you want gets me something I need."

"Like what."

Javi considered him over the rim of the glass for a second. His gaze lingered on Cloister's thighs and then the width of his shoulders. Then he shrugged and tilted his head back against the glass and drained the last of his whiskey. "That's what you have to work out."

Javi pushed himself off the window to get a refill. He lifted the bottle and tilted it toward Cloister in mute question. There was only tinted water left in Cloister's glass, but he shook his head and nursed the dregs.

"It's enough to merit a look," he said. "Just pull the case file from storage and have a look. What do you have to lose?"

"Time," Javi reminded him succinctly as he splashed a generous measure of whiskey into his glass.

The reminder that time was running out for Drew Hartley threw a pall over them both. They were entering the fourth day. There was still hope, but it was against all the evidence and statistics. Cloister propped the glass on his thigh and felt the damp chill through the denim. He reached for a reason that sounded like something Javi would say.

His stepdad had taught him the key to convincing people. They didn't want to hear you being clever. They wanted to hear themselves.

"If I'm right, you won't waste any more time on the wrong suspect," he said. "If I'm wrong, nobody can say you didn't consider all the angles. Either way I'll owe you."

Javi pursed his lips thoughtfully and then nodded. "Better." He walked across the floor toward Cloister. "But debts are only good if you can depend on them."

Ten years since he'd been home, and the answer still growled out of Cloister's chest like he'd never left. "Wittes keep their word."

"Really?" Javi braced his hand on the back of the chair, leaned over, and got into his face with the dark interest that had flickered in and out since the office. "What if it's something you don't want to do?"

"Like what?" Cloister asked. He could taste Javi as he inhaled— soap, lemon, and a clean, fit male smell. He absently swiped his tongue over his lower lip, and Javi dropped his gaze to watch the gesture with unabashed attention.

"I bet you can guess." Javi braced his other arm on the back of the chair and effectively pinned Cloister in place. "Towns this size, people talk."

"You'd be surprised what they leave out," Cloister said. Tension throbbed in his voice, dragging it down to a rough, throaty growl. He supposed it could be misconstrued, though.

Javi kissed him with a hard, impatient slash of mouth and tongue. He twisted a hand in Cloister's hair. His knuckles pressed against his skull, and he tasted of mint under the whiskey. So it *was* a seduction, Cloister thought smugly.

"Like that," Javi said as he pulled back. He sounded so controlled that it was cold, but his hand was still roughly twisted in Cloister's hair, and his breathing had gone ragged around the edges. "What if I asked you to do that? You still going to keep your—"

Cloister grabbed a handful of T-shirt and dragged Javi back down into the kiss. His teeth found the lush curve of Javi's lower lip, and he tugged. He felt the tickle of Javi's sharp intake of breath and surprise run through his lean, tense body.

For a quick count of three, Cloister was in control of the kiss. Then Javi tightened his grip on Cloister's hair and took it back, crushing Cloister down into the chair with a bruising, claiming kiss that left him breathless and hard.

CHAPTER TEN

THAT WAS the problem with a bad decision. Once you knew it was there, eventually you were going to make it. Javi couldn't even blame the liquor for it. He'd known what he wanted before he poured that first glass of gasoline Saul had been keeping in a whiskey bottle in his desk.

He shoved Cloister against the huge window, making it tremble, and bit hot, impatient kisses along Cloister's jaw and back to his mouth. Tomorrow it would be a disaster, so Javi had to make the most of tonight. And more than once, he'd entertained the fantasy of fucking Cloister against the wall of glass.

Cloister made a rough, approving noise into the kiss, grabbed at the hem of Javi's shirt, and tugged it up and over his shoulders. Javi dragged his mouth away from Cloister's long enough to pull the shirt over his head. He tossed it to the side and got yanked back into another kiss as Cloister cupped the back of his neck with a hard hand.

The scrape of callused fingertips against his sensitive skin and the scrape of stubble against his jaw bled heat down Javi's spine. It wasn't what he'd planned, though. He liked things to go as planned.

He grabbed Cloister's wrists, dug his fingers into the thick bands of muscle, and pinned him to the glass. Cloister flexed his long fingers and then clenched them. Javi could feel the play of tendons against his palms. They were nice hands, he noticed—long fingers, wide palms. His mother would have called them pianist's hands and bemoaned the scars and nicks. Javi imagined them on his cock and had to bite the inside of his cheek. *Want* grabbed a fistful of nerve endings and twisted.

"You want to fuck?" he said. "We do it my way."

They didn't exactly get on, so Javi supposed it wasn't so strange he'd never seen Cloister smile before. It was wide and boyish and carved a distracting slice of dimple down his cheek. It didn't repair the nose or heavy bones—Cloister would never be a handsome man—but with that smile, he didn't need to be.

"How's that?" he drawled as he curled his fingers in and wriggled his little fingers. "With our pinkies out?"

Javi shifted his weight and leaned into the hard line of Cloister's body. He could feel the hard bulge of Cloister's cock pressed against his thigh. The contact made Cloister clench his jaw and suck in a breath through his teeth. "You seem to be enjoying it so far," he said.

"In case you haven't noticed," Cloister rasped, the shift of his shoulders and shift of his feet somehow turning his pinned stance into something insolent, "I have issues with authority."

He wasn't smiling anymore. Javi felt a passing urge to change that, but it couldn't compete with the urge to focus on fucking Cloister senseless instead. The pulse under Cloister's jaw jumped, the skin pulled taut by the tilt of his head. Leaning in, Javi bit him hard enough to make him jerk, hard enough to leave a mark. Stubble rasped his lips. It was faintly dusty, the way everything was when the wind picked up, and Cloister pushed against his restraining grip. Not too hard.

"You were in the army, and you're a cop," Javi pointed out. "Odd choices for a free spirit."

"I got other issues too," Cloister said. The muscles Javi was exploring with his mouth moved in a way that suggested he was smirking again. "I'm a complicated man."

He said it as though it were a joke. It wasn't. Javi wasn't a profiler, but he wasn't blind either, and he'd been watching Cloister. If you wanted to have dark, detailed fantasies about someone, you needed to pay attention.

It was a shame. If he'd been easy, Javi might have been able to justify fucking him more than once.

"Well, it's simple," Javi said. His voice was low and sharp around the edges, control pulled tight from his jaw to his cock. "Do as you're told, and I'll fuck you against this window for anyone walking past to see."

Cloister swallowed hard. The sharp lines of his Adam's apple bobbed its betrayal. It wasn't exactly a surrender, but he stopped arguing. Good enough. Javi let go of his wrists, stepped back, and ran his tongue over his lower lip.

"Strip," he said.

Cloister dropped his arms from behind his head and hooked his thumb in the waistband of his jeans. As he unbuttoned them, he gave a slow once-over, his eyes following the flow of muscle down to the flat, taut plane of Javi's stomach.

"I like your body," Cloister said. He left the gaping jeans hanging on his hipbones and grabbed his T-shirt to pull it off. "I was worried those shoulders might just have been good tailoring."

"I'm glad I could clear that up for you," Javi said. "I'm sure it's been keeping you up at night."

"Among other things," Cloister admitted as he tossed the T-shirt. The worn cotton hadn't really hidden much, as the soft fabric clung to every dip and rise of muscle, and Javi had already seen it all the other day. It didn't matter. Seeing it still sucked the moisture out of his mouth.

It was the way Cloister *moved*. The rangy sprawl of muscle and scarred skin was elegant in motion—loose-limbed and sleek. He was like a big cat at the zoo, but he was one Javi would get to touch. The thought tugged lust down the shaft of Javi's cock, and a dull ache twisted in his balls.

Cloister shoved his jeans down and stepped out of the puddle of the denim.

Now *that* bit Javi hadn't seen before. He wasn't disappointed, although he'd have to adjust his fantasies for scale in future. Cloister's cock was bigger than he'd pictured it in his mind's eye—a heavy, fleshy shaft a few shades darker than his skin. The foreskin was trimmed back neatly, showcasing the tight, shiny head as it curved up toward Cloister's flat stomach.

"Your turn," Cloister said as he tilted his head back against the window and bit his lip. He wrapped his hand around his cock and pulled lazily on it with loosely clasped fingers.

Javi closed the distance between them, reached up to grab the back of Cloister's neck, and dragged him down into a kiss. There wasn't much height difference between them, but there was enough, and Javi didn't stretch to meet. He kissed Cloister deeply and shoved his tongue into his mouth. Then he shoved Cloister around to face the window. Cloister caught himself with his hands against the glass, and the muscles in his upper arms and back were tight and defined.

"Dim the lights," Javi said. The overhead lights dimmed to a shadowy twilight. Fucking Deputy Cloister Witte against a window was a fantasy. Having an audience in the street below would be a nightmare. He ran a hand down Cloister's back—the long, smooth lines of it were clammy with sweat—to the curve of his ass. Even in the dim light, he could see it was evenly tanned all over and dusted with freckles. He flexed his fingers against it to feel the hardness of muscle under the layer of soft skin. "Last chance to change your mind, Cloister."

He didn't want to make the offer, and it might have held more moral weight if he hadn't slid a hand between Cloister's legs to roughly squeeze his balls. Cloister made a ragged sound that turned into a curse, and his breath dampened the glass in front of him.

Since a *fuck* wasn't a *no*, Javi emptied the pockets of his exercise pants and then stripped them off. The condom and travel sachet of raspberry-scented lube punched another hole in his patchy excuse that it wasn't planned. He ripped the corner of the sachet open with his teeth. The intense, sickly smell of sugared fruit was faintly repulsive but also familiar enough that, in a Pavlovian sexual response, it made his balls drag up tight to his body.

He coated his fingers and worked the slippery gel into Cloister. He pressed his fingers past the tight ring of muscle and deep inside. Then he hooked his index finger and grazed the firm bump of Cloister's prostate. Cloister clenched his hands into fists against the window, and the knuckles pressed white against the glass. He swallowed hard with a noisy and wet-sounding gulp, and he rocked back against Javi's fingers.

"Just fuck me," he growled impatiently. The snap of command in Cloister's voice should have pissed Javi off. Instead it hit some strange button he didn't know he had. Maybe he knew he was going to fuck that starch right out of the good deputy.

He caught Cloister's hips in his hands and his fingers around the hard knobs of his hipbones and repositioned him. When he finished, Cloister was leaning on the window instead of just against it. The long muscles of his legs were clenched to keep his balance, and his ass and inner thighs were shiny with raspberry lotion.

Javi's cock was so hard it bumped against his stomach, and a dull ache worked its way through his balls and down his thighs. The desire to fuck Cloister, to *have* him against the damn window, was so uncomplicated he wasn't sure he trusted it. There was no denying it, though.

"I don't even know why I want to fuck you," he said as he worked the tight rubber of the condom down over his cock. The sheath was a slippery, wet look against the darker skin of his cock and snug around the base. "You aren't my type."

Cloister was thickly erect. Reflected in the window, his cock jutted at a proud, untouched angle between his spread thighs. "Yeah, well, I wouldn't ask you to prom either," he said. "But you're here, so...."

It was exactly the sort of emotional engagement Javi wanted. None. So he could ignore the ember of annoyance that itched at him. He tugged the firm, freckled globes of Cloister's backside apart and pushed his cock against the tight, puckered asshole. It stretched around him—a tight, gripping pressure on his shaft that popped fireworks of hot pleasure along his nerves and up his spine.

Moonlight picked out the bunched muscles in Cloister's back and shoulders in hard lines defined under his skin. He rocked his hips back, working Javi's cock half an inch deeper inside him. Javi leaned over, grabbed Cloister's shoulder, and dug his fingers into the heavy arch of muscle and used it as a handle.

He pulled back, which made Cloister groan, and then thrust into him again. Sweat and raspberry lube slid between ass and thighs, slick and wet. Cloister swore and begged. He gasped the words out between ragged breaths.

Javi stroked a hand down Cloister's side and over his stomach and felt the muscles clench and relax with each thrust.

"Do you want me to touch you?" he asked as he buried himself inside Cloister with one quick, hard shove. He splayed his hand out over that flat plane of stomach muscle, and his index finger bumped scar tissue. He pulled out and slammed back in again, clenching his jaw on trembling control. The need to fuck Cloister *into* the window pulsed between his ears and inside his balls, but he wanted this first. He spread his hand wider and dipped a slick little finger into Cloister's navel. It was sharply suggestive, enough to make Cloister squirm back against him. "Cloister, I asked you a question."

"Balls deep in me," Cloister groaned, his voice cracking and uneven. It was probably petty to feel smug that he sounded more... undone than Javi did. Javi felt it, anyhow. "And you're still a dick."

"Are you complaining about my dick?" Javi asked as he rolled his hips in a slow, hard thrust that rattled a shuddering, sucked-in "son of a bitch" out of Cloister.

He dropped his head and got enough breath and composure to grit out, "Not your dick, just you."

Javi moved his hand down and to the side, detouring around Cloister's thickly aroused cock to the thin skin at the crease of his thigh. His body was pressed against Cloister's back, and heat soaked between them. Javi could smell him—salt, dog, and sweat over the musky smell of healthy male body. It should have been a reek, but it was faded onto Cloister's skin, and the combination was aggressively masculine.

He pressed a sharp, openmouthed kiss to Cloister's shoulder and chewed that smell off his skin. He rocked his hips again and buried his cock deeper in that tight, hot ass. "You still haven't asked."

"Dick."

"I told you. Only if you ask."

"Touch me."

Javi snorted. "Ask," he said, "not tell."

The sigh reverberated all the way through Cloister, even the parts of him wrapped around Javi's cock. That was... interesting.

"Please," Cloister said. There was less pissiness in his voice than there would have been in Javi's in the same situation. Javi pressed another kiss to Cloister's throat to feel the heat he'd already worked into the skin, and he wondered if he could make him beg.

Maybe. Not tonight, though. His muscles felt leaden, clogged with adrenaline and endorphins, and he could feel his orgasm in a knot of pressure at the small of his back. He decided the *please* was enough and wrapped his hand around Cloister's cock.

It was heavy and hot against his palm—all soft, pliant skin and the throb of blood. Cloister jerked his hips forward into the touch, nearly pulling himself off Javi's cock. His breath was ragged, and it seemed like he couldn't even muster up a staccato swear word. The raw *need* trembling against Javi's palm was almost better than begging. Well, close.

He shoved his cock back into Cloister, twisting his hand back along Cloister's erection at the same time. That got an intelligible word out of Cloister—the gasped syllables of Javi's name. The last threads of Javi's control sliced out of his grip, and he let it go. He pumped his hand roughly along Cloister's cock and kept a counterpoint rhythm to the jerky, jarring thrust of his hips. Hand and cock were never quite in sync.

Cloister folded his arms under him, and his elbows clipped the glass as he ended up braced on his forearms. He managed to dredge a few swear words again and interspersed *fuck, dammit*, and *Javi* between low, throaty grunts.

Pressure built in Javi's spine, scraped up every misfiring, overstimulated nerve ending, and funneled it down into the hot, clenched sack of his balls. He buried his face against Cloister's back, keeping whatever spilled out of him mute. He mouthed against the tanned stretch of skin and hammered his cock into him.

He came, and for a second, the spill of come into someone else was all that mattered. The rest of the world, the Bureau, his career, and even poor, missing Drew Hartley faded into the background. The fulcrum of his world was the spot where cock met ass. Even the grunt and spill of Cloister's orgasm, semen half on Javi's fingers and half on the window, was a side effect.

It was why Javi preferred to keep his sex life and his life separate. Too distracting.

He pushed Cloister full-length against the window and pinned him there, which smeared Cloister's own come over his belly and thighs. His cock was still inside Cloister, and the electric jolt of overstimulation was enjoyable in its own way.

"Anyone could see you," he rasped in Cloister's ear. Cloister's haphazardly chopped blond hair tickled his jaw. "Fucked raw and sticky from enjoying it. What do you think they'd do then?"

Cloister rested his forehead against the glass to catch his breath. "I don't know," he said. "Probably take a picture."

He sounded unconcerned, but that was probably because he didn't think it was likely he'd see anyone he knew. If one of his neighbors did walk by, Javi doubted he would be so cocky. Not that it mattered anyhow, he reminded himself.

Exhaustion tugged at him. He felt wrung out of come, and he hadn't slept properly in a couple of days. The bedroom seemed unfeasibly far. If he didn't have company, he'd have folded himself onto the couch and napped. Since he did, and showing Cloister to the door would, as with bed, involve crossing a ridiculous distance, he idly considered various solutions.

The sound of a yawn that didn't come from either him or Cloister pushed fresh energy into his muscles. He pulled away from Cloister, the back of his neck raw with paranoia, and twisted around.

Instead of… whatever he expected… he found that damn dog stretched out on his leather couch and watching them with what could best be described as an unimpressed expression. As much as a dog could have an expression.

"Was your dog watching us fuck?" He dragged the condom off and bent down to grab his exercise pants off the floor. The dog dropped her chin to her paws.

"Well, it's not like she can turn on the TV," Cloister said mildly. That should have been the nail in his coffin. Somehow, when Cloister, through a jaw-cracking yawn, asked if he should go—

"No," Javi said, yanking his pants back on. His voice sounded dour, and he wasn't sure what he wanted it to actually sound like. More enthusiastic? Less? In the end he went with the familiar suite of emotions—frustration and banked lust. "It's late. You've been drinking. Stay the night, sober up, and you can go in the morning."

CHAPTER ELEVEN

THREE HOURS' sleep was not enough. Javi woke up groggily just before it turned five. He was facedown on his bed, sweating sex into sheets that smelled like fabric softener instead of bodies. Cloister had crashed on the couch, and his long legs dangled ridiculously over the edge. At the time, Javi was relieved. He preferred to sleep alone, especially in California. Winter in Minnesota could make spooning seem appealing. Midwinter in San Diego and you ended up glued to the other person like a sweaty thigh to vinyl.

But waking up alone and smelling of sex felt odd and empty.

He rolled over, sat up, and squinted into the glare of lights through the window. The waistband of his pants cut low across his stomach, baring the dark trail of hair that arrowed down to his groin. He scratched it absently as he listened for the sounds of someone moving about. Nothing. Cloister must still be asleep.

That was an… odd thought. Usually the only people there were Javi's housekeeper and, once a year, his family. The thought of someone new sleeping in his space felt more intimate than he was comfortable with. Of course, he thought with a jab of bitter self-mockery, sharing a coffee cup was more intimate than he was comfortable with.

He slid out of bed and grabbed his phone from the bedside table on the way by. It hadn't rung during the night, so nothing dramatic had changed in any of his cases. He flicked through his notifications anyhow, scanned the important ones, and logged the actions he needed to take.

An email from J.J. Diggs directing him to funnel all further communications with the Hartleys through him. It ended with an allusion to their onetime fuck that was so veiled Javi wasn't sure if it was a threat or an invitation. A text from Frome telling him that Reed would be available for an interview tomorrow afternoon at four, which would take some schedule reshuffling. He tapped over the screen and fired off a quick email to Debi to do that once she got in at eight, and he stepped into the main room.

He looked up and frowned as he hit send. The room was empty, the sex-smeared window wiped down, and the bedding he tossed to Cloister the night before neatly folded on a side table. No wonder the place was quiet. Apparently Cloister liked to get his walk of shame over with early.

"Son of a bitch," Javi muttered.

It took him twenty minutes to shower and get dressed. He shrugged his suit jacket on and ignored the drawling memory of Cloister admiring his body. The bedding and the crumpled-up towel he found under the TV—covered with dog fluff and slobber—he tossed in the laundry basket for the housekeeper.

On the way down to his car, he called Frome.

"Pull the case files on the Utkin disappearance for me?" he said when Frome answered. Frome had that "awake but low on coffee" scrape to his voice that meant he was either up early or up late. A less hot version of Cloister's rasp.

"Utkin? Why?"

"Call it a hunch."

"Okay. I'll have them sent to your office."

"I'll pick them up this afternoon," Javi said.

Frome grunted his agreement, and Javi hung up. He hesitated with the phone in his hand and wrestled over whether or not to call Cloister. He needed to talk to him and make sure they were on the same page about last night. But he also needed to get on the road if he was going to get to RJD Correctional Facility and back in time to look over the Utkin files.

He also didn't *want* to have an awkward conversation. So the phone went in his pocket, and he got in the car and switched the engine on with a touch of a button. The radio beeped gently as it synced with his phone, and his driving playlist queued itself up automatically. Javi canceled it midsong, glanced over his shoulder briefly as he pulled out of the space, and put the phone into dictation mode.

It was two and half hours to the State prison on a good day. Throw in at least one traffic jam, and Javi would have time to narrate most of the reports he'd put on a back burner during the week.

PRISONS ALWAYS smelled foul. It was a mixture of body fluids, boiled grease, and misery. The prisoners probably had more pressing issues to worry about, but it caught in Javi's nose whenever he had to visit.

He sat on the hard metal chair in the interview room with Branko Nemac's file open on the table in front of him as he flicked through it. The photo attached was of a smiling, middle-aged man with a nicely starched collar and a sharply trimmed beard standing in for an actual chin. The leader of a local Albanian gang, Nemac thought he was untouchable until Saul linked the murder of a young waitress to the outwardly affable gangster.

He killed her because he thought she spat in his food.

There were plenty of criminals with a reason to have a grudge against Agent Saul Lee, but Nemac was the only one with a grudge and the resources to do something about it. He wasn't the boss these days. That hostile takeover had left three people dead and Nemac short half a lung, but he still had contacts. More importantly, or so the FBI believed, he still had access to a significant amount of money he'd skimmed off the top over the years. In his circles the money meant more than the loyalty.

The shuffle-rattle of chains in the hallway distracted Javi from the file. He flipped the cover shut as he looked up and kept his face composed as the door opened and Nemac shuffled into the room.

The meticulously barbered beard was scruffier, and the affability had worn off. Otherwise Nemac hadn't changed. He still smiled too much.

"Agent Merlo. The pretty boy," he said. "I'd heard you stepped into Lee's shoes. Who'd have thought he had a heart, eh?"

The guards shoved him into a chair and cuffed his hands securely to the table. He went along with it genially and tapped his fingertips absently on the scuffed Formica. Job done, the guards gave Javi the usual list of rules and told him to yell if he needed help.

Javi waited until they left the room, and then he raised his eyebrows at Nemac.

"It sounds like you're still holding a grudge against Agent Lee," he said.

"Me?" Nemac asked. "He's dead. I'm not. I win."

"You're still in here."

Nemac shrugged. "And he's in the dirt. I still win."

"Winning seems very important to you," Javi noted.

Contempt twisted Nemac's face. "That's because I'm a winner." He slapped his cuffed hand on the table. "You know who says winning isn't important? People who don't win."

"So when Agent Lee arrested you, that must have been a blow."

A humorless smile folded Nemac's mouth. "Don't think anyone fucking enjoys it."

"True, but most people don't spend as much time boasting about being untouchable as you did," Javi pointed out. "What was it you said when you were sentenced? He'd regret it, that you'd take everything away from him...?"

Nemac sat back in the chair with his arms stretched out in front of him. The cuffs of his shirt slid back, flashing the heavy black iconography worked into the skin of his arms.

"And like I said, he's dead. I'm not."

"Agent Lee's grandson has gone missing," Javi said. "Eighteen-year-old waitresses and ten-year-old little boys—sounds like your speed, doesn't it?"

A muscle tightened in Nemac's cheek. It squirmed under the coarse, drink-veined skin. "Fuck you, Merlo."

That particular invective was a lot hotter when Cloister growled it. Javi ignored his brief mental digression and studied Nemac's face. He wasn't expecting guilt. Nemac once took his ex-wife, the mother of his son, to Nevada and left her in the desert in her underwear and bare feet. Or at least that's what they believed happened. Afterward, from her hospital bed, the woman insisted it was a tragic accident. She dropped the custody case against Nemac too.

The expression Nemac had in that second was what Javi was looking for—a repulsive sort of smug satisfaction that his entitled view of what he deserved was what he was getting—just the dead-shark blank of a man who didn't care about anything beyond his own skin.

"I imagine making good on that promise would impress your old associates," Javi pointed out. "It might convince them that you're not a has-been."

Nemac turned his head and spat contemptuously on the cheap tiles. "Who the fuck do you think killing a ten-year-old impresses,

Merlo?" He leaned forward, and his shackles rattled as he braced his hands flat against the table. His breath was sour. Javi glanced at the door and, with a slightly raised finger, dismissed the hovering guard's instinct to help. "If I'd done this, and I'm not saying I did, it'd make me look weak—like I was scared to do anything when Lee was alive—or mental. Neither makes me look good, does it? Taking the kid wouldn't profit me, and in case you haven't noticed, I'm not exactly in a position to go sneaking around some bitch's house at night."

He sat back, looked away from Javi, and stared at the wall as he sucked his cheeks in. After a second spent studying Nemac's pallid face over the beard, Javi gestured for the guards to take him away.

If it was Nemac, he wasn't going to admit or negotiate. But Javi didn't think it was.

The guards unshackled Nemac and hauled him to his feet. He leaned back against them, braced his feet against the floor, and smirked at Javi.

"Still," he said. "I hope the kid's still alive… and that someone real bad got him. I hope he dies hard."

BACK IN Plenty, Javi looked at the yellowed case file and wondered if Bridget "Birdie" Utkin had died hard. The picture in the file showed her wearing the height of fashion from ten years before, the gently dated image faintly sorrowful despite her grin. There were no updated pictures for the pretty blonde girl with the squint and the, according to the identifying features section of the old missing-person report, butterfly tattoo on her hip.

"I remember that case," the plump young woman who brought him the file said. After a second of drawing a blank, he remembered her fumbling a plastic bag and the wind taking it while she cursed. She'd had to get him another one. Tancredi.

She lingered in the doorway with her arms crossed and a frown pleating her faded red eyebrows together.

"I didn't know you were one of the PD's officers who stayed after the Bureau took over this office."

She shook her head. "I'm not. I lived in town for a while, though, when I was a teenager. My mom did some work for Mr. Utkin. She was a realtor. Do you think what happened to Birdie has something to do with the Hartley boy?"

Javi lifted his shoulder in a pleasant but unresponsive shrug. He had set up shop in the relatives' room with its tape-patched pleather seats, drinking coffee that hadn't got any better since the last time. The box file sat on the floor next to him, the cardboard dry and faded in patches.

"Do you have a minute to talk about it?" he asked and pointed at a chair opposite.

Tancredi glanced over her shoulder for a second and then nodded and stepped inside. She closed the door, sat down opposite him, and rested the heels of her hands on her knees. "I didn't know her that well," she said. "She was younger than me…. I didn't really think about her at all until she disappeared."

"I have the case files." Javi tapped a finger against the manila folder that rested on his knee. "I know the details of the case. Tell me what the town was like at the time."

"*Tense*," Tancredi said, exaggerating the shape of her mouth around the word. "It was meant to be safe in Plenty, you know? Open space for kids to play, no crime, friendly neighborhood police…."

She trailed off with a sardonic twist of her mouth. That last expectation, at least, had ended with disillusionment and scandal.

"I remember that my mom wouldn't let me do anything for the rest of the year," Tancredi went on. "She thought she'd been snatched. Some people thought Birdie ran away. Nobody ever knew, though. Not for sure. I always figured she ran away. A lot of those kids did, you know."

"What did you mean about her family wanting to keep her out of trouble?"

"Oh, she'd been hanging out with some local kids," Tancredi said. "Looking back, they were just petty crooks. They did drugs in derelict houses, and they vandalized the new builds and got into fights. Back then, though, we thought they were gangsters. I heard that Birdie was hanging out with them, but her parents put a stop to that."

"What about the boyfriend?" Javi asked.

Tancredi pursed her lips. "Umm, I didn't know him. He was…." She blinked as her memory finally caught up with her. "He was a Hartley, wasn't he? John Hartley. I'd forgotten that. It probably doesn't mean anything. I mean, there's a lot of them in town."

There were. Javi had done his research at a roadside stop with his phone hooked into a McDonald's Wi-Fi connection after he accepted that Cloister's hunch had moved into his brain. Plenty of Hartleys, but there were only a few degrees of separation between John and Drew Hartley. They were cousins. It would have been enough to tag the man as a suspect, if John hadn't moved to Australia to go to college and not been back since.

"How did Birdie and her boyfriend know each other?"

Tancredi shook her head slowly. "I don't know," she said. "I mean, Kelly Hartley—Ken Hartley's aunt, the bank president? She was friends with the Utkins. My mom said she was always up at the house in those days. Maybe that's how."

She paused with the tip of her tongue caught between her teeth and her nose scrunched up.

"What?"

"Mom used to say a lot. She thought Mr. Utkin and Kelly were having an affair," she said almost apologetically. "Mom was a bit of a gossip."

"In our line of work, gossips can be useful," Javi said. "Thanks for the background, Deputy."

She took the hint, stood up, and headed for the door.

"Look," she said as she hesitated at the doorway. "I don't know if this has anything to do with it, but Witte's right."

"He is?" Javi said, irritation sharpening his voice more than the helpful Deputy Tancredi probably deserved. It made her wince, and she hunched her shoulders as though she were weathering a blow, but she forged on.

"There's no way we missed that phone," she said. "People underestimate Witte all the time, but he's damn good at his job. We all are. Even if one of us, *somehow*, missed an iPhone right in the middle of our search area? No way we all did."

She looked earnest and intent, determined to defend the integrity of her department. She probably knew Cloister better than he did. Fucking a man didn't give you a shortcut to his inner self.

"I'll bear that in mind, Deputy," he said.

She grimaced an awkward smile and closed the door behind her as she left. Javi went back to the files and shuffled through the stacks of reports and crime-scene photos as though they were a stack of cards. That two members of the same family were involved in similar disappearances a decade apart was... thin.

On the other hand, it wasn't nothing.

That was the status quo for the next half hour as he hunted through the old investigation for anything he could use. He found nothing that actually demonstrated a link, but just enough to sustain that bit of suspicion that there might be *something* to Cloister's hunch. The memory of the night before sidled through his brain to remind him Cloister *had* said he'd still owe him. The thought hung around his brain, all sticky, sly temptation as he hefted the box in his arms and headed out. He had no intention of indulging it. The fallout from their one-night stand was still to come, and he didn't need to pencil in new fuckups, but his libido didn't seem to care.

The silent shudder of the phone in his pocket dragged him out of the mire of distracting lust and badly written notebooks. Javi straightened up, craned his neck from one side to the other to make his vertebrae crackle, and tugged the phone out.

A quick glance at the screen confirmed it was the lab calling. He quickly swiped Accept on the call and lifted the phone to his ear.

"Merlo," he said. "Do you have the results on the bottle?"

"Yes. Yes, we do," the voice on the other end said. The remnants of an old stutter caught between the words. All the syllables got out, but with odd gaps between. It was worse in person. If Fletcher could see your eyes, he could hardly get the words out. "Whoever blended this together was *not* looking for a good trip. It's a blend of Red Bull, dipt... diisopropyltryptamine—an hallucinogen—and, in a blast from the past, mephedrone."

"Foxy has been on the rise in Southern California," Javi pointed out absently as he tucked an evidence bag back into the box.

"I know," Fletcher said. "I've seen it coming through the lab a couple of times this year, although Plenty is still predominantly meth. I've never heard of it being mixed like this, though. Besides, this mephedrone is an old chemical composition that used to turn up in Bath Salts."

Javi paused and tapped the top of the box absently with his fingers. "How old?"

There was a pause and the sound of keys clacking quickly in the background. "Like I said, it's an old composition. Most of the drugs in the US used MPDV. Mephedrone was used mostly in Europe. I guess 2004 to 2008?"

"Has it ever turned up in Plenty before?"

"Possibly, but like I said, Plenty's always been a meth town," Fletcher said. "And not always great with keeping records. Sorry."

"No," Javi said. "That's really useful. Thank you."

More than useful. Fletcher's call had finally tipped Cloister's hunch enough toward likely to warrant further investigation. Not that Javi was going to acquit Billy Hartley just yet—the boy was clearly hiding something, and he was the last person to see his brother—but if a thirteen-year-old were going to drug someone, he'd use his mother's valium or take a drug dealer's free meth sample, not a drug that was popular back when the missing Birdie was hanging around with drug dealers.

He forced the lid back onto the box, stood up, and tucked it under his arm as he headed down to the back office. Mel looked up from the computer as Javi set the archive box on her desk. A flick of sharp blue eyes behind cat-eye glasses acknowledged he was there, and an uplifted finger told him to wait. She gave clipped orders in a brisk voice and then pulled her headphones down to hang around her neck.

"What?"

Either Mel had been on dispatch long enough to adopt the staccato rhythm of police radio in her everyday speech, or she just didn't care for being disturbed.

"Detective Sean Stokes," Javi said. "You remember him?"

She arched her straight, peppery brows curiously. "I do. Good detective. Bad taste in friends."

That meant he'd only been passively corrupt—blind eyes instead of kickbacks.

"Is he still in town?"

Mel nodded. She click-tapped her fingers over the keyboard of her computer, and a frown pinched the line between her eyebrows deeper. She grabbed a pen and scribbled an address down with writing that ran diagonally over the Post-it.

"Here," she said and held it out.

She hung on to the corner as Javi tried to take it. "He never liked the Feds. It would have driven him to the brink having a resident agency here."

Her piece said, she pulled her headphones back on and went back to work.

Javi checked the address and mentally revised his opinion of Stokes—blind eyes and *some* kickbacks. A local cop didn't buy a house in Spruce Groves on his salary alone.

CHAPTER TWELVE

THE RETREAT had opened its rec hall to the search effort and piled up hi-vis vests and hastily laminated maps on trestle tables along one wall. Groups of people clutched whistles in sweaty hands and listened to quick and dirty instructions on good search protocol while news cameras filmed from the sidelines and, with the Hartleys leaving their lawyer to talk to the public, pulled out random people for heartrending interviews.

Cloister grabbed a bottle of water from one of the ice chests. There was plenty to go around. The Retreat's lanky groundskeeper had been hauling in buckets of ice and crates of water once or twice an hour. Cloister didn't know if Reed had approved it or not, but Matt gave him an awkward, crooked smile when he asked.

"I know what it is to be thirsty," he said as he wiped a condensation-wet hand over the sun-scorched back of his neck.

One of the reporters had come over to ask him questions then, and Matt made himself scarce. So it wasn't just handsome FBI agents who made him uncomfortable.

Cloister twisted the lid off the bottle, poured it into a bowl for Bourneville, and presented it firmly under her nose. She sneezed into it, turned in a fretful circle, and stepped over the leash like it was a jump rope. Given the option, she'd rather run herself into heat exhaustion than get pulled from a hunt with nothing to show for it.

It was a good trait when they were actually tracking, but they weren't even sure Drew was still in the area. Most of the deputies had been pulled away, leaving SAR volunteers to beat the bushes and canvas neighboring farms and businesses. Cloister wanted to bring the boy home too, but he wouldn't run himself or his dog to death to do it. He caught Bourneville's collar and showed her the water again.

"Drink," he ordered.

She sighed, and her ribs heaved under her dusty coat. She stuck her nose into the water.

"Here," a teenager said as she handed Cloister a bottle. She was wearing a badge with Drew's face on it. Most of the new volunteers were. Cloister had no idea who organized that or when. "You look nearly as thirsty as she does."

"Thanks." Cloister nodded at her. She smiled back and then looked guilty about it.

While she handed out more bottles around the room, Cloister took a drink, and the cold hit his sternum like a heart attack. It made him grimace, but he kept drinking. The dull headache that had been dogging him for the last hour eased off, and the scratch in his throat disappeared. Maybe Bourneville wasn't the only idiot with a tendency to overcommit.

He squatted against the wall with his head tilted back and the water bottle dangling between his knees. The back of his neck felt hot and itchy with sunburn, and sweat and dust had turned the morning's pleasant ache into a chafed itching. None of which he'd care about if it weren't for the heavy feeling of futility lodged in the pit of his stomach.

The pitch of the room changed abruptly, and the soft murmur of emotional interviews was replaced with sharp, overlapping questions.

"...questioned the family...."

"Is there any chance of finding Drew Hartley alive after...."

"...respond to theories that Drew's disappearance is linked to the recent arrival of immigrants...."

Cloister knew who'd arrived even before he heard Javi's low, measured tones responding to the questions with reassuring but uninformative sound bites. His voice reached under Cloister's skin and tweaked at the nerve bundles.

It had always done that, of course. The difference was that, instead of thinking Javi was a dickhead, Cloister was thinking about Javi's dick.

He lifted his head off the wall and watched Javi deal with the press. It was "too soon to know anything" and "irresponsible and inaccurate to jump to those conclusions," and a promise to update them the minute they knew anything. He looked around as he talked, and he scanned the room until he finally caught slight of Cloister. When he did, he narrowed his eyes slightly and inclined his chin in brusque acknowledgment.

It was hardly the warmest greeting, but Cloister's cock still twitched with the memory of Javi's hand on him and the rasp of that controlling voice in his ear. He mentally told it to behave, which worked about as well as it usually did, and he pushed himself up the wall. Bourneville looked up at him, and water dripped from her chin as she cocked her head.

"Not yet," he told her.

Javi extracted himself from the journalists and strode over to Cloister. "I need a local officer to take point on an interview."

"You'd be better off with Tancredi," Cloister said. "She's sharp."

"I don't need sharp. I need…" Javi paused and chewed over the word choice. "…approachable. I've already cleared it with Frome."

Approachable? Cloister wasn't sure he appreciated that description. For most of his life, looking like the guy most likely to throw a punch had helped him avoid having to throw any punches. He caught himself scowling and pulling his eyebrows down in his best off-putting brood. Javi looked unimpressed.

"I guess I don't have a choice, then," he said.

"It was your hunch," Javi said. He glanced down at Bourneville and frowned. "We can take your car too. It already smells of dog."

The dull, guilty feeling that had been gnawing at Cloister since he rolled off Javi's couch took its teeth out of him. He pushed himself off the wall and held his tongue on the questions he wanted to ask. The media already had too many theories about the case. They didn't need any more.

"So you're not straight," Javi said. He'd rolled the window down and laid his arm along the edge of the door. Black-lensed sunglasses hid his eyes. Glancing over at him, Cloister wasn't sure that being able to see his eyes would help. Fucking Javi hadn't made him any easier to read.

"Yeah, no shit, Sherlock," he said as he swung his attention back to the road. A crow sat in the road ahead of them, pecking and pulling at sun-dried roadkill. Whatever it was had been there long enough and gone under enough tires that all he could say for sure was that it was once brownish in color. The crow waited until it was dangerously close to joining its dinner before it took off and half flapped and half hopped to the side of the road to wait for them to pass. Bourneville ruffed at it through the back window with her "I'm in the work car, so I gotta behave, but I see you" bark. Cloister reached back one-handed to give her a pat. "I can see how you got into the FBI."

He didn't need to look at Javi to know he was being glared at. He could feel it on the side of his face.

"I never said I was straight."

"You never said you weren't."

"That's because that would be weird," Cloister said. He tugged the hem of his shirt. He'd changed into the spare gear he kept in the car, but it covered over a morning's worth of dust and sweat. It itched. "What did you want me to do, pull you aside in the middle of a manhunt and say, 'By the way, I like cock'? Besides, if you thought I was straight, what exactly did you think was going to happen last night?"

There was a pause, and then Javi snorted. "Ninety percent chance of an ugly scene, 10 percent chance of 'I was bi all along,'" he said. "Either way, I'd get to stop wondering what you'd do if I stuck my cock in you."

The mirror at the Rottsdown Road blind turn caught the sun, and the flash of reflected light made Cloister squint. He took the turn and slanted another look at Javi once the road straightened out again.

"I'm a redneck and a police officer," he said. "What if I'd pulled a gun?"

Javi snorted.

Cloister wasn't sure if he should take that as an insult or not. Maybe it was because he was "approachable." He sneered at that idea from inside his head.

"For the record," Javi said, "it won't go beyond me. If you aren't... out, I mean."

"I've been out since I was fourteen and my stepdad caught me masturbating over a Colin Farrell photospread in a magazine."

"Awkward," Javi said. His voice sounded careful—the tone you took when you weren't sure if you were poking a raw spot or not. "Did he... react badly?"

"Fucker laughed at me," Cloister said. The old indignity still stung, but that wasn't entirely fair, not to his dad. "No. I had my problems with him, but he never gave a crap about me being gay."

"You're lucky."

Cloister laughed, but there wasn't much humor in it. "Not often," he said. "So I guess I was owed something."

That seemed to dry up the conversation. For the next half mile, the only sound in the car was Bourneville panting in the back. The suburbs grew up around them as they drove. Dusty scrub and lizards gave way to artificially verdant patches of lawn and neighborhood watch signs.

"So, if you aren't in the closet," Javi said, sounding like he resented spitting the words out, "how come you made yourself scarce this morning?"

He sounded like he didn't want to ask, and Cloister didn't particularly want to answer. There were a load of reasons why a man crawled off a sofa after two hours' sleep and let himself out, from a lifelong problem with affection to a need to take the dog out for a crap.

"Your couch is uncomfortable," he said instead, picking the most innocuous truth. "Besides, admit it, you were relieved. If you had any more commitment issues, a flag saying 'no strings' would have popped out of your cock when you came."

"I don't have commitment issues," Javi said.

Cloister swung his black Tacoma into the curved, cobblestone-paved driveway and parked behind a row of cars. The house was long, low, and white as a seashell—one of the sprawling plantation-style buildings that supplanted the modernist boxes that used to dominate the suburb. They had a dog. Cloister could hear it barking its shrill displeasure at their arrival.

"We had sex, and you told me to sleep on the couch," Cloister said as he turned the engine off.

"I didn't want to get fleas in my bed," Javi said, his voice clipped with annoyance.

"Seriously?" Cloister asked, raising his eyebrows. "So instead of commitment issues, you'd rather people think you're a snob with a taste for rough trade? Not what I'd pick, but up to you."

He got out of the car, slammed the door on Javi's spluttered protest, and got Bourneville. She hopped out, shook herself, and shed a cloud of dust and hair.

"I meant the dog," Javi said over the roof of the car. He'd taken his sunglasses off, and he folded the legs to tuck them into his pocket as he spoke. His dark eyes squinted against the sun. "Where you go, it follows."

"You don't like dogs?" Cloister asked.

"I like them fine," Javi said as he gave Bourneville an uncomfortable look. Cloister was pretty sure it was a lie. "They just don't belong indoors. That's why we invented kennels."

Cloister cocked his head to the side. "You did *not* have a dog when you were a kid, did you?"

"We moved a lot," Javi said. "Pets were an extra responsibility my parents didn't want. Why?"

"Explains a lot," Cloister said.

"No. It doesn't."

He didn't sound amused, so Cloister dropped it. But if Javi made *that* face over Cloister's trailer, he'd have to take him by his childhood home sometime. Working dogs stayed in the kennels, but old dogs made the move to being pets, and his mom had bred a small pack of bad-tempered Pomeranians that chased dust bunnies like they were a wolf pack. Cloister hadn't seen a cushion that didn't have a layer of dog hair on it until he was ten.

His good sense jerked the reins on that because Javi wasn't going to be around long enough to get used to the trailer. Even if he were, one mind-blowing hour against a window was not a good reason to plan a trip home to meet the parents. Not after so many years.

No falling in love, Cloister reminded himself as they walked up the drive to the shiny blue front door. No getting overattached like a stray dog shown some affection. Javi Merlo was just a hot asshole who got under Cloister's skin, not the next ex-boyfriend he was going to disappoint.

He fell easily. It didn't mean he was any good at it.

BEHIND THE bright blue door, Sean Stokes made them coffee. It was black and thick enough to stand a spoon up in but not nearly as bitter as the man who made it.

"So what is this?" he asked as he poured a shot of whiskey into his coffee. It was, Cloister supposed, past noon. From the backyard, Sean's dog—a perpetual-motion spaniel—barked itself into a confused frenzy of adoration and hatred over Bourneville, who ignored it gamely from where she sprawled. "The Feds couldn't get anything on me back then, so now you're back for a second bite of the apple?"

Javi smiled like a shark. "Why? Is there something for me to find?"

It was hard to tell if Javi was playing up the antagonism as "bad cop" or just acting according to his nature. Cloister leaned forward to pick up his cup. The ceramic was hot against the palm of his hand.

"You've seen the missing kid on the news?" he asked.

Sean sniffed and leaned back against the kitchen counter. It might be past noon, but he looked like he'd just gotten out of bed in boxers and a faded T-shirt. His hair hadn't been brushed yet, and his eyes were still bloodshot from last night's hangover.

It didn't look as though early retirement suited him.

"News, Facebook, telegraph poles, pinned up at Whole Foods," he said as he drank his spiked coffee. He squinted, seemingly balancing pain and curiosity. "Only place I haven't seen him is on the back of a milk carton. I'm sure they'll get there, though. What's it got to do with me?"

"Birdie Utkin," Cloister said. A muscle clenched in Sean's jaw and bulged under the skin at the name. "You were the detective on her case."

The coffee was hot enough to scald, even with milk and whiskey in it. Sean drained his cup, grimaced around the burn, and set it down with a clatter in the sink.

"I was the detective on a lot of cases," he said. He cut his gaze across to Javi. "Until the FBI got me canned."

"The Plenty police force was corrupt," Javi said.

"I wasn't."

"Yet you seem to have something to hide."

Sean snorted. "Time for you to go."

"Wait." Cloister raised his voice. "Look, this isn't anything to do with corruption. We just want to know about the Utkin case."

Sean looked sour. "I thought you said it wasn't anything to do with corruption." He stalked out of the kitchen, his bare feet slapping against the wooden floor.

It wasn't the sort of thing someone said when they weren't going to talk to you. Cloister glanced at Javi and raised his eyebrows. He got a mouthed "go" in answer, set his coffee down, and followed Sean. Javi stayed behind with a reproachful-looking Bourneville.

The house was all white plastered walls and pale wood floors. There wasn't a lot of furniture. Sean slouched in the one chair and scowled out at the spaniel that was spinning around the garden, barking manically through the sliding glass doors, and then doing another lap.

"It's not even my dog," Sean said without looking at Cloister. "My ex's. Took the furniture, left the dog."

"After you lost your job?"

"After I lost my wedding ring in a hooker." Sean pulled a rueful face and then shrugged it off. "You wanna know if Hartley had anything to do with the first disappearance?"

Cloister nodded. Sean stared at him and idly scratched at the scruff of silvering stubble on his jaw.

"Well, case has been a long time closed, but hypothetically? Couldn't tell you," Sean said. He shoved his hand through his hair, making it stick up in all new directions. "First day the case came over my desk, Captain told me to close it as soon as possible. Just another runaway, he said. No need to make waves."

"Who was pressuring him?"

"Couldn't swear to it," Sean said, "but the Utkins were telling everyone that we weren't doing enough to find their kid. I got letters from the mother right up until the time the FBI turned me out of my desk. Poor old girl is probably still sending them. Besides, by that point, the captain had some expensive tastes to keep up, and the Utkin coffers were dry."

"They were broke?"

Sean waved a hand at the empty room, the scuffed marks on the floor and brackets on the wall mute testimony to what used to be there. "Not broke like this," he said. "I got a reverse mortgage, and I'm still paying for the TV my ex is watching football on. The Utkins had a shitload of property they'd brought up but no ready cash. Unlike their good family friend, who also happened to be a very overprotective mother."

"Kelly Hartley."

Sean made a gun with his fingers and cocked it. "She was all sweetness and light around the Utkins, but the minute she had me alone, she was singing the same song the captain was—just another runaway. And it was probably true," he said. "No one dragged her out that window. She went under her own steam. Things were bad at home between her parents, she'd had a huge fight with Hartley Junior, and her friends said she'd been back in touch with her ex. Whatever happened to her happened later. Thing was, no one cared enough to find out. Including me."

His self-loathing settled like beer, and he seemed to wait expectantly for someone to absolve him of blame. It wasn't going to come from

Cloister. Angry words were hooked into the back of his tongue. He wanted to tell Sean that he didn't get to sit in judgment of the captain's corruption. He'd been just as bad, just cheaper.

It wouldn't help.

"What was your theory?" he asked instead.

Sean huffed out a sigh and scratched his jaw again. "She'd been IMing one of her friends that her ex wanted her to hook up again. Said that *of course* she wasn't going to, that she had a boyfriend." He shrugged one shoulder. "I think she was lying and that she went to see him that night. If she ever got there or not, I don't know."

Javi interrupted as he leaned against the doorframe with Bourneville skirting around him. She padded over to Cloister and leaned against his leg, pointedly not looking at him. "What did the ex-boyfriend say? Or did you even talk to him?"

Sean tried for a sneer. The expression didn't get any traction. His grudge against the FBI slid off his guilt. He leaned forward and rested his elbows on his knees.

"I spoke to him a couple of times," he said. "He was homeless. Cute enough to pass for a bad boy instead of a loser. Did pot instead of meth. Night that Birdie disappeared, though, he was in the hospital getting his scalp stitched back on. One of his friends had taken a bottle to his head. Besides, he seemed genuinely devastated. Altered but devastated."

"What was his name?"

Sean pulled a face and rubbed his hand through his hair again as though he could massage the memory back to the surface. "It was ten years ago," he said.

"You let Birdie Utkin down," Cloister said. "You remember that."

"I doubt it was even his real name," Sean said after a second. "Umm, Hector something. Hector Andrew? Anders? He was sixteen, seventeen? A few years older than Birdie was. Just another kid. He lived in his car, an old '69 Charger, but it was mostly primer and rust by then. It'd be dust on the wind by now. Look, what happened with Birdie was shit. She got brushed under the rug to keep the Hartley kid out of the news and to stop the bottom falling out of the real estate market. Didn't want any of those nice San Diego professionals getting cold feet about the move, right? Still, I don't see how my case is connected to the missing kid. There's a lot of Hartleys in town. Bad things have to happen to them sometimes, right?"

Javi pushed himself off the door. "It's not your case anymore," he said. "It's mine. Thanks for your help, Mr. Stokes. We'll let ourselves out."

He left. Cloister went to follow him and nudged Bourneville with his knee to get her to stop ignoring him. She grunted, stood up, and pointedly stretched her forelegs out.

"Wait," Sean said. He shoved himself up out of his chair and patted his thighs with his hands until he seemed to remember he was just wearing boxers. "Shit. Hold on."

He loped into the kitchen, came back out, and caught Cloister in the hallway.

"Here." He shoved a dog-eared card into Cloister's hand, the edges of it grubby from being shoved in a wallet. It said *Stokes Investigations* on the top in stark black lettering. "If you find anything out about Birdie, anything, let me know? I was a good detective. It never sat right with me, the way I let her down."

Cloister's chest was still tight with anger, but he knew what it was like to not get answers. He inclined his head in a tight nod, tucked the card into his back pocket, and followed Javi out the front door.

It was bright enough to make him squint, and the spaniel was still shouting at Bourneville from behind its fence. Javi stood next to the car. He was on the phone.

"...Tancredi," he said as Cloister walked over, "where did Birdie and those kids used to hang out?"

CHAPTER THIRTEEN

IT MIGHT have been a Charger once. That would be down to the lab to confirm once they scraped off the char and rust and rebuilt the bits that had rotted away. It smelled like mildew and piss, layered over the particular rancid aroma of cooked vermin. The back seat was shredded, the stuffing gutted down to the springs, and the tires were naked, scuffed rims in pits of melted tarmac.

"You'd think someone would have towed it," Cloister said as he wiped rust and sticky grease on his jeans.

"It's on a private plot, not a public road. No one has to take responsibility, so no one will," Javi said. He pushed his sunglasses up onto the top of his head. He narrowed his eyes, not quite squinting as he looked around. "It seems to be the general approach people take to the area. From the looks of it, there hasn't been any work done here since Birdie disappeared."

A block of houses had been chopped out of the neighborhood, caged off behind wire, and left to rot. Faded signs declared, under bars of blue and yellow graffiti, that Mallard Park was an urban regeneration project, bringing luxury residential accommodations and green space to revitalize the area. Suburbs with an urban edge. Instead there were empty buildings, half of them gutted and sagging like damp houses of cards, the others half-built and angular like an interrupted game of Tetris. The only green space was a field of broken bottles in front of a listing wall.

"Some of the local developers got overambitious," Cloister said. "They thought there'd be a market for professional urban living. Turned out, if you're commuting two hours so you don't have to live in a one-bedroom box in San Diego—"

"You don't want to live in a one-bedroom box somewhere less exciting," Javi finished for him. "Who owns it?"

"The bank now, most of them," Cloister said. It was the sort of common knowledge that you never really thought about. It was only after he said it that he remembered. "Kelly Hartley's bank, I guess."

Javi lifted his eyebrows toward his hairline, notching a row of four V-shaped wrinkles into his forehead. "The coincidences are starting to stack up."

"When does it become evidence?" Cloister asked.

"I'll let you know," Javi said. He turned in a slow circle and searched the buildings. "I hoped there might be someone here we could talk to. A resident or one of Hector's homeless friends."

"Ten years," Cloister said.

"Humans need homes," Javi said. "Even if it isn't a *house*, people want to stay someplace familiar. Usually."

"Every now and again, the bank and the developers send people down to run them off," Cloister said. "The sheriff's department too, whenever someone sets up a meth lab or a grow house. It can't hurt to look around, though."

He ignored Javi's skeptical grunt and headed back to the car. Bourneville was pancaked out in the backseat, looking bored. Her ears pricked up as Cloister popped the trunk, and she scrambled to her feet when he dragged her dress-up box out over the wheelwell.

"What are you doing?" Javi asked.

"There's a lot of glass," Cloister said. He whistled through his teeth and signaled for Bourneville to get out of the car. She jumped out, waited, and lifted her paw up like a furry Cinderella as he crouched down next to her. He slid the heavy-soled sock on and secured the Velcro around the top.

"Bootees?" Javi said.

Cloister twisted around and squinted one eye shut as he looked up at the lean silhouette. "You want to walk around here barefoot?"

"I'm not a dog," Javi said.

"Neither is Bourneville," Cloister said. "She's a sheriff's department deputy, and it costs more when she's on sick leave than it does when you are."

Javi snorted like he didn't believe that. He'd obviously never seen a vet bill.

Cloister finished getting her booted up, and he stood. First couple of times he tried the shoes on her, she went stiff legged and reproachful like he'd strapped bees to her feet. Now she knew it meant they were going to be doing something interesting—either search and rescue or body retrieval.

And after ten years, Cloister didn't think Birdie Utkin needed rescuing. Just finding.

Cloister grabbed the T-shirt bone out of the car, stuffed it into his back pocket, and tossed the keys to Javi.

"You can wait in the car if you want," he said.

"I've come this far," Javi said. "I might as well see it through."

Cloister smirked and stooped over to unclip Bourneville's leash. He could feel her quivering with pent-up energy as she waited for the command.

"Bourneville, find RJ," he barked. "Where's RJ?"

It was kinder than *corpse* if the family was there, or the press, and Cloister was the only one who knew what it really meant. Besides, it worked. The minute he let go of Bourneville's collar, she was away.

She trotted the first couple of yards, sniffed around, and doubled back on herself. The burned-out car pulled her over, and she circled in twice on big, gloved feet.

"She smells the raccoon," Javi said impatiently.

"No," Cloister says. "She can tell the difference."

Something had happened in the car, but between the weather, the years, and the fire, it wasn't enough to hold Bourneville's nose. She snorted, abandoned the car, and made a beeline for the splintered front door of one of the nearby houses. Like the car, someone had put a match to it at some point. The roof was caved in, and the windows were smoke-stained shards of glass.

There was enough of a gap at the bottom of the door for her to squirm through. Cloister loped after her and caught up just as her tail disappeared into the dark. The door had been broken up previously. Twisted metal popped out of the charred wood of the door. Cloister shoved it open. A drift of trash behind it scraped over the floor, and he found a room that looked like somewhere you'd find a dead body.

Profanity was scraped into the walls, stained bedding was shoved into a corner, and discarded balls of tinfoil threaded the vinegary bite of heroin through the piss-and-smoke stink of the place. Bourneville was already gone, though, and the indistinct smudge of gloved paw prints were left in the sooty residue on the ground.

There was someone dead nearby, and the scent had to be strong.

Cloister broke into a run. All those late-night sprints down the beach weren't just to wear himself out until he could sleep without dreaming. Dogs that had gotten the scent rarely remembered their handlers were stuck on slow human legs. He spent a lot of time trying to keep up with her.

He went through the kitchen, scrambled over the cracked beam that had come down and crushed the sink, and ran across the alley at the back. A disgruntled, scrawny tabby cat, still arched and bristly from an unexpected encounter with a big dog, hissed at him from the top of a broken wall.

Bourneville wove through rubble and unfinished buildings. She went in one door and came out another, doubled back on herself, and crisscrossed over her own path. Occasionally she'd stop and look around to check that she knew where Cloister was.

"Has she lost the scent?" Javi asked when he caught up with Cloister. They were both sweating, Cloister's T-shirt was stuck to him, and the stiff collar of Javi's shirt was damp and out of shape. Javi wasn't quite as out of breath as Cloister might have expected, but then—Cloister hitched in a quick breath—he *had* seen the hard lines of muscle hidden under the sharp tailoring.

"No," Cloister said. He pulled the neck of his T-shirt up and wiped his face. "She's… triangulating."

A sniff at the base of a pallet of bricks, and Bourneville took off again. She arrowed in a mostly straight line down the sketched-out street and into the shell of a building that never got beyond the ground floor. At one point the walls had been plastered and the roof intact, but years of sand and the elements had worn both paper-thin and pocked. The windows were intact, and the protective film still clung on in shreds.

Bourneville flopped down on the floor, chin on her paws, and whined. Her eyes were flat and her tail clamped in around her haunches. It was her tell, but Cloister could never shake the feeling that she felt bad about not finding the corpse while it was still alive.

"Good girl," he said as he took a knee next to her. He fussed over her until she relaxed, uncoiled from her tell posture, and sat up. Cloister pulled the T-shirt bone from his pocket and tossed it across the room for her. She skidded after it, nearly went headlong into the wall, and flopped down to slobber on it. While she was occupied, Cloister tapped his knuckles against the sheet of chipboard flooring. It was dry enough to rattle under his knuckles.

There was no smell. No stain.

"Did you see a crowbar outside?" he asked. When Javi just snorted at him, he shrugged and fished in his pocket for the chunky rectangle of his old Swiss Army Knife. The cover was chipped and battered, and grime was worked into the hinges, but it was the closest the Wittes had to a family heirloom—three generations, two sets of initials, and taken apart at least twice to get the blood out before it rusted.

He hooked his finger in the groove and pulled the knife blade out.

"Maybe it's not her," Javi said. He had his phone in his hands, and the flash blinked as he snapped a picture of the floor.

"It's still someone."

Cloister supposed they could call it in and wait for the CSI team to excavate the area properly. Except he wasn't keen on swallowing the jeers if it turned out to be a bag of pork ribs a builder had dumped in the foundations instead of the garbage can. Besides, if this was Birdie Utkin, she'd been in this sad, sour place long enough.

He dug the knife into the chipboard, which cracked and broke under the digging point. He wriggled the blade around until there was a hole big enough to get his fingers in. The sharp edges dug into his skin as he wrenched at it, and the sheet of wood bowed up under the pressure. Two nails popped out of the floor, screeching out of the wood, and a chunk of the chipboard snapped off.

"Shit," Javi said. "You were right."

The flash went again, the bright light harsh on the plastic covering the dry, wizened face of a girl who'd been too young to end up lost under a floor. She was curled up on her side, hugging herself with wiry, jerky-tanned arms. Her hair was a brittle, wispy halo, more dust colored than anything else. But it had probably been blonde.

"It's her," Cloister said.

"We don't know that. Not yet," Javi said. He tapped Cloister's ankle with his foot and stepped back as he called the discovery in. "Don't touch anything. We need to get the forensic teams in here… see if there's anything useful left. How the hell did they miss this the first time? I thought the Plenty police force were corrupt, not incompetent."

He stalked out of the dusty box of a room to bark orders down the phone.

Cloister folded the knife back in and stuffed it into his back pocket. His hands shook as adrenaline worked its way down into the tendons. He already knew he'd have the nightmare tonight, but at least one family would have an answer.

"Time to go home, Birdie," he said.

CHAPTER FOURTEEN

THE DEAD girl looked very small as they carried her out of the building on a stretcher. Under the white sheet, her dried-out corpse looked more like a child or an animal. Nothing but bones and weathered skin.

"I can't tell you anything until I've finished the autopsy," the coroner said. She wiped her glasses with her thumb, pushed them back up her nose, and squinted through the greasy smears until her eyes adjusted. "In my opinion the corpse was moved here after she'd already been dead for a while."

"How long is a while?"

Galloway sighed. She was a colorless woman with dishwater-blonde hair and washed-out blue eyes. Even her skin had that oddly sallow effect that came from spending most of her life under florescent lights. She was good at her job, though.

"I prefer not to give my opinion until I've opened them up," she said. Her blanched-out eyebrows lifted. "Do you really think I'm going to do guesses?"

"Is there anything you can tell me?"

She pursed her lips and picked distractedly at a bit of dried skin. "No obvious cause of death," she said. "It looks like she was held somewhere before she died. Her fingertips show signs of damage." She hooked her fingers and scratched at the air to make her point. "That *could* have been predation, though. I will know more when—"

"You finish the autopsy," he finished for her.

Galloway gave him a dry smile and turned to go. Before she could, Javi tapped his finger against her elbow to reclaim her attention.

"Can you put a rush on it?" he asked. "Front of the line?"

"I could," she said, but she moved her arm away from him. "Why should I?"

Javi hesitated. The evidence of a connection between the two cases was reaching a tipping point, but Javi wasn't sure he wanted to commit his name to it yet. Haring off on wild-goose chases, even ones that proved fruitful, didn't look good on an agent's record or when they got to court. Let J.J. Diggs at a case based on gut feelings instead of evidence and investigative procedure, and he'd have a field day.

"It could be connected to another case," he said. "Maybe."

Galloway grimaced. "Lara's little boy?" she asked. Of course she knew the family, Javi realized. There weren't that many doctors in Plenty, and the county coroner's office dealt with deaths at the hospital too.

"It's not confirmed," Javi said. "And I do not want it getting back to the Hartley family. Not yet."

That got him a scathing look. "She's a professional acquaintance, not my 'bestie,'" Galloway said dryly. "But I'll make sure I examine this body as soon as I can."

Javi let her leave. As she oversaw loading the body into the back of the coroner's van, Javi pinched the bridge of his nose between his fingers and squeezed as though the pressure might help make the current situation simpler.

If the two cases *were* connected, how? If the Utkin family finally worked out that Kelly Hartley had put pressure on the investigation, they might have snatched Billy as payback. But despite Utkin's reputed connections, that seemed a severe jump in antisocial behavior for a SoCal builder with no criminal record.

Except they still didn't *know* the corpse they'd found was Birdie Utkin, he reminded himself. Until they did he might as well put a pin in the question of how and deal with the situation at hand.

Cloister was off playing fetch with the dog, and the news crews had joined the crowd of rubberneckers gathered outside the wire fencing. The deputies on duty were trying to keep them back, but a mixture of nosiness and concern made them press closer.

He walked to the perimeter and into a battery of questions.

"Is this connected to the Hartley case?" a vaguely familiar woman asked as she tucked her hair behind her ear. It took a second, but Javi put a name to her—Harriet Green of the local television station.

"Have you found Drew Hartley's body?" a more direct man asked. He had hipster black glasses and a laptop bag. Newspaper or blog. "Do you have a suspect?"

"This is a separate case," Javi said. "At the moment we have no reason to connect this to the missing local boy, Drew Hartley. We have every hope that we'll be able to return Drew home happy and well."

It had been *confidence* in the first hours after Drew walked out of the Retreat and didn't come back. The more time passed, the more he had to manage expectations. There was no kindness in keeping hope alive after a certain point.

"Who was found? We saw them bringing a stretcher out," Harriet asked again, leaning forward to get the microphone in his face.

Before he could say anything, one of the CSI techs yelled for him.

"Agent Merlo. There's something you need to see." Over the collar of the man's white coveralls, his face was grim with concern.

"I'm not able to share any more information at this moment," Javi said smoothly. "As soon as we have more, we'll let you know. Thank you."

He turned and walked away quickly, ignoring the questions tossed at his back. The CSI tech was already walking back toward the building as Javi approached.

"What is it?" Javi asked.

"Bad news," the man said. "We pulled up the floor to get the body out. She wasn't the only thing under there."

The image of a dozen sad, curled-up brown corpses flashed into Javi's head. He ground out a curse and stretched his legs. He ducked through the plastic sheet they'd tacked up over the door. The area was gridded off with yellow tags and cameras. There were no bodies. It would almost have been better if there were. At least it would have been a clear situation.

Five plastic bags had been unearthed from under the floor. Each was full of a set of neatly folded clothes, down to a pair of shoes neatly placed on top.

"Son of a bitch," Javi said through stiff lips.

"Look at this," the tech said as he stepped around Javi. He picked his way over the wooden framework on the ground, shuffling in his oversized boots, and crouched down to pick up one of the already tagged and photographed bags. He tilted it toward Javi. Even through the glaze of milky plastic, Javi could see the faded red fabric of the T-shirt and the Avengers' logo screen printed on it.

Captain America was Drew's favorite, Kay told them when she gave them the description, but he loved the Avengers too.

"Get them back to the lab, process them, and get me the report before the end of today," he snapped. Habit made the tech start to hedge, but Javi cut him off impatiently. "This missing-child investigation is about to be reclassified to a serial offender. Get me that report."

The tech pinched his mouth—either in resentment or understanding of how the case had escalated, Javi didn't care—and nodded.

"Agent."

Javi took one last look at the room, fixed it in his mind for later when he would need to make sense of it, and then headed back outside. It was time to tell Cloister his hunch had become a theory. It looked like Drew's disappearance and Birdie Hartley's *were* connected. Javi thought about the other little bags of clothes they'd unearthed and tightened his mouth into a grim line. At *least* those two cases.

WHEN BIRDIE went missing, so did whatever held the Utkins' marriage together. Heather Utkin divorced her husband within the year and moved out of the city. Out of state, in fact.

"She went back to Illinois," Lew Utkin said. Shock had knocked the confidence out of his voice, leaving it vague and distracted. He was a big man, although he'd run to fat a bit across his stomach, and probably still handsome usually. Today his face looked like it was slipping a little on his bones, sagging as though grief had a weight. He sat on the cheap metal chair and fiddled with a plastic cup of water. "I don't have her number, but, umm... I have her sister's address. I can get in touch. Are you *sure* it's Birdie?"

It was the fourth time he'd asked that question. Javi wasn't sure what answer he was looking for.

"We're waiting on getting the DNA tests back from the lab," Javi said. "That's one reason we asked you to come in, so we could get a sample from you for analysis."

Lew nodded before Javi even finished speaking. "Of course," he said. "I... anything I can do to help."

"We also have some of her effects...."

"Can't I just see *her*? I'll know if it's my daughter. It's been ten years, but I'd know my own daughter."

Javi mentally overlaid the pretty, smiling girl in the photo over the dead girl's half-mummified face, her eyelids sagging over empty sockets and lips peeled back from a yard of hard gum and broken teeth. He didn't think there was anything there to recognize.

"It's been ten years, Mr. Utkin," he said. "Let the lab do their job first."

Lew closed his eyes. "Did someone hurt her?" he asked.

"We don't know anything yet. Would you feel comfortable looking at some of the items we found with her, to see if you can identify them?"

The nod took a bit longer that time. Lew finally nodded stiffly and clenched his jaw until Javi thought he could hear his teeth grind. He got up from the chair as though he were much older than his face indicated. "Let's get it over with."

Javi walked him down to the evidence room, where the tech swabbed his cheek. Then he brought out a clean metal tray, carefully laid with the items they thought belonged to Birdie. A yellow shirt and a grubby rag of a top that had probably been floaty, hippy muslin at some point, flip-flops with brittle plastic straps, and a pair of tarnished-to-dullness silver earrings. There was a thread of hair still caught in one— frizzy and crooked in the bright light. Finally a set of keys, all different acid-bright colors, with a tangle of age-yellowed Zac Efron pics attached as key rings.

"Take your time," Javi said as he discreetly watched Lew's face.

It crumpled in around his grief. Lew reached for the tray but pulled his hand back before Javi had to say anything to him. He rubbed it roughly over his face instead and dug his fingers up into his graying, well-cut hair.

"The, umm... keys are hers," he choked out. "The earrings look like hers too. Little birds. She always wore those. I don't... I don't know about the clothes. She liked yellow. She was always wearing yellow. I, ah, I think I need to sit down."

"That's fine," Javi said. He gave a quick nod of thanks to the tech and showed Lew back out into the hall. There was a long bench halfway down with an empty Coke can sitting on it, and he helped Lew to it. Lew sat down hard, folded over, and pressed the heels of his hands roughly against his cheeks.

"Maybe she was robbed," he said. "That could have been what happened. She was robbed and maybe hit on the head? That would explain why she never came home."

"Mr. Utkin—"

Lew straightened up and scrubbed his sleeve over his mouth. "I know," he said. "I do know, but I don't *have* to know yet, right? I can *not* know."

He sounded desperate for Javi to give him permission, and his face pled for that small kindness. Javi wanted children—or expected children—but the idea of being that vulnerable to something you couldn't control terrified him.

"We'll know more once they do the DNA test," he said.

Lew nodded.

"Can you tell us anything that you didn't tell Detective Stokes during the first investigation—"

"Investigation? Is that what you call it?" Lew asked bitterly. "They didn't care about my daughter. They just wanted to write her off. You know how much money I donated when we were campaigning to unincorporate? A fuckload. Just so I didn't have to see that uniform every day, remember how they let Birdie down."

"Anything," Javi repeated patiently. "Even something that didn't seem like anything at the time. What about Birdie's boyfriend? She was dating one of the Hartleys, wasn't she?"

Regret pulled at Lew's face. "I thought it would be good for her. He was a good boy—smart, ambitious, respectful. Kelly saw to that. Birdie said he was boring—she was probably right—but I pushed it. Not just me, her mom too. We thought he'd calm her down." He hesitated, and his eyebrows burrowed together over his nose. "You don't think he had anything to do with it? They said he had an alibi. Kelly—"

"I'm just trying to build a clearer picture," Javi said. "Sometimes people leave things out because they think it's irrelevant, or they worry that it might show the victim in an unflattering light."

"She was fifteen," Lew said. "The worst thing she'd ever done was skip curfew."

"Her other boyfriend?" Javi said. "The one you didn't like?"

"Hector?" Utkin shook his head. "I didn't *trust* him. In my line of work, Agent Merlo, you meet people that aren't... nice. You get to know the signs. Hector Andrews was bad news, and he would have hurt her one day, but not that night. Somebody had put him in the hospital."

"Somebody?"

"One of his lowlife friends," Lew said. There was a challenge in his voice, the expression his eyes somewhere between defiance and smugness. "That's the thing about lowlifes, Agent. They'd stab you in the back for fifty bucks."

"That the going rate for a bottle to the head?" Javi suggested quietly.

Lew pulled up short of a confession. He turned the corner of his mouth up in a sour, brief smile. "Let's say that I wasn't sorry to hear about it."

"Do you have any idea where Hector is now?"

Lew grimaced and pulled his chin back into his neck. "I didn't know where he was then. He was homeless. His family had lost their house and left, but he just hung around. I told Birdie. Something's wrong with a man whose own family don't want them. She didn't listen."

That was when Lew's ability to lie to himself visibly ran out. He hunched in on himself, suddenly looking lost in his skin, and closed his eyes. His mouth folded down as he sniffed in a deep breath. No tears, but if Lew was having an affair with Kelly Hartley, he'd be crying on her shoulder later after a bottle of whiskey.

"I, umm… I should call my wife," he said and wiped his hand over his mouth. "My ex-wife. Book flights for her and… and everything. Do you need anything else?"

"Not right now," Javi said.

Lew nodded and stood up slowly. "You'll let me know if…."

Javi nodded and put a reassuring hand on his arm. "We'll let you know as soon as the results are back. Take care."

"Why?"

CHAPTER FIFTEEN

JAVI ASKED a passing deputy to escort Lew Utkin out. He wasn't sure Lew would have actually left otherwise. Then he headed for the bull pen. There were four deputies at their desks and two teenagers and a biker sitting on the bench against the wall. The biker had his arms crossed and his eyes closed. It could have been a front, but Javi thought the man was actually catching a nap.

The missing-in-action blond Javi was looking for was the deputy sitting in the back-left corner under the window. Cloister had the courtesy to look embarrassed when he realized he'd been caught. He scrabbled at the desk and grabbed hopefully at the scattered paperwork with his big scuffed-up hands.

"I told you I wanted you to sit in on Lew Utkin's interview. Not"— he plucked one page from Cloister's hands, glanced at it, and hitched an eyebrow in pointed surprise—"expense claims for dog food and vet bills?"

Cloister scratched the back of his neck. The black sleeve of his T-shirt slid back from the hard bulge of his tricep. It was more distracting than a few inches of skin should have been.

"Bon hurt her foot finding the phone. Better safe than sorry," he said.

"Until Frome tells you different," Javi reminded him. "You're mine."

Something dark slid under those words, thick and heated and demanding. More than Javi meant to put into his voice. He bit the inside of his cheek in annoyance. Someone sniggered. It was probably louder than expected, from the way it choked off, and almost welcome as an external irritation to aim his temper at. Javi clenched his jaw hard enough to pulse pain up into his skull, and he breathed in. Before he could settle on a response, Cloister jabbed his middle finger in the direction of the snicker. Its source was, Javi discovered as he turned around, a meaty-looking young man with fading acne scars and the look of a high school athlete.

"He knows I'm gay, Collins," Cloister said. "So now you just look like an asshole. And in front of our ticket-dodging guests."

Without opening his eyes, the biker snorted.

Meaty young Collins squirmed in place for a second, then muttered something that might have been an apology and hunched over his desk. His neck was flushed dully red all the way up into his scalp, visible through his close-cropped hair, and the pen scratched industriously at the paper. Javi allowed himself the spiteful thought that he was surprised the jock could read. He would have been even more cruel, but it wasn't the time.

"I'm not telling you to do things for the sake of hearing my own voice," he said. "So leave the expenses and come with me. I've finished with Utkin, but I need you to run some other errands...."

Cloister scowled at the "errands" snark but did as he was told and pushed himself out from the desk. Apparently the dog had been under there with his knees. It scrambled out after him, panting gently. Javi rolled his eyes. It was like having a chaperone, but he supposed the dog had been useful so far.

"Is its foot all right?" he asked as she padded out of the room with them.

"Her," Cloister corrected him. He reached down absently and ruffled the pricked ears. "And she's fine. She just got jabbed by a bit of wire, and I wanted to make sure it was clean."

Out in the hall, Javi glanced sideways at Cloister.

"So I really am the only one who didn't know you were gay?"

Cloister shrugged. "Pretty much." He hesitated and dropped his hand to Bourneville's head again. "I should have been there to speak to Utkin. I'm sorry."

As apologies go, it was unremorseful, blunt, and to the point—rather like Cloister in that way. It was annoying that Javi still found both of them appealing.

"Nobody likes notifying the next of kin," he admitted. After a second he went on, the memory of Utkin's blank "why" in his ears. "To be honest, I wonder if he'd have been happier not knowing. He could have kept that 10 percent chance that she'd run away for a new life somewhere. In that situation I don't know if I'd want the truth."

Cloister didn't say anything. The silence dragged on long enough that the moment passed, and Javi cringed, not sure why he'd exposed that much of himself. He swallowed mortification—it was dry and sandy—and tried to change the subject.

"Maybe he—"

"It's not 10 percent," Cloister interrupted. His voice was low. "With no body, parents are 90 percent sure their kid is still alive—maybe living a new life, but more likely hurt and afraid. It's still grief, but you're afraid as well."

This time it was Javi's turn to not know what to say. It felt as to the point as the apology, and it was too honest for him. It was easier if Cloister stayed big, blond, and fuckable, with nothing as inconvenient as feelings. Discomfort itched under his skin, and instead of asking Cloister who he'd lost, Javi veered back onto safer ground.

"Next time I have to deliver bad news, I'll lead with that," he said because apparently *asshole* was his go-to safe space.

Bourneville whined and stuck her nose into Cloister's hand, her tongue pink as she licked his fingers because she was more emotionally mature than Javi. They reached the doors, and Javi shoved one open, his irritation making him thump it harder than he needed to. It was still warm out, but the winds had finally dropped. There was a dampness in the air that hadn't been there before, and it was softer on the throat as you breathed in.

"Right now I want you to go and talk to the Hartleys. Let them know we aren't looking at Billy anymore. It'll come better from you," Javi said. "Take the phone with you—the techs haven't managed to unlock it yet—and get it opened. However the phone got there. Find out what Billy is hiding and who he's protecting."

"Why me?"

Javi glanced down at the dog pressed devotedly to Cloister's leg. "Dogs like you. I bet children do too."

"He's not a child. He's a teenager."

"Same difference," Javi said. He shrugged. "Of course, if you'd rather, you can come with me to the records office to go through the property register. I want to see who used to live in that house we found the bodies in."

He was fairly sure it was going to turn out to be the house that Hector Andrews's family lost to the bank. If it was, that was a coincidence too many to ignore because of an alibi.

Cloister made a face at that idea because significant periods of Plenty's official records hadn't been reliably computerized. Extensive corruption among the town's public officials meant a lot of people had things they didn't want easily searchable. In addition to the incriminating evidence, a lot of fairly prosaic records were elided as well to make it harder to pinpoint what was being hidden. So it was going to be a few hours of arguing with the librarian and chasing red tape through old archival boxes.

"I'll take the teenager," Cloister surrendered. Then he hesitated and shifted his weight uncomfortably. He looked off-balance, unsure of himself. It was the first time Javi had seen that. Whatever else was going on around him, Cloister always seemed confident in the space his body inhabited.

"Look, last night…." Cloister let that hang.

It was the perfect opportunity to brush him off kindly but firmly. Javi didn't do relationships. He had a career plotted out, and you didn't make assistant director by crafting emotional compromises and weathering bad breakups. He already tried that. It ended badly. Predictably but badly. A ridiculously attractive smile that didn't belong on that rough face or the spray of freckles on a nice ass weren't good reasons to change that policy.

Except… an arrangement wasn't a relationship. It was obvious that Cloister wasn't the type to get attached. He was a grown man with a substantial paycheck who chose to live in a house that could be towed away. That screamed flight risk.

"Last night was—" Halfway through the sentence and Javi wasn't *sure* what way he was going.

Before he had to make up his mind, Tancredi burst out of the doors behind them and into Cloister's back. It didn't move Cloister much, but the impact made Bourneville jump. Her ears went down, giving her narrow skull a snakelike look, and her lips wrinkled back in a snarl that bared a lot of very sharp teeth.

For a second, Javi felt a visceral cringe that started in his gut and went up into his chest. His imagination had run ahead of itself, already a minute in the future with Tancredi's face degloved and half-eaten, and he wasn't sure if calling for an ambulance would be a kindness or not.

Cloister jerked Bourneville's lead back, choking off the snarl, and snapped out, "*Lass es*. Bourneville, Lass."

The dog visibly unclenched at the command, and the quivering violence drained out of her lean, heavy body. She unflattened her ears and whined apologetically at Cloister.

Javi felt heat twist in his groin. The contrast between the hard command in Cloister's voice *now* and the easy submission of his body *then* tugged a wire of want through him. The dark, honeyed idea of him surrendering even wriggled through his head, rough hands and rougher commands on his body as Javi just... unclenched.

The brief image was unexpectedly potent—a shot of heat straight to his groin. It wasn't something he'd ever do, but he still stored the brief fantasy away for later.

"What the hell, Tancredi?" Cloister said. He sounded annoyed, but not nearly scared enough to Javi's mind. "You want sick leave while they stitch your fingers back on?"

Tancredi took a discreet step back, her face a bit paler than usual. "No... umm... sorry. We just got a call, though, I knew you'd want it."

"What?" Javi asked.

She looked at him, and regret and interest jostled for primacy over her expression. "It's the Hartleys. They were getting ready to leave the Retreat, head back home, when Billy Hartley went missing. They've been looking for hours, but they can't find him."

JAVI BRACED his arm against the dashboard as Cloister hammered the gas along the rutted country roads. The car swung around one corner tightly enough that he felt the tires jolt off the road as sandy dirt sprayed up against the paintwork.

"Are you sure she's secure back there?" Javi asked, pitching his voice over the wail of the siren. He cocked his head to check the sliver of rearview mirror he could see. Bourneville's harness looked more secure than his seatbelt, but he could still see the imagined ruin of Tancredi's face in his mind.

Maybe his sex life was limited enough at the moment that he was considering an arrangement based on nothing but geographical proximity. His libido stirred back there with the disturbing, sticky fantasies of heavy scarred bodies and various shades of surrender. It mocked him, but that would change. He didn't want to try to negotiate the queer dating scene with a face that looked like a badly put-together jigsaw puzzle. He didn't have the personality to get away with not being pretty.

"She's fine," Cloister said impatiently. He took his eyes off the road long enough to look over at Javi. "Bourneville wasn't going for Tancredi."

"Not what it looked like to me."

"If she'd been attacking, it wouldn't have been so easy to pull her back," Cloister said. "Tancredi startled us. Bon went on the defensive."

"So there was no danger?"

"Of course there was," Cloister said bluntly. "But there's probably less danger with Bon than with your neighbor's ill-trained Labrador. The sheriff's department has spent a lot of money on training her not to attack unless I give the nod. She's still a dog, though, and dogs can bite."

"Jesus," Javi muttered. He didn't take the Lord's name in vain often—adult atheism had no traction against a childhood spent threatened with a bar of soap—but it felt appropriate. "You make pet owning sound like running a gauntlet."

"Bon's not a pet." Cloister shrugged. He broke off for a second as they took another turn, and he spun the steering wheel. "She's a good dog, and she's never bitten anyone outside of the job, but it would be irresponsible of me to tell you she's never going to. It would be like saying that if I've never shot anyone, it would be safe to leave my gun lying around the house."

Javi snorted.

"I think I'll stick to guns," he said. "They're more predictable and don't need to be walked."

This time the press had gotten there first in network affiliate vans and old cars. In response the Retreat had closed their gates, which pushed the reporters back onto the road. Reed had sent Matt down to stand guard. He looked hunched and uncomfortable as he pulled his hat down and tried to avoid the reporters' attention.

Cloister pulled in behind a dusty FOX news van. The man standing next to it, slotting batteries into transmitter packs, scowled at them. "Hey!" he protested, waving a hand at the nonexistent gap between bumpers. He looked stocky, but that was an optical illusion caused by the heavy pocket-hung vest he had on. "How am I supposed to get in to get my gear?"

Javi flashed his badge through the windshield. There was no way the man could have identified the FBI seal through the dust and mud and glass between them. All he saw was the gold shield, the heavy black wallet, and a good reason to mind his own business. Still scowling, he threw his hands up in surrender and backed off. Javi opened his door just in time to catch the muttered, "...assholes."

Two squad cars arrived while Cloister was getting Bourneville out. Javi waved one of the deputies over.

"Take over at the gate." He pointed toward the cluster of bodies blocking the road. "I don't think the country needs to know what the Prom King of Plenty thinks about this case."

The woman nodded briskly. "I'll get on that, Agent Merlo."

While she did that, Cloister and Javi ducked through the gauntlet of the press. Javi fended off questions with the brisk reminder that he'd only just arrived and they'd know more as soon as he did.

Matt had already unlocked the padlocks and dragged the gates back as they approached. He let them duck through and then locked up again.

"Mr. Reed sent one of the ATVs down for you," he said. He pointed over to a red buggy parked at the side of the road. He faltered as the math of one buggy with two seats settled in. "You could drive up yourself? It's easy enough...."

"I'll walk." Cloister gave the buggy a jaded look. "It won't take me long."

A bone-rattling ride later and a spring intimately acquainted with his ass, Javi thought Cloister had probably made the right decision.

"Have the media been causing problems?" Javi asked.

Matt shrugged with his mouth and shoulders. He freed one hand to scratch at the welt on his neck. "Not for me. They don't care much what I think," he muttered. "Had a couple of things happen up here. Never had so many show up before."

"Children tug the heartstrings," Javi said.

Matt snorted. "Not met some of the ones up here," he muttered. "Spoiled brats. No idea how lucky they are."

"Like Drew?" Javi asked, suspicion tweaking at the back of his brain. The sheriff's department had run background checks on all the

Retreat's staff. Nothing had come up that raised suspicion, and they'd all had alibis of varying strength.

Matt pulled up in front of the Retreat's main office. He turned the engine off and gave Javi an abashed look.

"No, he was just a kid. The little ones are okay," he said. "It's the older ones, like Billy. He was always going behind his parents' back, picking on the other kids, getting in people's way. They come up here and act like we're servants, here to run around for them."

Javi delayed getting out of the ATV. "Did the staff have a lot of problems with Billy?"

"Not before." Matt pulled the key out, fiddled with it, and twisted his fingers around the metal ring. "This year he just came up with a bad attitude. I caught him smokin' out in the forest. Told him he could start a fire. He told me to mind my own business."

"Teenagers," Javi said lightly. "They grow out of it."

"If someone shows them the way," Matt said. "Let me know if you need a ride back down, Agent Merlo."

It was difficult to scramble out of a buggy with any elegance. Javi extricated himself and fastidiously dusted his trousers down. He made a mental note to review Matt's background check, just in case, but it was probably just service burnout. If Javi had to work with children all day, every day, he'd sound bitter too.

Javi thanked Matt for the ride, and when he turned around, he saw Reed jogging across the courtyard toward him.

Finally. Tranquil had made himself scarce since the night Drew disappeared. The ex-hippy mouthed all the right sympathetic platitudes to the department when they called, but stopped short of actually coming in for an interview. Javi assumed he was trying to dodge a lawsuit. With two missing children and a body in the morgue, he wondered bleakly if Reed had been afraid of something else.

"Special Agent Merlo," Reed said as he reached him. He stopped and smoothed his graying hair back from his face. He was wearing jeans and a plain white shirt instead of his hippy costume of linen and approachable wrinkles, and his mask of affability had worn thin. His mouth was tight and his eyes hard as stones. "This is untenable. My business is disrupted, and the press is implying this is somehow my fault—"

"Is it?" Javi asked.

Reed stopped. Calculation made him narrow his eyes as he tried to measure just how serious Javi was.

"Of course not," he said. "I've always tried to make the Retreat safe for my guests. It's part of the ethos we've always had here. Since I opened my home to—"

"Then, when we find these missing children, your reputation will be cleared, won't it?" Javi asked. He wasn't in the mood, but for the sake of smoothing out the interaction, he added some honey. "The FBI will certainly make it clear how grateful we are for your help."

Quid pro quo was something Reed understood. He smoothed his shirt down again and put his salesman face back on.

"Of course," he said. "You're right. I'm sorry. It's just been such a shock that this happened here. The Hartleys are in my office, Agent Merlo, if you want to come with me?"

Javi hesitated and glanced back at the road. He would have preferred to let Cloister take point with talking to the Hartleys, use that sincerity of his to undercut the family's resentment. There was no sign of him, though.

Apparently he was telling the truth when he said he had a problem with authority. Javi would have to deal with that. He swallowed to work the dry mix of frustration and lust out of his mouth and nodded to Reed.

"Of course."

CHAPTER SIXTEEN

FOR ONCE it wasn't Bourneville who found the missing boy. Cloister would give her the credit, though.

He hunched down, tilted his head to the side, and looked under the cabin. The thick stilts driven into the rocky hill to hold up the porch created a shaded slice of pseudobasement. The rocks had slid down the hill, leaving a bed of fine dirt. It smelled of beer and teenage sweat. It was just the sort of place two boys would turn into a den away from their parents, and the last place a parent convinced a predator had snatched their son—or convinced their son *was* a predator—would look for a missing child.

Billy Hartley was hunched as far back into the space as he could get, sneakered feet wedged against one of the struts.

"I'm not leaving," he said when he saw Cloister. His voice cracked with defiance. "You can't make me. *They* can't make me."

He was wrong about that. Cloister supposed he should try diplomacy first, even though the strategic application of force would be easier.

"We know you didn't hurt your brother," he said. "If you come out…."

Billy curled his lip in a sneer. "I already *knew* that," he said. "They're the ones you should be telling."

"Your parents?"

The sneer stayed. Billy hunched down farther, shoved his hands into the pockets of his hoodie, and folded them across his chest.

"They want to send me to some sort of special therapist," he said. "They think I did something to Drew and that I have to go and get *fixed* before I start burying little kids in the backyard. But *they're* the ones that want to leave. Just leave him behind and go back home."

Billy's voice wobbled and cracked with a sour mix of adrenaline and fear. He didn't look much like Cloister had at that age—not even if someone stretched Billy out a few inches and packed on a few pounds of resentment muscle—but the hurt and antipathy had a sharp and unwelcome familiarity.

The sun was beating down on the back of Cloister's neck, stinging the prickle rash from where he'd clipped his hair short, and the backs of his thighs ached.

"What good will staying here do?" he asked.

Billy looked up, his dark eyes red rimmed and puffy. He swiped his sleeve over his face and gave Cloister a glare that challenged him to notice the tears.

"You said you'd bring him home," he said.

"I said I'd try," Cloister said. "I haven't given up. You?"

"I'm not the one trying to leave."

"Come on out, kid," Cloister tried. "Your parents are worried sick."

It would have worked on a little kid. They looked at Cloister and saw someone trustworthy. Cloister didn't know what Billy saw, but apparently it merited another sneer and a snarled "Fuck off." So much for kids and teenagers being basically the same thing.

Cloister pushed himself up, brushed the sand off his hands, and looked up. On the cabin's narrow porch, Bourneville looked down with pricked ears and head-tilted interest. Her tail swished over the wood and stirred up a small cloud of dust. Her ears tilted forward, and their tufted tips trembled.

He snapped his fingers—the crack of callus on callus was loud in the still air—and pointed under the cabin. "Bourneville, bring."

She scrambled over the edge of the wood, squeezed her lean frame between the slats, and leaped down. Long black fur floated as the wind caught it, and for a second, she looked elegant. Then she hit the ground hard, her clawed toes dug ruts into the dirt, and she went scrambling into the dark, restricted space.

Billy started to swear before the dog even reached him. He kicked up divots of dirt as he worked his way farther back into the space. That only worked as long as there was space to go back into, though. His back hit the wall, and Bourneville latched on to the leg of his jeans. She dragged him back out, and the reinforced denim cuff held as it caught between her teeth. Billy spat out curses and grabbed at the struts. His knuckles showed white as he tried to hang on, but that was just another game of tug-of-war for Bourneville. Her head went down, and the heavy muscles in her shoulders bunched under the thick ruff of fur.

It was a short war. Billy's fingers slipped, a yelp escaped him as he probably picked up a few splinters, and she triumphantly hauled him out at Cloister's feet. Sobbing in frustration and probably grief, Billy pulled his leg back and aimed his sneaker at Bourneville's head.

"Don't kick my dog," Cloister warned him and caught his foot. The rubber sole smacked against the palm of his hand. A terse whistle between his teeth called Bourneville off, and she let Billy's leg drop as she backed up to behind Cloister. "She won't like it. Neither will I."

He let Billy have his foot back and nudged Bourneville with his knee. "Good girl," he praised her and dug his fingers into her ruff approvingly.

Sprawled on the ground, Billy glared up at him. Frustrated, resentful tears dripped down into Billy's ears, cutting trails through the dirt on his face. He scrubbed them away on his shoulder and scrambled up onto his knees.

"If my grandad were still here, he'd have found Drew by now," he said, his voice breaking. "He wouldn't have wasted time blaming me."

Cloister held his hand out and waited. After a second, Billy grabbed it, and Cloister hauled him to his feet. He staggered, caught his balance, and pulled away. He clenched his hands into fists, and his knuckles poked bony divots against his skin.

"Why can't you just leave me alone?" Billy asked bitterly. "What do you want from me?"

He was angry. That was obvious. Under that, though, was guilt. Javi had seen it and thought it was because of what Billy had done. Cloister had too, at first. Now, though, he thought it was because of what he hadn't done, or what he thought he hadn't done.

"Whatever it is that you don't want to tell us."

The defiance in Billy's eyes flickered, and he looked away. His shoulders, sharp and too broad as he waited for the next growth spurt, hunched up under his hoodie. "Don't know what you're talking about," he said.

"Yeah, you do," Cloister said. He reached back and shoved his hands into the back pockets of his jeans. The denim was rough against his fingers. A breath pulled at his chest and pressed against his ribs. "I did."

That got Billy to look up from the ground and search Cloister's face suspiciously for something. "Huh?"

Cloister looked around. He squinted against the glare and nodded toward the path he'd taken uphill. "C'mon," he said, starting back that way.

As usual Bourneville padded along in his shadow. After a second so did Billy—more from a lack of anything better to do, Cloister suspected, than any real desire to know Cloister's story. That was okay. The lack of questions gave Cloister time to work out how to say what he needed. In the end it was easy. The story wasn't that involved. It wasn't even that unusual. It was just his.

"When I was younger than you, my brother went missing too."

"Younger brother?"

"Older," Cloister said. "Not by much, but he never let me forget it."

"What happened to him?"

"Don't know," Cloister said. "Probably never will."

It took a second, but eventually Billy grunted. Not quite sorry, but at least acknowledging that his wasn't the only family shitty things had happened to. That didn't remind Cloister of himself at all. He'd been a miserable bastard.

They reached the hill behind the campground—a scrub of trees growing raggedly in the stripped-back dirt. It was steeper than it looked. Cloister had skidded down it earlier. Momentum was the only thing that kept him from sliding on his ass. Now he kicked his toes in, dug out short-lived, crumbling footholds, and went up with even less grace.

Bourneville lunged past him, back legs kicking the dirt, and showed him her furry ass as she scrambled to the top of the hill. She flopped down to wait and stuck her head over to watch him intently with pricked ears and a lolling grin. Some of the dog handlers Cloister had worked with warned against giving your dog too much credit, like assigning the dog brain with human intelligence or motives. Cloister didn't care. He could tell when he was being laughed at.

He gave Bourneville the finger—it made him feel better, whether she got it or not—and grabbed a low-hanging tree branch to pull himself over a loose patch of dirt. The bark dug into his palm as the branch bent and pulled away from the trunk as it took his weight.

"My mom never believed that, though." He glanced around at Billy. "She figured I knew something, had seen something, and I was lying."

"Why?"

Cloister let go of the branch and scrubbed his sap-sticky palm absently against his thigh. "I don't know. Because at least if I were lying, there was something she could do? There was an answer out there if she could just get it out of me." He shrugged and hesitated for a second. It was harder to talk about than he expected. The story of his brother's disappearance had been told so many times—by Cloister and to Cloister—that it didn't really hurt anymore. There was just the memory of when it had. Like a hole where a tooth had been.

His mother wasn't someone he talked about. Not really. Not often. When he was a kid, he figured he'd grow up, get out, and get over it. He'd done the first two, but he thought the fact that his mother hated him would sting until the day they tossed the dirt on top of him. He'd never been able to do anything to help her, but maybe he could help Lara Hartley.

"I guess because, at least if I were lying, she still had some control," he said. "If she could make me talk, then we could find him. If I'm telling the truth, if there's nothing I can tell her, then what else can she do? Me lying is all she has."

Bourneville got up as Cloister reached him, and Cloister let her lick him and then turned and grabbed a handful of Billy's hoodie to steady him up the last few feet. He put him back on his feet and then gripped his shoulder and felt the bones and wiry muscle under his fingers. Billy looked up at him, chewing at his chapped lower lip with sharp teeth, and his eyes were desperate for Cloister to not say what he was going to say.

"You do know something, and you need to tell us what it is," Cloister told him. "There was nothing I could do to help my mom. You can, and you have to."

Billy sagged. He looked a lot older than thirteen. Adult fear gave his features an adult cast. He sniffed and wiped his nose on the back of his hand.

"She's gonna hate me," he said.

"She'll be angry at you," Cloister told him and squeezed his shoulder gently. "Maybe she'll be angry at you for a real long time. She won't hate you."

A sigh, another sniff, and then Billy nodded. "Okay," he almost mouthed, his voice was so low. "Okay, but I don't even know if it'll help."

Cloister didn't lie often. Dogs and the bereaved didn't understand the idea of a white lie, or best efforts, or optimism. They just saw that you'd promised something and then not given it to them.

"It will," he said, and he hoped it was true.

The search party, a shrunken version of the one that was still looking for Drew, was just about to head out when Cloister dragged Billy back into the Retreat. When Lara saw her son, her face lit up with relief that spread down from her eyes to the corners of her lips. It took her three long steps to remember that she thought he might be a murderer. Her face closed over and turned cold, and her outstretched hands trembled and then dropped back to her side.

"Where was he?" she asked and swallowed hard. It was obvious she half expected the answer to be something horrible, something incriminating.

"He just lost track of time," Cloister said. He nudged Billy forward a step. "He's all right now."

A half-hearted mutter of relief spread through the crowd of searchers. The fact that Billy was—had been—a suspect obviously wasn't a secret anymore. One of the women stepped forward to put an arm around Lara. Her "you must be so relieved" wasn't any more convincing than Lara's delayed agreement.

"Of course," she said.

Three men pushed their way through the crowd. Ken ignored his son and went straight to his wife and tried to pull her into his arms. She shoved at him impatiently and thumped the heels of her hands against his chest as she tried to keep him at arm's length. When that didn't work, she hissed something angry enough to make the woman trying to comfort her go round mouthed and round eyed—scandalized, delighted, and guilty all at once. It made Ken back up. He dropped his empty arms to his side as though he didn't know what else to do with them.

The other two headed straight for Cloister, and he braced himself for a scolding.

"Where the hell have you been?" Javi gritted out, anger smeared like two lines of red paint across his cheekbones. The man with him stepped in front of Javi, ignored his low snarl of irritation, and asked sharply, "More importantly, what the hell are you doing with my client?"

That let Cloister put his finger on his name, or at least his profession—the lawyer Lara had called in when they brought Billy in for questioning. Diggs. He was dark and pretty, with expensive hair and a suit that made it look like he shopped in the same store as Javi. It was stupid to be jealous, but Cloister felt the emotion latch on anyhow. It sank its teeth into the back of his tongue, and reminding himself that he had no fucking claim on Javi or any reason to think the lawyer did have a claim didn't do anything to dissuade it. Cloister rolled his shoulders back and tried to work the tension out of the muscles.

"You'd mislaid him," Cloister reminded Diggs flatly. The edge to his voice could probably pass for a cop's easy dislike of a defense lawyer. "Maybe you should be more careful."

Diggs took another step forward. He pulled himself up to his full height, chin up and black eyes snapping. He was nearly half a foot shorter than Cloister, but that didn't seem to bother him.

"You were told that any future contact with my clients had to be done through me," he said. "If you ignored that and interrogated my *underage* client, then I'll get anything said thrown out of court."

He lifted a finger and poked Cloister in the chest to underline his point. Maybe Javi had been telling the man that Cloister was approachable. Down by his knee, Bourneville picked up the bleed of tension through Cloister's muscles. She growled, and the sound was low and nasty in her chest.

To his credit Diggs had the good sense to take that as a sign he should step back. Cloister dropped a hand to Bourneville's head to reassure her he wasn't in danger.

"Don't poke me," he said bluntly.

"Then don't try to do a side run around me to get to my clients," Diggs snapped back. "Billy's parents and I have made our position perfectly clear, and we expect—"

"We talked, that's all," Billy said. His voice cracked with nerves, or puberty, as he glanced over at his parents. "I want to talk to them. Okay?"

It started as a statement, but by the end of the sentence, it was a question. He desperately wanted them to make the decision for him.

"Maybe that's a good idea, as long as—" Ken started to say. His attempt at conviction faltered and dropped away the minute his wife interrupted him.

"What if we don't want him to?" Lara asked. She glanced at Billy and then away, and the line of her jaw pulled sharply under stress-dull skin. Her voice was very small as she quietly added. "What if I don't want to know?"

This time when Ken reached for her, she let him pull her into a hug. It didn't look like affection to Cloister, just that she didn't have the energy to keep fighting him. Families fractured over lesser things than a missing child, but maybe he was wrong.

Healthy emotional relationships weren't his area of expertise.

"You need to know," he told her. "One way or another, you need to know. Trust me."

She'd trusted him once, and he told her her son had been taken. Cloister didn't know if she had it in her to do it again. But after a second, she nodded against her husband's shoulder.

"Okay," she said. She extracted herself more gently from Ken and held her hand out to Billy. He stared at it as though he expected a slap but finally shuffled forward and let her grab his fingers. She squeezed tightly and left white divots on the back of his hand as she dragged her chin down in a sharp nod. "You can talk to them if you want, Billy. No matter what, I *do* love you."

Cloister's mom had said that too. He really wanted to make sure that, for Billy, it didn't have to be a lie.

CHAPTER SEVENTEEN

REED WAS feeling cooperative for the first and probably only time in Cloister's acquaintance with the grasping ex-hippie. When they asked he was only too glad to let them use his office. He would probably have preferred to stay and watch the interview, but Javi coldly but politely closed the door in his face.

Like the linen clothes, the office reflected Reed's public persona of aging hippy. The sofa was worn, the fabric threadbare on the arms and along the front of the cushions, and the desk was a repurposed kitchen table with graffiti scarred into the wooden surface. The top-of-the-line safe and the glossy curve of the MacBook Pro charging on the filing cabinet were the only things out of place.

Those and the people.

Billy sat in the corner of the battered couch and picked nervously at the stuffing with his fingernail while his parents hovered and Diggs talked with quiet intensity to all three.

"How did you convince Billy to talk to us?" Javi asked Cloister as he grabbed his elbow and pulled him into the corner.

"I asked him to."

Javi hissed out a sigh between his teeth. "Did you threaten or intimidate him in any way?" he asked. "He's not a suspect anymore, but with J.J. involved, we *need* to stick to—"

Two hours before or two hours later, and Cloister would have let the comment roll off his back. He knew what he looked like. Back home there were plenty of men who looked like him. Between fifteen and seventy-five, the Witte men looked like bad news, and Cloister hadn't fallen far from the family bad-apple tree. Javi had just picked the wrong time for that particular criticism while Cloister's skin was still raw from those old truths.

"You're the one who wanted me to talk to the kid," he growled, and he could feel the rasp of it in his throat. "Don't complain about it now that I have."

Javi narrowed his eyes but let it go. He turned his back on Cloister and looked at Diggs.

"Well?" he said. "Do you have any objections to us speaking to your client?"

"Plenty," Diggs said. He smirked acknowledgment of the pun as he made it. The flicker of shared, dry amusement between him and Javi made Cloister clench his jaw. Diggs didn't even acknowledge his presence as he went on. "But on the understanding he isn't a suspect, and since both he and his family insist, I suppose I have to allow it. However, if I don't like the direction this conversation is going... that could change."

Javi grabbed Reed's office chair, pulled it from behind the desk, sat down in it, and leaned forward. His shirt pulled tight over his shoulders as he rested his elbows on his knees and linked his hands together in front of him. Hunched against the arm of the couch, Billy tensed visibly. Lara reached for his arm, hesitated, and then completed the gesture.

"So talk," Javi said.

The calm direction made Billy, braced for interrogation, blink in confusion. He licked his dry lips and glanced at Cloister, clearly seeking some sort of support. Cloister didn't know what he had left to offer, but he gave Bourneville a nudge with his knee. She got up, padded over, and put her chin on Billy's knee. He grabbed a handful of her ruff and seemed to soak up confidence from the coarse fur and warm weight of the dog.

"I was supposed to be meeting a girl," he said.

"Allison," Lara said. "You told us...."

Color crawled up Billy's throat and picked out the scabs and spots of encroaching puberty. He swallowed hard, and his Adam's apple bobbed jerkily under his skin.

"No, she was someone I met online," he said. "We were going to... she said she wanted to do... y'know."

He trailed off awkwardly, still flushed miserably up to his ears. Despite the obviously exhausted fear that dragged at Lara, she reacted to the familiar fear of internet predators. She slapped Billy's shoulder.

"You were going to meet someone you met online? What have I told you about that? You don't know who they really are, what they really are. Just because they say something, doesn't mean that it's true. They could be anyone. They could be—" She stopped suddenly and pressed her fingers against her trembling lips. Her horrified eyes sought out Javi as her voice spiraled up, shrill and scared. Ken put his hand on her shoulder, but she ignored him. "Do you think that's what happened? Did this *person* that Billy was talking to, this pervert, did they take Drew?"

"We don't know anything yet, Lara," Javi said as he raised his hands in a stilling gesture. "Let Billy finish. Who was this girl? And how long had you been talking to her?"

"Bri," Billy said. Despite everything that had happened, a dreamy, lovelorn expression swam across his face as he said her name. "We were both into geocaching, y'know, like treasure hunting. She kept beating me, like all the time, and then we started talking online. We... she didn't have anything to do with this. I... Mom was right. It was my fault."

The sound of Lara's indrawn breath was sharp. A hard look from Javi made her bite her lip, fold the full curve of it between her teeth, and hold her tongue. She clenched her hand into a fist on her knee, and her fingers dug into the flesh through her trousers.

"Why?" Javi asked patiently.

Billy looked down and stared intently at his hands as he petted Bourneville. She was panting patiently, not relaxed, but easygoing.

"I was supposed to meet Bri that night," he said, not looking up. "I know I was dating Allison, but... Bri is beautiful and smart, and I just wanted to meet her. She told me that she'd come to the party, that we could meet there. Drew wanted to come with me. He *always* wanted to come with me. I told him not to. I told him that he couldn't, and that he was a stupid little kid...."

There were tears in his eyes and snot wet on his upper lip. "I didn't *know*," he said desperately. The tears dripped down onto Bourneville's head, leaving wet commas on her fur and making her ears twitch. "How could I have known? He should have stayed at the cabin. He should have been okay."

"Did you meet Bri?" Cloister asked. The scrape of his voice sounded harsh as it cut over Billy's muttered confession.

Billy wiped his face again and shook his head. "She didn't turn up. I guess her parents stopped her, maybe. She was gonna sneak out." He looked around the circle of grim faces and seemed to realize what they were thinking. "No. No, you don't get it. It wasn't Bri's fault. It was *mine*—"

Diggs put his hands on Billy's shoulders and squeezed warningly. "I think that's enough. My client—"

Billy ignored him and tripped over his words as he sped on. "If I hadn't argued with Drew, if I'd gone back to the cabin with him, it would have been okay. It was *my* fault. Bri's not some sort of pervert, not some sort of creeper. I know her."

The indignation in his voice cracked with adolescent certainty. Cloister remembered when he'd been that sure about things. Sometimes he'd been right, but never about the things he wanted to be right about. Javi glanced up at Diggs and traded a reassuring look with him when he reluctantly backed off a step.

"I'm sure you're right," Javi said patiently. The tone made Billy glare at him and hunch his shoulders defensively. "But we need to check. You understand that, right?"

Lara squeezed his knee. "He does, of course," she said firmly. "Whatever you need, he's going to tell you. If this... person... took Drew, they'll have kept him... safe, right?"

Alive was the word she meant but didn't want to say. The shitty hope at the bottom of the box that whoever took your kid had their own twisted reasons to keep them breathing. No matter what else had happened. With Birdie's tight, sunken face still fresh in his mind, the tiny bones of her wrists looking breakable, Cloister wasn't sure they even had that.

"I'm sure they will, Lara," Javi said. "We're still looking for him."

She stared at his face for a second and visibly decided to believe him. She dipped her chin in a nod and pushed Billy's shoulder. "So you tell them," she said. "Everything this person told you."

"Bri," he said stubbornly. "Her name's Bri. She's not some old perv. I'd have known. I'm not stupid. We're friends."

"Do you know where we can find her?" Javi asked.

Billy opened his mouth and closed it again. He twisted his hands in Bourneville's ruff again, worrying her hair into nervous elflocks. "She...

her dad hasn't bought a house yet," he said. "They had one, but it fell through. They've been staying in hotels with friends and stuff."

"What does her dad do?" Javi asked. He sounded interested, almost casual.

"Building," Billy said promptly. He looked relieved to have a question he could answer. "He's a developer. That's why it's funny he can't get a house. You know?"

Javi just nodded. "Do you have a contact for her?"

"On my phone," Billy said. "We talked on Skype and Facebook mostly."

Still hovering behind the couch, Ken frowned. "That's not possible," he protested. "We have access to his social media accounts. We check them once a week, make sure everything is aboveboard."

Lara took a deep breath. "Don't be stupid. He had another account, didn't he? One we didn't know about?" She looked at Billy and waited for an answer. Instead of giving her one, he hunched over and tucked his chin in guiltily. When that was all she got, Lara turned a flinty expression to Javi. "He'll give you the code to his phone and his secret accounts. Everything."

It took two sides of a sheet of a paper for Billy to scribble down all his passwords. He underlined the last string of random words and numbers, which bisected the back half of the page, and held it out.

"You'll see," he said defiantly. "Bri's real. She's sent me pictures and everything."

It was almost poignant and definitely enough to make Cloister feel even worse for Billy. The quick flash of knowing heat that passed between Diggs and Javi—the sly looks of people who had naked pictures—almost didn't bother him at all.

An hour later, in Javi's office, the contents of the phone opened up across the curved screen that had higher definition than Cloister's TV back in the trailer. By *sent*, it turned out Billy meant uploaded to a friend's locked Instagram account.

On Javi's computer the pretty blonde girl grinned out of the screen, stared pensively into the distance, crossed her eyes, and stuck her tongue out over a Starbucks cup. Shiny, delicate earrings sparkled in her ears in every picture, and she had freckles that death had scraped off.

Apparently the '80s had been back in fashion ten years ago too.

"Why use her?" Cloister asked as he leaned his arm on the back of Javi's chair. He could smell the sharp gingery smell of Javi's skin, the hint of lemon caught in his dark, dense hair. It tickled the back of his tongue and made his mouth dry, but he tried to ignore it. "If Billy had shown that to his father, there's every chance that Ken would have recognized her. Even though he was older than her, Birdie dated his cousin and then disappeared. It was memorable."

Javi snorted. "He knew that wasn't going to happen. Billy was already lying to his parents about his use of the internet. He wasn't going to snitch on himself just to show his dad a picture of a girl he liked."

He tapped his finger on the mouse, flicked one picture aside, and pulled up another—a landscape. The caption claimed it was a "site my dad's going to buy!" The picture was a familiar mix of half-finished and rundown buildings.

Technically Birdie was in that picture too. Cloister picked out the building they'd found her sad little corpse in.

The grim mockery of it made both men fall silent for a second.

After a moment Javi closed the files. "Taking everything else into consideration," he said. "The risk might have been the point. Until we know more about the other effects found in the house, we can't say for sure, but I think it's obvious that the Hartleys weren't chosen at random."

The cold shadow of old dread crawled out of the basement of Cloister's brain. He could feel the heat of that long-ago run, the sweat of it itching under his arms. It wasn't that he didn't remember his childhood. One of his therapists told him once that the memories were there, but he didn't let them out. Just the nightmares and the dread.

"Why take Drew?" Cloister asked. His voice was a rough scrape that made Javi look curiously at him. Clearing his throat, he tried again. "It wasn't Drew that our killer was grooming, it was Billy. He's the one who was in contact, and he's the same age as the killer's first victim. So why change?"

Javi pulled up another file scraped from Billy's phone and maximized the window. It was a log of text messages sent the night Drew went missing.

Bri: Don't want to go to party. Just wanna c u. Can we do that?
Billy: You sure? I haven't washed in days.

Bri: Don't care. Are you alone?
Billy: I got, like, no friends.
Bri: U've got me. Meet me at the road.
Billy: K!

It was almost funny for a second. The "not washed in days" remark nearly dragged a laugh out of Cloister's throat. Then the tragedy of it all wrapped back around it, and he didn't want to laugh anymore.

"Drew wanted to embarrass his brother," he said. "So he stole his phone."

"And while Billy was waiting for his Bri at the original meeting place, Drew walked into the trap. And once he turned up, the killer had to adapt," Javi said. He had restless hands and fidgeted with the keyboard and tapped the end of a pen against the desk. It was a bit distracting. Cloister kept catching himself watching Javi's hands as though the long fingers—all straight and unscarred—were doing something more erotic than fussing. "Drew wasn't the one he wanted, but he couldn't just try again. Not once Drew told his brother that his girlfriend was a man. That could be... bad."

Cloister could see that. Panic made people stupid, and serial killers probably didn't react well to pressure. But panic was immediate, powered by that first flood of act-first adrenaline. And they'd found a bloodstain, not a body.

"It might work in his favor," he said. "If this guy wanted Billy for some specific reason, then maybe hurting Drew won't do what he needs it to."

The sudden stillness of Javi's hands was oddly jarring. He spun the chair to the side and looked up at Cloister with pursed lips and narrowed, thoughtful eyes. You could practically see his brain working behind the shield of short, thick lashes.

"Maybe," Javi said slowly, drawing the word over his tongue. "And if you're right, and you didn't miss the phone during the initial search—"

"I am. We didn't," Cloister said.

"I can accept that," Javi said. "That means that our kidnapper planted the phone. He didn't need to do that, and he knew it. This isn't the first time he's done this. So that means he wanted to frame Billy, and that means he might not be able to let go of his initial plan. He might not be done with Billy yet."

The speculation was clear. It was Cloister's turn to narrow his eyes and clench his jaw until he could feel his teeth shift. He wanted to get Drew home. Needed to, if he wanted to sleep anytime soon. Yet he could still see Billy's pinched face and the fear that stripped the adolescence away to leave the kid underneath exposed. He could see himself there too.

That was what decided it for him. He'd never had much sympathy for himself.

"We're going to use him as bait," he said.

The slow smile that crawled over Javi's face was hard, with sharp edges under the prettiness of his mouth. "Yes," he said. "We are. Do you think it will work?"

"Maybe," Cloister admitted. "Will the family agree to let him?"

Javi didn't hesitate. "They will," he said. "Billy isn't exactly in their good books right now, is he? Besides, he won't be in any real danger. We'll be there."

The careless tone put Cloister's teeth on edge. It was like Javi only saw the solution to a problem, not the boy who'd already taken on too much blame. Was Cloister any better, though? He saw the boy, and he was still willing to go ahead with it.

"And since you already have a connection with Billy," Javi added, "it will be even easier to convince them to go along with it."

That was right. Javi was the asshole. Cloister really needed to keep that in mind. Maybe it would stop him worrying about Diggs and his expensive suits.

CHAPTER EIGHTEEN

DOCTOR GALLOWAY smelled of carbolic soap and lavender hand cream. She pushed her glasses up onto the top of her head, where her pale hair tangled around the funky pink arms of her glasses, and rubbed her eyes. The small office was dim. The only light came through a narrow window high on the wall, and the light from her computer made her look even paler than usual.

"There's only so much I can tell you," she warned. "The poor girl's been dead a long time."

Javi nodded. Pathology was always presented as though it were as linear as mathematics, but anyone who'd had to decipher conflicting autopsy reports knew it was half formula and half flair. Mistakes could be made, assumptions influenced decisions, and experience varied. Give a corpse a couple of days in a body of water, and a stab wound and animal predation could be hard to tell apart. A ten-year-old corpse meant things were even more complicated.

"What do you have?" he asked.

She sat back in her chair, which made it creak under her shifting weight, and reached for the mug on top of an anatomy book.

"There's no evidence of any gross trauma to Bridget Utkin's body," Galloway said. She took a drink of coffee, tipped the mug right back for a swig, and grimaced at the taste as it hit her taste buds. "Cold," she explained as she put it back down in the existing coffee ring. "She had some superficial injuries to her wrists, indicating some form of restraint, and I have sent the trace evidence extracted to the lab. The staining to the occipital bone of the skull also indicates a superficial injury, probably a blow to the head, prior to death. None of those were likely to be the cause of death, though."

"So what was?"

Galloway folded her lips together and pressed them into a thin, pale line. For a second Javi thought it was uncertainty or an unwillingness to commit to an idea, but it was more like... distaste for what she was about to say.

"I can't, at this stage, make a definitive statement on the cause of death." She reeled off the ass-covering disclaimer without bothering to give him time to respond. "However, based on the evidence of autolysis to the organs, discoloration to the lower extremities, and the fact that I found strands of Utkin's own hair under her nails... I suspect she died of a combination of dehydration and hyperthermia. It's possible the tissue samples I've sent to the lab will contradict that, but... I know the signs."

She did. There'd been three infant deaths from hyperthermia in Plenty in the last year. Javi had been called in on one of the cases when the evidence mounted that it hadn't been a mistake. Mostly it was just tragic.

"How long would it have taken?" Javi asked. "Birdie Utkin was a teenager, so her ability to regulate her own temperature would have been established."

Galloway nodded, picked up her mug again, and grimaced around another gulp of cold coffee. "It depends on where she was being kept. It could have been a couple of hours, or a couple of days."

With babies it was always cars. Javi didn't believe in hunches, but he remembered a burnt-out car and the desiccated leather-and-rag remains of a raccoon in the backseat. If their suspect was Birdie's boyfriend Hector, he'd been living in his car. It would have been the only place he had control of.

"If she were in the trunk of a car?"

Galloway pulled that unhappy face again, got up from the desk, and squeezed around it to get to the coffee machine on the filing cabinet. She topped up her mug with the dregs sizzling in the bottom of the stained glass carafe.

"Under an hour," she said. "It would have been like being in a crockpot."

It was the mundanity of the image that made it so macabre, Javi thought. His brain queasily revisited the slow-broiled tilapia he had made last week—the curled edges and wet, slipping flesh. He blocked his imagination from developing the idea any further, not that it needed to, and swallowed the sour acid taste on the back of his tongue.

"After this period of time," he said. "Would it be still be possible to detect drug residue in her system?"

Galloway raised her pale eyebrows at him, wrinkling her forehead. The gesture seemed to remind her she was still wearing her glasses on her forehead, and she tugged them down. Her fingers left more smudges on the lenses as she settled them on the bridge of her nose.

"Assuming she ingested the substance shortly before death, there might not have been time to metabolize it," she said. "In that case, for some chemicals, we might be able to find traces. Why? What should I be looking for?"

"Psychotropics," Javi said. It was possible the killer used the same cocktail in every murder, but if he was also a drug dealer, then it was possible drugs were just a weapon of opportunity. "Mephedrone."

Galloway gave him a curious look. When he didn't explain any further, she nodded and squeezed back behind her desk. She drank her coffee absently as she typed one-handed on the computer.

"I can do that," she said. "I already sent tissue samples, so I can just append these tests for the lab. Anything else?"

Javi shook his head and got up, ready to take his leave. He changed his mind as something occurred to him. It was possible that losing a house and ending up homeless when your family left the area was enough of a trigger for a fragile personality. It removed the constraints of socially encultured behavior and gave a direction for their anger and delusions.

It didn't feel like the focal point of the crimes, however. The drugs in the bottle Cloister had found weren't just to disable Drew—or Billy, as the initial target. There was a reason behind them.

"Could you check back in the records ten or twelve years?" he asked. "Any death involving cars, drugs, and a teen male survivor or next of kin."

Galloway snorted at him. "You don't want much," she said. "Lucky for you it's a slow day."

"Really?"

She laughed. It was a big, braying sound from a woman who usually looked like she should be on a vitamin drip.

"No," she said. "I'll see what I can do, though."

Javi nodded his thanks. "Forward anything that you find to my office," he said. "I appreciate it, Doctor Galloway."

"My birthday's in a couple of weeks," she said. "I like Amazon gift cards and coffee."

He quirked a dry smile. "We'll see what your search turns up," he said. "Coffee is for winners."

That earned him another snorting laugh and a toast with the coffee cup. He left her to it.

"WELL?" JAVI asked without preamble. He flicked the radio down as the Bluetooth kicked in. He was sitting on the road back into Plenty, stationary in a sea of tired commuters on the way home from San Diego. The rows of cars crawled when they moved at all. Javi was already irritated when he got in the car—Reed had begged off his interview at the station due to "unavoidable business commitments"—and the smell of gasoline and hot tarmac wasn't improving his mood.

"They've agreed to make contact online," Cloister said. There was a roughness to his voice, a rasp hiding under the easygoing drawl. It got stronger when he was turned on. When Javi's hand had been wrapped around his cock, Cloister's voice was hoarse and ragged. "Parents draw the line at an actual physical meeting."

"We can work on that," Javi said.

Even without seeing Cloister's face, Javi could tell he wasn't completely comfortable with that idea. It was probably good that he was on the dog squad instead of homicide. He was soft.

Not all the time, his brain took the opportunity to remind him. He flexed his fingers around the steering wheel, and the tips of his fingers prickled with the memory of hard flesh and silky skin. Javi grimaced. It would be a lot easier to stick to his rule about keeping Cloister a one-night stand if his cock and his libido would play along. Or if thinking about the naked, growling Cloister weren't a lot more pleasant than the image of Birdie Utkin baking to death in a car.

With Galloway's crockpot analogy back in the forefront of his mind, the distraction of Cloister's whiskey-and-sex voice in his ear faded. A bit. Javi nudged the car forward and gained speed as the cars ahead of him started to move.

"According to Galloway, Birdie's COD was hyperthermia," he said. "Probably from being locked in a car. I'm having samples tested to see if Birdie was dosed with the same drugs that we found in the desert."

There was a snort in his ear. "We?"

Javi ignored that. "I'll get one of the computer techs to head over to the Hartleys'. They can set up everything we need to monitor any contact Billy makes. We aren't going to put him in danger."

"Yeah, usually people don't mean to let the shit hit the fan," Cloister said. "It does anyhow."

"Well, that's… homespun."

The sun hit the canted window of the sports car ahead of Javi, making him squint even through his sunglasses. The driver kept veering in and out of his lane with abortive attempts to nudge between the cars.

"I just don't want that family to lose two kids," Cloister said. He sounded tired suddenly, like a truckload of lost sleep had just settled on his shoulders. "Two days in a car trunk, hot as it's been…."

It didn't matter. They both knew what he'd been going to say. There came a point when hoping for the best was more delusional than optimistic.

"Doesn't change our job," Javi said. "We'll catch who did this."

"That's your job. Mine is to bring Drew home."

"I hate to be the one to disillusion you," Javi said dryly, "but you're still a police officer. Arresting criminals is part of your job description."

The douche in the sports car nearly clipped a battered pickup in his latest attempt to change lanes. Javi flinched back between the lines at the near miss while the driver of the pickup rolled down a window to give sports douche the finger. In the back of the car, a big white dog scrambled to its feet and swayed with the motion of the vehicle as it barked furiously. Slobber dripped from its jowls and matted the fur on its chest in wet, white strings.

At least Cloister's dog was better behaved than that.

"Are you still at the Hartleys'?" Javi asked. There was an exit coming up five miles ahead. If he took it, he could get to the Hartleys' address in about forty minutes by the back roads.

"Yeah," Cloister said. "But I'm going to head back to the station. Unless you need me for something?"

"Not so far." Javi put more bite into the dig than was entirely fair. It had just thrown him, the pinch of disappointment he felt when he realized he wasn't going to see Cloister. It wasn't devastating. He'd seen the man a few hours before, for God's sake, but it stung enough to make it impossible to deny he wanted to see Cloister. "More vet bills?"

"Something like that," Cloister said. "There's some stuff I want to follow up."

"What?"

"Stuff."

He sounded obdurate, like the dumb, drawling hick Javi judged him for originally. Now that he knew him better, well, Cloister was still a drawling hick—which was apparently Javi's type these days—but he wasn't stupid. Inarticulate but not stupid.

"You've got another hunch."

There was a pause and then a reluctantly muttered "Maybe."

"Okay," Javi said. He wanted to know the details, to control the threads of the investigation, but pushing Cloister in that sort of mood just ended with fuck-offs and disciplinary action.

Or fucking, Javi supposed. Sometimes it ended in fucking.

He took a deep breath, tasted dust and exhaust fumes, and tried to judge where his professional responsibility to manage the investigation ended and his personal need to control his environment began.

"I'm going to go to the Hartleys', get the tracking software installed on their computer, and make sure they understand the limitations of what they can communicate," he said. "Once I'm done, you get to fill me in on where this hunch is going. Understood?"

"I'm not an agent," Cloister growled. "I don't answer to you."

"Really?" Javi said. "Last night you did exactly what you were told."

Heat licked the edges of the voice, sweet and fizzing against Javi's lips. It didn't matter. It was still flirting, however the words came out. The silence on the other end of the phone managed to sound somehow strangled. Javi assumed Cloister was trying to decide if he was furious or just embarrassed.

Before he could decide, Javi continued. "I'll see you in about two hours, Cloister. I expect words by then."

He tapped the earpiece, and the connection went dead. Ahead of him the sports car had finally managed to squeeze between lanes and was trying to change again. Javi leaned back in the soft leather seat and wondered idly what Cloister looked like when he blushed. It passed the time until he reached the cutoff and peeled off the main road onto the narrow, cracked tarmac.

CHAPTER NINETEEN

"WHEN WAS the last time you slept?" Tancredi leaned on Cloister's desk. Her sleeves were rolled up, and the skin on her forearms was freckled and pocked with old scars. He'd never asked about them, and she never talked about them. But they were old, so whatever it was, she'd dealt with it.

Cloister snorted and sat back in his chair. It creaked under his weight and wobbled as the loose castor clacked and slid against the linoleum.

"I got a couple of hours sleep last night." It wasn't exactly true—not quite a lie either, more of an exaggeration—but he didn't think anyone had ever given an honest answer to that sort of question.

Tancredi wrinkled her nose at him. "You need to learn how to lie better."

"What I need is to find Drew Hartley."

The mention of the boy made her wince, and the teasing slid off her face to leave her looking somber and regretful. She pushed herself off the desk and folded her arms tightly over her chest.

"Don't remind me," she said, and she pursed her lips unhappily. "A serial killer in Plenty. That's all we needed to round out the hand of drug dealers and wife beaters. Did Merlo tell you?"

His blank look was enough answer.

"You know I knew Birdie." Tancredi hesitated and folded her mouth down at one corner in a self-mocking grimace. "That sounds like we were best friends. I saw her in town. I remember her face in the paper and on posters. I thought she'd run away. I never thought she was dead. God. And how many other people has this guy killed? *Children*."

Cloister glanced at his computer screen. A dozen missing-person reports were lined up in overlapping windows—a dozen different names and a dozen outcomes that announced whomever it was had been found. All of them stamped as *No Further Action Required*.

The crime lab had techs analyzing the packets of clothing they'd found and hunting through cold-case files for missing-person reports that matched. Thing was, once a person was found, they weren't a cold case anymore.

"Maybe he didn't kill them all," he said slowly.

"He killed Birdie."

"I know. She was the only body we found, though."

Tancredi looked skeptical but tried to play along. "So what is he doing, then?"

"I don't know," Cloister admitted.

"You know I'm joining the FBI," Tancredi said. "Well, that I want to. I've read a lot of textbooks about aberrant psychology, and that isn't how they work. They don't retreat after the first kill. They embrace it."

She was right. Not that Cloister had read the books, but he knew how violence worked. Even for normal people—if you could find one— it got *easier*. Just like anything else. The kid who puked his ring up after his first fight might not fight again, but if he did, he wouldn't puke. Eventually even the weird pop-yield of a broken nose under knuckles wouldn't bother him much.

Except… he still had a *hunch*. Nothing he could put a finger on, nothing he could pin down and point out. It was like trying to pass someone a handful of frogspawn. The data was there in squishy little pods, but the slime of connective instinct made it hard for someone else to get to.

It was just easier to get on with whatever he needed to do and let people fill in the gaps for themselves. That way everyone was happy— more or less.

"Yeah, you're probably right," he said.

Tancredi cocked her head to the side and squinted at him suspiciously. "Yeah," she said as she rolled the word over her tongue. "You really need to learn to lie better. Let me know if you need any help."

She left, twisting her hair back in a braid as she walked away, and Cloister went back to staring at the computer.

The transcripts of the 9-1-1 calls weren't much use. It sounded as though someone had given each caller the same script to read from. The names were different, the locations, but they hit all the same points. Someone had gone missing, it wasn't like them, they wouldn't do this to whomever was calling and/or their mother, and they knew something had happened.

It didn't mean anything—their fear just had a lot of things in common—but it made it hard to pick out any that might be relevant to his case. The distinct details, what they had of them, got lost in the noise.

By the time he finished, his back ached, his skull felt like someone had it in a nutcracker, and he had a list of five names that might be connected to the Hartley case. Three boys and a girl, all between thirteen and fifteen, all disappeared at the same time of year, all of them with a new boyfriend or girlfriend who couldn't be tracked down. All their parents, with the exception of one boy whose father was a firefighter, worked in either banking or construction.

Now all he had to do was pick one of them and hope they were the one who could confirm his theory before he had to hand Javi a handful of frogspawn and no evidence.

SIX YEARS ago the Szerdos' housekeeper had called the police to report that the family's fourteen-year-old son hadn't come home. His mother was too distraught to make the call. According to the police report, Leo Szerdo was the sort of golden boy that Cloister imagined Javi had been. He was moderately athletic and had excellent grades and a college recruiter's wet-dream list of extracurricular activities. His mother thought he was an angel, his father thought he was a chip off the old block, and the housekeeper thought he was a spoiled brat.

Sometime between being found and the present, the luster wore off for his family. He had a criminal record for drug possession and the occasional bout of disorderly conduct. At the address on file for him, his mother claimed they were no longer in contact. Eventually—reluctantly—she handed over the address where he was staying.

The twenty-year-old was slouched on the bed in the hotel room his parents had to be paying for. One tattooed arm was slung over the cushions. His hair was ratty with grease, and a cold sore scarred the corner of his mouth. It cracked and bled as he spoke.

"It was a long time ago," he said. "I was a stupid kid. I ran away from home, and I was so grateful when my parents found me. That what you wanna hear?"

The words singsonged out of him. He was long past bothering to make them sound believable.

"Is it the truth?" Cloister asked. He sat on an office chair dragged away from the computer desk. Apparently Leo didn't have many friends over. Bourneville lay on the ground next to him on a short leash as she fidgeted and grumbled into her paws. Her tail tip tapped the floor in irritated thuds.

Leo rolled his eyes. "Who cares?" he said. "It's what I'm supposed to say, isn't it? Good boy gone bad? Stupid, ungrateful boy who doesn't appreciate his parents' sacrifices? What do you care, anyhow? It was years ago."

"It's in connection with another case—"

"The Hartley kid," Leo said. "Right?"

He made a scoffing noise at Cloister's blink and leaned forward to grab a pack of cigarettes off the table. His fingers were roughly tattooed with black lettering, and they trembled as he tapped out a cigarette.

"I'd rather you didn't smoke, Mr. Szerdo," Cloister said.

"Yeah? Well it's my home, and I can do what I fucking want," Leo said harshly. He hitched his hips up and worked his hand into his jeans to pull out a lighter. He spun the wheel with his thumb, which made the flint spark. He was doing it too hard and fast for it to catch. Giving up for a second, he plucked the cigarette from between his lips and pointed it at Cloister. "It's a fucking shame about the Hartley kid, okay? It's got nothing to do with me. I don't know what my goddamn parents told you, but the only person I hurt is me. Okay? I'm not some pervert."

He tried to light his cigarette again. He managed it, and the paper flared as it caught. The smell of burning hung in the air, undercut with the bitter smell of nicotine. It put Cloister's teeth on edge. He'd never liked the smell.

"You're not under suspicion, Mr. Szerdo."

"Fuck I'm not," Leo spat. He leaned forward abruptly, and smoke drooled from his mouth. "Why else would you be here?"

"Did you know Birdie Utkin?"

There wasn't a lot of color in Leo's face. He had the greasy pallor of someone who'd been treating themselves badly for a while. But what there was leeched away and left the spots and scars stark against his coarse skin. He licked his scabbed lips.

"How…? Who told you…?" He stopped and clenched his jaw, and the muscles bunched like ropes in his cheeks as he stood up abruptly and pointed at the door, the cigarette pinched between his fore and index fingers. "Get out. Unless you're going to arrest me. Get the hell out of my house, or I'm calling a lawyer."

Cloister could taste the nicotine in the back of his throat—a musty, clinging smell that would be with him the rest of the day. He could have tried to calm Leo down, explain what he needed, and that he wanted to help. Instead he let Bourneville's leash slip through his fingers. She lunged up from the ground and glanced at him for her cue.

"Get it," Cloister whispered and snapped his fingers.

Bourneville barked her acknowledgment and stalked around the apartment nose-first. She skirted the bed, and sniffed the crumpled, sweaty sheets with interest and under the window. The stiff-legged, deliberate stalk covered more ground than you'd expect, and she looked as though she were heading off to murder something.

"Hey, wait. What the hell is she doing?" Leo protested. He took a step toward Bourneville. She ignored him. Cloister got up and blocked him with one arm. Despite the concern twitching at the corners of his eyes, Leo backed off. He sniffed and tried to front up some confidence as he looked at Cloister and squared his shoulders. "You can't do that. You don't have a search warrant."

"I don't need one," Cloister said. "A sniff test from a trained K-9 dog is probable cause for a search, Mr. Szerdo. Why? Is there something you don't want found?"

Leo chewed nervously at his lips and watched as Bourneville barked sharply at the curtains but abandoned them to go into the bathroom. She barked again, more insistently this time, and Cloister guessed it was probably at the toilet. Drug dealers knew better, but it was amazing how many users thought the tank was a good place to hide their stash.

"Mr. Szerdo?" Cloister said. He tilted his head and caught Leo's nervous, bloodshot eyes. "Should I go look in the bathroom?"

Leo twisted his mouth into a bitter smile and crossed his arms. "Do what you want. My mom will get me a lawyer, and I'll be out by tomorrow."

"If that's how you want it," Cloister said. He grabbed Leo's shoulder and pushed him back down into the couch. "Stay here. If you run, the dog will catch you."

He went into the bathroom. Bourneville was standing with her front paws on the toilet, staring at the tank with intense interest and barking every two seconds. Cloister caught her collar and pulled her down off the toilet. He pulled a toy from his pocket for her and praised her enthusiastically. She looked pleased with herself and took the toy off him delicately with her front teeth.

Leaving her to chew on it, Cloister snapped his gloves on and lifted the cistern. It smelled of standing water and old bleach, and a double-bagged package of white powder was taped to the back of it. Cloister pulled it free, went back into the main room, and let it dangle between his fingers.

"Mr. Szerdo," he said. "You're under arrest."

CHAPTER TWENTY

THE LAWYER was waiting for them when they got back to the station. Cloister supposed that, at this point, Leo's mother knew what her son was like. On the plus side, at least it wasn't Diggs. While he talked to his client, Cloister got to talk to his boss. And the guy who seemed to think he was Cloister's boss.

The only one missing was Bourneville, who was getting her dinner in the K-9 kennels.

"Tell me, Deputy Witte," Javi said through clenched teeth. He closed Frome's office door behind him. "What exactly made you think it was a good idea to take a break from our investigation to arrest a councilman's son?"

Sitting behind his desk, anger turning his temples red, Frome tapped a pen irritably against the table. "Couldn't have said it better myself, Agent Merlo," he said. "Witte. Thoughts?"

Javi snorted. "That would be a new experience for him."

He stalked over to the window and jerked the blinds closed. The wooden slats rattled against each other.

"I wasn't taking a break," he said. "I was… following a lead."

Javi turned on his heel to glare at him. "You don't do detection, Witte," he said. "You do dogs, remember? Stick to what you know."

Fine. Cloister dredged his best shit-eating grin out of the back of his brain. "Sure thing, Agent," he said. "Fuck you."

Frome slammed his hand down on the desk. "Witte. That's enough." He swiveled his chair to look at Javi and included him in the rebuke. "You too, Agent. We appreciate your assistance in this matter, but my deputies do *not* come under your authority."

The muscles around Javi's mouth pulled his lips into a bitter line. "As far as I can tell, Lieutenant Frome, they don't come under yours either."

Red spread down from Frome's temples, and his nostrils flared as he took a deep breath. The room felt muggy with testosterone and tension—too small and getting smaller. It reminded Cloister of home. That was never good.

"My mom set fire to her car once," Cloister said.

Both Javi and Frome gave him frustrated, incredulous looks, like he was talking gibberish. "What the fuck, Witte?" Frome asked as he shook his head.

Fucking frogspawn. Cloister shifted in his chair and forced his back out of the sullen slouch it wanted to be in. He squared his shoulders and forced the rest of the words out, past his mother's old advice to "better to be thought a fool than open your mouth and remove doubt."

"Wasn't her fault. She'd *meant* to throw the cigarette out the back window, not into the backseat," he explained. "Dad didn't care. He just got her a new car."

Javi snorted softly down his nose and crossed his arms. His shirt pulled tightly over his shoulders. "Heartwarming tale of redneck love," he said.

Frome gave him a hard look. "Pushing your luck, Agent," he said. Then, just to spite him, he nodded to Cloister. "Go on. And have a point."

"She was the only one who brought it up all the time. Five years later someone mentioned a burn in the backseat, and she would bristle that we were blaming her because of the Chevy. I figure that's what this 'Bri' is doing with Birdie. Killing her was an accident, and that's why he's always the first to bring her name up. Name, photo, all of it. That's why we've had no other bodies. He doesn't wanna kill them."

Frome sat back in his chair and looked dubious. "Serial killers don't—"

"They don't," Javi agreed. "However, Witte might have stumbled onto his one idea of the year. I don't know if this killer, or 'Bri,' cares much if his victims live or die, but you don't dose someone up with psychedelics if death is all you're after. Easier ways to kill people."

"And if we're right about Hector, he was in the ER that night too," Cloister said. "You said that Birdie would have taken a couple of hours to die in that car. He'd have missed it all. That's not what someone like that wants."

Frome coughed—a crackle of nervous sound in the back of his throat—and reached for a glass of water. "That's supposition. You don't know what goes on in the head of someone like—"

The sound of knuckles on glass interrupted. He fired the door an irritated look, but in the middle of a missing-child investigation, he couldn't ignore it to finish dressing Cloister down. Frome tossed his pen onto the table with a huff of impatience.

"What?" he barked.

The door opened, and Tancredi stuck her head in.

"Sir?" she said. "I was talking to Deputy Witte about his theory earlier, and… I thought it was wrong."

"Well, that's helpful," Javi said dryly.

Tancredi glanced at him and flushed awkwardly. "I mean, I thought that earlier, sir. *I* was wrong."

She held out the sheet of paper she was holding and aimed it diplomatically between Javi and Frome. Javi was the one who stepped forward and took it, and he flicked his eyes down the page. "While Witte was going to pick up Leo, I went to check the evidence room for the bags you found at the body-dump site. According to his missing-person report, Leo went missing wearing jeans, a high school sweater, and a dog tag necklace with his birthdate on it." Tancredi craned her neck and reached over to point at something and tapped her nail against the paper. "Package three. Witte was right."

"Well done," Javi said.

Tancredi gave him a quick, relieved smile and exhaled quickly. "Thank you, sir." When she glanced at Cloister, the expression faltered and her smile pleated apologetically in the middle. She cleared her throat and looked around the room. "I don't understand, though. Why was Szerdo down as just a missing person? Even after he got away?"

Cloister shrugged. "We'll need to ask him that."

He waited. In the end Frome sighed and gave up. He took another drink of water and wiped his hand over his mouth when he swallowed. "Fine, we talk to Leo. However, Agent Merlo will lead the interview. Witte, stay out of the way. You've already alienated him enough."

That was fine with Cloister. He shrugged, got up, and drawled out a *sir* as he let himself out. The door slammed shut behind him on its own, which didn't give the same satisfaction as banging it yourself. He was halfway down the hall when he heard it creak open again.

"Witte, wait," Tancredi said. She half jogged the short distance he'd covered and hesitated and grimaced unhappily. "Look, Agent Merlo asked me to sit in on the interview. I'm sorry."

"Why?"

"Well, it was your instincts, your hunch," Tancredi said. She shrugged uncomfortably and hooked her fingers in her pockets. "I didn't mean to… steal the credit."

That was a lie. It was in the nervous movement of her fingers and the faint pink that stained the skin under her freckles. It didn't matter. It left a bad taste in Cloister's mouth, but it didn't matter. Tancredi was ambitious, and he wasn't. She needed this, and he didn't.

"Don't worry about it," he said. "Good work."

She nodded and bounced absently on the balls of her feet. "Thanks. A recommendation from Agent Merlo couldn't hurt, right?"

Cloister shrugged. "Hell if I know," he said. "He's a bit of a prick. Maybe people at the FBI don't like him more than people here do."

That made her snigger and check over her shoulder guiltily to be sure Javi hadn't heard. Cloister wished her luck and went back to his desk. He quickly typed up his report and filed it, shoved some papers into the locked drawer, and killed time to see if anyone came out of the interview room. When they didn't after half an hour—just low voices mumbling through the heavy door—he gave up and headed to the locker room.

There was dust in the creases of his elbows and knees, and sweat rubbed his ass raw. Cloister stripped down to bare skin, cracked his neck, blinked away the tears that brought to his eyes, and weighed the benefits of having a shower against just dragging on his jeans and going home.

In the end the promise of cold water won. He grabbed one of the hard, bleached towels from the rack and padded into the wet room. One benefit of taking over from a corrupt local police force—they had good amenities. He slung the towel over a hook, turned the water on without turning the heat up, and let it beat down on his shoulders.

Chilly needles hammered his tense shoulders and made him jerk despite the fact that he expected it. He felt his body temperature drop. It felt cold, and the pressure jolted the sullen resentment out of his brain, or at least battered it down away from the surface of his skull.

Cloister dropped his head and soaked his hair and the back of his neck. He braced both arms against the wet tile, and his muscles tensed from his wrists to his shoulders. He sighed and blew drops of water off his lips. It felt good.

He closed his eyes and waited for the clatter in his head to go numb.

It worked well enough that the warm hand pressed against his back jolted him out of a shallow, unsatisfying daze. He spat out a curse. The welcome chill suddenly was freezing, and he slapped the shower off. The water managed to get a few degrees colder before it finally drizzled off. He wiped his arm over his face and turned around.

He hadn't expected to see Javi standing there, but on some level, he wasn't surprised either. Cloister combed his fingers through his wet hair and plastered it flat to his head.

"What?"

"I was going to ask you to step into the interview," Javi said. "But if you're napping in the shower, maybe it's time for you to go home."

Cloister scrubbed his hands over his face and chafed away the last sleepiness. "I'm fine," he said. "What happened to keeping me out of the way?"

For a second, as he studied Cloister's face, it didn't look like Javi was going to buy the assurance. Then he grabbed the towel from the hook and shoved it against Cloister's chest.

"He's not cooperating," he said as he leaned back against the door. He dipped his eyes for an efficient once-over of Cloister's wet body and then fastened them back to his face. "Even if you do antagonize him, at least we might get *something* other than smart remarks out of him."

Cloister dragged the towel over his arms. It had been bleached to the point that it wasn't really absorbing water, just scraping it off his skin.

"I don't get it," he admitted. "If I'm right, what's he got to hide?"

The corner of Javi's mouth tilted up, and he shrugged. "Sometimes it's easier to be an asshole than admit you've screwed up."

Cloister wiped his face and then between his legs. "Is that an apology?"

Javi raised his eyebrows. "For what?"

"Dick."

He looked down Cloister's torso to the heavy dangle of flesh between his thighs. Javi tilted his head to the side. "That it is."

Cloister balled up the towel and tossed it at Javi's starched white cotton shirt, and Javi caught it just before the wet fabric hit his tie. The urge to turn it into an argument scratched at the inside of his chest, but... he knew what Javi was like. It worked for him for now. Hell, when it went down in flames, maybe it wouldn't even be Cloister's fault for once.

"Have you talked to his housekeeper?" he asked as he stepped around Javi. Despite his irritation and the lingering chill from the shower, being naked around Javi was giving his cock ideas.

"Housekeeper?"

"His parents think—thought—he pissed champagne," Cloister said. He tugged his locker open and scuffled around inside for something clean. Mostly clean had to do as he pulled on black cargo pants and a T-shirt. "When she was interviewed, the housekeeper thought he was a little brat, but she was worried about him anyhow. So he probably spent more time with her."

Javi shrugged. "Worth a try if you can't help us get him to talk," he said. "Shoes would complete that look, by the way."

He hadn't forgotten. Cloister stepped into his boots. The leather scraped his damp feet, and he crouched down to straighten the tongue and dry the laces.

"Like I said, I'll see what I can do," he said.

The smart remark he was expecting didn't come. Cloister glanced up from his laces and caught a distracted expression on Javi's face. The *what* almost made its way past his lips. Then he glanced down slightly and realized he was eye level with Javi's belt. On his knees. Well, it was good to know he wasn't the only one whose cock kept trying to distract him. He looked back up and didn't try to hide his smirk.

"Shut up, Witte," Javi growled and licked his lips. He absently folded the towel that Cloister had tossed him, squared it neatly, and dropped it onto a chair. "Now come on, before his lawyer marches him out of here."

CHAPTER TWENTY-ONE

BEING A fuckup from a good family had its advantages. Leo Szerdo had an addict's acne, but his teeth were still good, and his skin wasn't covered in sores. Not yet. Unfortunately he also had a good lawyer, if not quite as prestigious as J.J. The difference between good family and Hartley money, Javi supposed.

Javi sat back down and hit Record on the machine again.

"Special Agent Merlo, resuming the interview at—" He glanced up as Cloister pulled out the spare chair and folded his lean form down into it. "Deputy Witte has joined me."

Leo crossed his arms and pursed his lips. "The other one was prettier," he said. Snottily.

"Most people are," Cloister said mildly.

At the same time, the lawyer put a manicured hand on Leo's arm. "Let me do the talking, Mr. Szerdo."

Leo hitched his bony shoulders and slouched back. He picked absently at his nails while he waited and peeled away threads of picked-off cuticle. His lawyer watched him for a moment, and then—once he was sure Leo was going to obey the order to stay quiet—switched his attention back to Javi.

"My client was arrested for possession of a controlled substance," he said. "I'd prefer to keep this interview relevant to that arrest, not a few days of missing time six years ago."

"A week of missing time," Cloister said.

The lawyer made a dismissive gesture with his hands and flicked away the correction as irrelevant. It made Leo pick harder at his nails.

"Mr. Park," Javi said. "Your client has information that could be relevant to an ongoing investigation. If he would cooperate with us, it could make his current situation significantly easier."

"His situation, as you call it, is about to go away," Park said briskly. "It was a 'bad bust.' You had no warrant."

Cloister shifted in the chair and leaned forward to put his elbows on the table. He ignored the lawyer, his attention on Leo.

"There's a little boy *missing*," he said in a rough, frustrated voice. "His brother is blaming himself, his mom's devastated, and that little boy is scared out of his mind. How can you *not* want to help him?"

It was vicious because it wasn't. The anger in Cloister's voice, in between the cracking honesty of it, just sounded confused. Like he didn't understand how someone could turn their back. It made Javi feel a pinch of guilt for every ass-covering, career-oriented thought he'd had since Drew Hartley first slipped out of sight.

Tancredi was an able interviewer. A little stiff—she'd obviously read more books than she had experience—but with solid technique. She made a good cop. Cloister was like being punched by six foot one of principled redneck.

Park rapped his finger on the table. "That's enough, I think," he said firmly. "My client is not responsible—"

"No one helped me," Leo muttered, barely moving his lips.

"Someone should have," Cloister said.

Leo hesitated. For a second the hard shell of smarmy, entitled bad boy hung by a thread, and something raw and terrified was underneath. Then he pulled the mask back on and shrugged irritably.

"Even if I wanted to help, and like I said, it's nothing to fucking do with me, I can't," he said. "So just charge me and let me get on with my life, okay?"

His voice was careless, but he had moved on to chewing the skin around his nails. He'd worried them raw, and beads of blood oozed from the quicks. Javi caught Park's gaze across the table and raised his eyebrows.

It was enough. Park leaned into Leo's side and whispered intently into his ear. Javi idly tried to read his lips. *Demonstrate good faith. If you know anything.*

"He's *ten*," Cloister interrupted impatiently.

Javi grimaced but resisted the urge to kick him under the table. He opened his mouth, ready to smooth things over, but Leo had flinched. He blinked hard and swallowed.

"Ten?" he said.

"You didn't see the news?" Javi asked.

A bitter, self-mocking smile stretched Leo's mouth. "I don't really keep up with the news. I knew a kid had gone missing. I didn't...." He stopped and worked his jaw from side to side as though he needed to loosen up the muscles before he spoke. "Even if I wanted to help, I don't think I can. It was...."

He stopped and blinked again.

"Anything you can do," Javi said. "*Anything* you can tell us."

Leo took a deep breath and wiped his nose. "And you'll let this drugs thing slide?"

"We can discuss it," Javi said.

"It was her," he said as he eyes flicked toward Cloister. "Birdie. No one believes me, but it was."

They hadn't released the name of the dead girl they'd found in the construction site. Not yet. Javi paused and felt the case shift in his brain like a puzzle.

"You knew Birdie?"

"We weren't friends. I talked to her a couple of times," Leo said. He bit his lip and chewed at the rough skin. "Everyone thought I was making it up, that I was mad or a dick or something. Mom said I was hallucinating, but it was her. That's why I went to meet her. She emailed me, said that she'd run away—we all knew she'd run away—but that she was worried about her mom. I tried to talk her into coming home, but I was a kid. What did I know about shit, right? She told me about all the bad things her dad had done, like stealing from people and beating them up? She said he used to come into her room at night and, you know."

The words shuddered out of Leo, spat out one after the other with no pause to catch his breath. There was a brittle defiance to them, as though he were daring them not to believe him. It wasn't a story that gelled with any other version of the Utkin family's dynamic. The case files portrayed Utkin as a demanding but doting father, and Javi hadn't detected any false notes in his grief over the dead girl. That didn't necessarily mean anything, of course, but the fact that Birdie was dead when she told Leo cast the story into doubt.

"You became friends?"

"We talked on AIM. She texted me sometimes, but—" Leo paused to shrug. "—she was scared of people finding her, her dad finding her."

He stopped and pressed a finger between his eyebrows and rubbed the skin in tense circles. His lawyer touched his arm and leaned in to murmur something in his ear. Leo shrugged him off and nodded.

"I remember this," he said. "This bit I *do* remember, but no one believed me."

"We believe you," Javi said. "So you were talking to Birdie. Did she ever ask you to meet her somewhere?"

Leo shook his head. "No. That was my idea. She needed money, and I… I thought that she might, that she was pretty and might…." He shrugged his shoulder with a teen's awkwardness. "So I said I could get her some. Dad keeps a stash in his safe in case of emergencies. The combination was my birthday. Used to be. So I grabbed it and went to meet her."

"You met her?" Cloister said.

The hint of disbelief in his voice was enough to make Leo look up angrily and sniffle back snot as he insisted that "Yes! I met her," Javi bumped Cloister's knee with his under the table—a mute signal to be quiet.

"Where did you meet her?"

"Don't remember," Leo said.

"You do," Javi said. "Think."

Leo hissed out a frustrated sigh. "I *don't*. My memory's fucked, okay? It was some garage, all right? Mom had dropped me off at the movies. I walked there. It was dark. Birdie was waiting for me. She'd gotten me a slushie. She—"

"Did she look different?" Javi asked.

"Yeah. She looked like shit. Her teeth were gone, she was all sores, and…." Leo swallowed and glanced down at his hands, with their scars and swollen, chewed-at nails. "She looked like me. If I hadn't known it was her, I wouldn't have recognized her. Didn't wanna fuck her anymore. I didn't even want to take the slushie. I'd never thought about it before, you know, how shit your life could be and you still think it's better than something else."

"But you're sure it was Birdie?" Cloister said.

"Yes!" Leo bristled. "Fuck sake, how many times do I have to tell you? You *said* you believed me."

Javi put his hand on Cloister's thigh and squeezed. The length of hard muscle clenched under his fingers, but the heat and the rough scrape of denim were a pleasant sensation he put away for later.

"We do," he said.

"Tell him that," Leo said, jabbing a finger at Cloister. "He's got *no idea* what my life is like. No idea what you're asking me to do. And he's sitting there sneering at me?"

"I just don't get it," Cloister said, ignoring the fingers that dug into his leg. "You said you hardly recognized her that night. How did you *know* it was her?"

"She was…. She said…." Leo stumbled over the sentence like a bad starter motor, catching for the conviction and then losing it again. Despite the bad years Leo had on Billy, there was something painfully familiar about them in that second. "It was her AIM. Her profile was a selfie. It was… she said it was her. Who'd lie?"

Javi wasn't interested in answering that question just then. He dodged it instead and dragged the conversation back to the path he wanted to be on.

"What happened after you gave her the money?"

Leo closed his eyes. They looked bruised and older than they should. "It was really weird. She made me take the slushie. I didn't want to. There was lipstick on the straw. It was gross. *She* was gross. But she was getting upset, so I took it, and I had a drink, and she said she'd drive me back up to the movie theater."

"She had a car?" Cloister asked.

"Yeah. No. There was a guy with her. I know I shouldn't have gotten in the car with him, but the wind was so bad, and I didn't want to walk back in the storm. I don't remember much after that. I think I was sick. The guy said I'd been sick. Nothing after that… nothing that makes sense."

"Did she get in the car?" Javi asked.

"Yes," Leo said. Then he opened his eyes and squinted. "Or… no? I don't think she did. I didn't see her again."

"Doesn't matter. Go on," Javi said. "What happened next?"

Leo hunched in on himself, wire tight with the strain of remembering. "I don't remember. Really. It's just—" He thumped the heel of his hand against his temple hard enough that they all heard the impact. "—noises. It was hot and it was noisy—so noisy I couldn't think. Someone was talking, but it was like God screaming at me. I knew it was important, really important, but I couldn't make out the words. I was out of it for over a week. A trucker found me a week later in a truck stop begging for water. There was a fountain right *there*, but I kept asking people to let me drink."

He laughed, although there was no humor in it, and did jazz hands around his face.

"This is your brain on drugs, kids," he mocked as he mugged a dull expression. Then all the energy soaked out of him, and he slouched down in his chair and supported his head on his hand. "I was lucky, I suppose. Guy who found me called the cops. The cops called my mom. They thought I'd been doing drugs and had a bad trip."

"How were you physically?" Javi asked.

"Okay. I was really dehydrated, high as a kite, and I was sunburned really badly—but I wasn't dead, and I didn't have sexually transmitted diseases, which my mom kept going on about. So I was in peak physical form." He sniffed and snorted the breath out in a dry little laugh. "Hell, couple of years later, and it would have been a normal weekend for me. So I suppose it can't have been that bad."

It fit. The pieces were twisted and stained, but they fit. Javi pushed a pad of paper over the table to Leo.

"Write down anything you can remember. Times, people, locations, *anything*," he said. Leo looked daunted and wiped his hand over his face. "You've already been very helpful, Mr. Szerdo, and we appreciate it. Just a few minutes more. If there's anything you can think of that can help. Anything at all."

Leo pulled his lower lip between his teeth and chewed on the skin. "There's nothing," he said, but he pulled the pad toward him. The lawyer gave him a pen.

"You know, you didn't actually do anything wrong," Cloister said as he stood up. He hovered with his fingertips braced against the table as Leo looked up at him.

"What?" Leo asked, squinting uncertainly up at him. The nib of the pen scrawled to a stop on the page and left a line of text unfinished.

Cloister shrugged and pushed himself up straight. "It's just that I'm not sure why you're still punishing yourself."

The pen didn't start moving again between Cloister's statement and him joining Javi outside the interview room. Javi waited until the door swung shut.

"You were right," he said. "We don't have a serial killer. Birdie's death was an unintentional consequence. Probably an accident."

Cloister gave him a guarded look, his light eyes unreadable. "Well, at least I saved my one good idea for the second half of the year," he said lazily.

Ah, yes. That. The taunt had felt satisfying, if petty, in the moment—a passing slice at a familiar target. It had slipped Javi's mind that it wasn't an entirely appropriate way to talk to someone you'd fucked. Not if you wanted to fuck them again.

He probably *shouldn't* fuck Cloister again, of course, but that didn't mean he wanted to take the option off the table.

"Well, if you've been good, maybe Santa will bring you one for Christmas," he said. It was meant to be disarmingly flirtatious. Even to Javi's ears, it sounded more condescending. He shrugged mentally. What else was he going to do? Apologize? Hardly. He left the awkward moment hanging, swung back to the case, and talked briskly as he walked down the hall. Cloister couldn't have been that offended because he strode along with him. "Tancredi said you had a list of the other possible victims. Send it to her so we can get to work on finding our actual victims."

"I can—"

"You can go and get some sleep," Javi said. A sidelong glance showed a sullen expression on Cloister's face, or it might have been sullen. It mildly peeved Javi that he could already guess at how to get Cloister to do what he wanted, and that it *wasn't* seduction. "How many hours should a dog's shift be?"

He took Cloister's guilty frown as a surrender.

"I'm not sure what good finding Leo did, though," Cloister said. He rubbed his eye and ground the heel of his hand into the socket while he dug his fingers into his hair. "We didn't learn anything useful."

Javi pressed his lips together. A better man probably wouldn't have been tempted to leave Cloister with that conclusion. He wasn't a better man, though, and finding Leo had been a nice bit of detective work he knew Cloister would never capitalize on. After a brief battle, his conscience won out.

"That's not entirely true," he said. "We know that the point of our suspect's crimes isn't murder. We know where he's been operating, and we know that six years ago, he was working with an addict who got a dose of whatever he used on poor Leo. Which means *she* probably ended up in the hospital."

CHAPTER TWENTY-TWO

OR THE pen. That would have been Javi's second choice. It was Tancredi who brought him the file, but she didn't know the subject of it. So that meant a call to the other ex-cop in town.

"Alice Murney?" Sean said through the phone's speaker. There was a blur to his voice. He was at least a couple of beers to the wind. "That's a blast from the past. What does a hot-shit special agent like you, Agent Merlo, want with a sad little crack whore like Alice?"

Javi took a swig of an energy drink. The liquid was cold from the vending machine and tasted like artificial blueberry and the bitter, flat aftertaste of taurine. He was using Frome's office since the lieutenant had gone home for a couple of hours. So far he'd approved a press release on the search's progress, which underlined their continued faith in Drew's well-being, gotten an email about their suspect from Doctor Galloway—they were still waiting on the lab for the breakdown of the chemicals in Birdie's corpse—and left an urgent message for Luna McBride to call him back from her university in Philly. She was one of the lost-and-found children. The other boy, the firefighter's son, had committed suicide a year and a half earlier. Javi was tired, and his tolerance for bad coffee had worn out two hours ago. So taurine aftertaste was the go-to drink.

"Six years ago she was pretending to be Birdie Utkin," Javi said.

There was a pause. When Sean's voice came back, the blur was almost gone. He sounded sharp. "She wasn't your snatcher, Merlo. Alice would have stabbed her own mother for a fix, but once she came down, she'd have turned herself in. Half the things we collared her on, she confessed to. She was a nice kid with a bitch of an addiction."

Javi picked up his suit jacket from Frome's chair and pulled it on. "We think she was working for our suspect," he said. "Do you know where I could find her?"

"Now?" Sean said. "Probably in the ground. Like I said, bitch of an addiction. If she's not dead, ask her mom? Not sure where Betsy's living these days, but I could find out, if you want."

"I do," Javi said. "Do you remember Alice being pulled in six years ago? She was picked up down around the Mercado on a disorderly conduct."

"I was a detective," Sean said, putting the emphasis on the last word.

"So you say." Javi ignored the "asshole" that Sean snorted at him. "She'd have been tripping, hallucinating, and hearing things."

The pause was longer that time. In the background of the call, Javi could hear football on the TV and someone asking if Sean wanted the leftovers.

"Yeah," Sean said slowly. "I'd almost forgotten that. She was yelling abuse at everyone, accusing them of talking behind her back and taking her kid from her. It gave her the horrors all night long. In the end they had to send her to the hospital. Thing is, she didn't even have a kid. Not one her medical records knew about."

Javi picked up his phone and flicked the speaker off. "When you get her mother's contact details, let me know."

"Sure," Sean drawled. "And don't worry about owing me. The chance to enjoy your delightful company again is payment enough. Although, if you're feeling generous, send your hot friend round with some good whiskey. He can leave the dog at home."

With a dirty laugh, Sean hung up before Javi could do the same to him. Javi curled his lip in a sneer and dumped the phone in his pocket.

"Shows what you know," he muttered. "He never leaves the dog at home."

IT WAS late, and Javi was tired despite the buzz of Red Bull jittering under his skin. So he should have been on his way home to quinoa salad leftovers and his own bed, not driving an hour through the city to find the street where the Filling Station had its parking spot for the night.

Yet there he was.

The powder-blue-and-white food truck was parked outside the Gas Station, a classy nightclub close enough to the bad part of town to give it a certain scandalous cachet. The old neon *General Gasoline* sign was the only bit of the original lot left, but it was in pride of place over the door.

Javi stood in a line that was two-thirds giggly, altered-state clubgoers and one-third people who really wanted roast goat tacos at past midnight. The grinning teenager on the counter handed out Styrofoam boxes and paper bags of takeout with the confidence of practice. Some of them he just tossed out into the crowd, shouting the order as a heads-up for whichever customer had wandered away from their station.

It was controlled chaos. Javi struggled with the urge to make it controlled order. All it would take was two straight lines of people, lining up at one side to order and the other for pickup. Tidy, efficient, and not in the way of everyone else on the street. Javi sidestepped around a tottering couple not paying attention to where they were going as they tried to Uber while tipsy.

On the small TV set up on the corner of the counter, small men in brightly colored uniforms chased an even smaller ball across a field.

"¡Eeeh puto!" one of the men at the front of the line whooped drunkenly as the goalkeeper got the ball. He stuck his fingers in his mouth and whistled wetly.

The slur made Javi itch. He wasn't the only one either. A mutter of disapproval eddied through the crowd.

"Shut up, dude."

"Fuck sake."

"There's always one."

The teenager at the counter huffed a sigh. He stopped in the middle of dousing the tamales with western sauce, grabbed the remote, and changed the channel with a scrape of static. The footballers disappeared, and the familiar, earnest face of the local newscaster appeared instead.

"...Amber alert is still ongoing for a missing local boy," she said, mugging sadness with her eyebrows and the corners of her mouth. An out-of-date picture of Drew flashed on the screen, and the emergency number scrolled under it. "Drew Hartley has now been missing for over—"

The kid flicked the TV to another news station. This time to footage of—according to the ticker at the bottom—the San Francisco band Crossroad Gin's resurrection tour. The men on stage looked too young to have gotten to the reunion stage of their careers, but maybe when you were that pretty, things moved faster.

The mundane chatter of his brain couldn't distract him from the weight of the Hartley investigation. When Saul revived Javi's career by inviting him to Plenty, he probably hadn't imagined Javi would pay him back by failing to rescue his grandchild. The fact that Javi found Birdie Utkin's corpse after all these years probably wouldn't console Saul either.

Maybe if it were guilt, it wouldn't be so bad. But Javi couldn't pretend he didn't know it looked bad for his prospects. Not career ending, not yet, anyhow, but not good either. His first high-profile case since Saul's death, his first investigation as the lead agent, and while he was confident it would end with their suspect in jail, that wouldn't matter if they brought home a body to bury instead of reuniting a little boy with his family.

The girl ahead of him got her order, ripped it open, and dug into the taco as she turned around. Sucking sauce off her fingers, she sidled around him. The kid behind the counter gave Javi an easy smile, offensively chipper for the time of night.

"Hey," he said, squinting at Javi in recognition. "Back again? What can I get you this time, sir?"

He was young enough, and Javi was just about old enough, that the sir made him flinch inside a little. Ignoring that, Javi glanced over the kid's shoulder at the specials scrawled in white and blue chalk on the blackboard.

"Four tacos de tripa and four tacos de buche."

"Guess you're hungry," the kid said. "Good to see. It won't be a minute."

He took the cash Javi handed him, shoved it into the apron tied around his waist, and passed the order down to the older man doing the carving. It took over a minute, but not by much, for them to finish the order and swing it over the counter in a heavy, damp paper bag.

Javi tucked his hand under it as he took it and felt the heat of it against his palm. It smelled of sweet meat spiced with oregano and cumin. Like the stained Tupperware boxes his grandmother would bring home when she went to visit her friends and tipsily shared with him as she condemned his mother as a bad cook—which was the pot insulting the kettle, of course.

It was comfort food, nostalgia masquerading as appetite, and he'd ordered far more than he could eat on his own. He pretended to weigh his options as he walked back to the car. He could freeze the food, he could give it to a homeless person, he could leave it to stink his apartment out with the smell of last night's takeout—but he already knew what he was going to do.

He was tired and frustrated, and his nerves were twisted so tightly he could feel his skin scraping against them. Fucking was a good way to unwind. Food was a good way to apologize for the "one good idea" crack without actually having to do the grunt work of regret. So why not?

HE DID feel a bit bad for waking Cloister up. After all, Javi was the one who told him to go home and get some rest. Yet there he was, hammering on the tin side of the box until Cloister rolled out of bed and answered the door. Javi probably would have felt worse, but his cock demanded a lot of his attention.

Cloister leaned one arm against the door and knuckled a yawn off his mouth with his free hand. His hair was bedhead scruffy, and all he was wearing was a pair of faded boxers he hadn't noticed he'd pulled on backward. There was a layer of sweat clinging to his skin, caught in the smooth dips of muscle and asymmetrical knots of scar tissue over his ribs. His black ink looked very dark in the dim light.

"Did something happen?" he asked. His voice was raspy with sleep, but he didn't sound foggy or as though he were struggling to wake up. Just tired. "Did the kidnapper respond to Billy?"

"Not yet," Javi said. He held up the bag of food. It wasn't quite as hot as when he started, but it still smelled good. "I thought you might be hungry."

Cloister picked the sleep out of his eyes with a thumb and forefinger. "What time is it?"

Javi looked up at the black, star-freckled sky and then back to Cloister. "Morning?" he said.

That got him a snort, and Cloister stepped back from the door to let him in. The trailer was dimly lit by moonlight through the uncovered windows. From the tangle of blankets—and the black dog slowly stretching out into the available space—it looked like Cloister had been sleeping on the couch. The place smelled vaguely of wet dog and strongly of sweaty man. Not a smell Javi would want to live with, but he couldn't deny the tug it sent through his stomach.

"Do you even have a bed?" he asked.

Cloister turned on the lights, which made Bourneville whine and shove her nose under a sheet.

"I know you don't eat in bed, Javi," he said as he held his hand out for the food.

He didn't. It was disgusting. Javi handed over the bag of food and watched as Cloister unpacked, unwrapped, and set the tacos out on paper plates. Of course he had paper plates. Javi didn't know why he expected anything else.

His balls were aching and heavy, and lust poked at the back of his brain, but he kind of liked watching Cloister move. It was all economy of motion and no notion of self-consciousness.

"The firefighter whose kid went missing," Javi said. "He retired the year before, opened his own construction company."

Cloister raised his eyebrows and pushed Javi's share of tacos and a glass of soda toward him. "Damn. Guess they get paid better than deputies. Maybe I picked the wrong career."

Right then the only thing Javi was hungry for was tawny skin and the salt-sweet tang of sex. His stomach, on the other hand, growled until he picked up a taco. The first absentminded bite reminded him he hadn't had anything to eat since a snatched sandwich at lunchtime.

"He's doing well," he said. He picked up one of the napkins that came with the order, folded it, and wiped tidily at the corners of his mouth. "Does a lot of work for Utkin."

"It always comes back to the Utkins," Cloister said.

There was a soft thud behind Javi. He glanced around. The black sprawl of Bourneville was gone from the makeshift bed. He looked down into soulful brown eyes and a dangling pink tongue. Bourneville wagged her tail slowly without taking her attention off Javi's face.

"Your dog wants something," Javi said uncomfortably as he shifted sideways on the stool.

"Okay, you didn't have a dog. But did your parents not let you watch movies about dogs?" Cloister asked. He made it sound like a flaw, but Javi didn't think there was actually anything in the dog-POV film oeuvre he was missing out on. "She wants your taco, but she's not getting any."

"Is it bad for her?"

"I live in a tin box," Cloister said. "Feeding the dog spicy food would be bad for everyone."

He picked up his taco and cupped one hand under it as he lifted it to his mouth. It was weirdly distracting to watch him eat. Or maybe not. Cloister did have a nice mouth. By the time he dragged his attention back to his plate, he'd absently eaten another taco. He brushed the crumbs from his fingers and glanced at Cloister.

"So I've bought you dinner," he said as he leaned back and gave Cloister a lazy up and down. "Now it's time for you to put out."

Cloister leaned over the counter and curled a hand around Javi's neck. He pulled Javi into a kiss. Yes, Javi decided, Cloister definitely had a nice mouth. He caught the lower lip of that nice mouth between his teeth and bit down hard enough to make Cloister hiss, and then he laved the pinch with his tongue.

Cloister pulled back and dabbed his tongue at the red graze on his lower lip.

"Does that mean we're dating?" he asked, all earnest curiosity.

Brief panic bloomed in Javi's stomach. It faded when Cloister's smirk got away from him and conjured up a shadow of those ridiculous dimples. Javi shook his head.

"Shut up," he told Cloister. "And this time the dog doesn't get to watch."

Cloister cracked up, and his dimples woke up at last. Laughter wasn't a usual element of Javi's sex life. He liked his encounters to be planned, intense, and mutually satiating—not funny. So he was surprised at how hard the rough growl of Cloister's easy humor left him.

He didn't like surprises, so he dragged Cloister around the counter and shut him up with a rough, scraping kiss. The tickle of laughter lingered on his tongue for a second in the tilt of Cloister's mouth and the hitch of his breath, and then disappeared under the hungry bite of want.

Better.

CHAPTER TWENTY-THREE

THERE WAS a hook on the back of the bedroom door. Usually Cloister's dress uniform lived there between outings, pressed and vaguely ominous in its dry-cleaning bag. Now it was crumpled on the floor, and both of Cloister's hands were clenched around the hook.

"Don't move." Javi had kissed the order into his mouth as he wrapped Cloister's hands around the hook. Cloister hadn't moved. That nagged at him like a pin in a freshly opened shirt and poked at him every time he almost lost himself in the flood of sensation that threatened to take his knees out from under him. Hot mouth, eager tongue, the damp chill of spit drying on his hard cock. It needled— enough to stop him losing himself in the slick pressure on his cock and the wet fingers kneading his balls—never quite enough to actually turn into movement.

Cloister clenched his jaw, tilted his head back, and pressed his skull hard against the door. His breathing was ragged, and his body was stretched out long and lean against the wood. The muscles in his thighs clenched, taut under the skin as he braced himself.

"Fuck," he groaned. He arched his hips up from the door, and his shoulder blades dug into the wood as Javi worked his tongue against the underside of Cloister's cock. His balls felt like rocks, dragged up tight and aching between his thighs, and if he wanted, he could just let go of the hook.

He didn't.

Javi drew back and let Cloister's cock slide out of his mouth. It tilted up toward Cloister's stomach, the head tight and shiny with Javi's spit and a gloss of precome. Javi threw his head back and tracked up Cloister's ribs to his shoulders and upraised arms.

"Got over that problem with authority?" he asked.

"No," Cloister rasped. "Not entirely."

"You're not moving, though," Javi pointed out. He stood up. His shirt hung loose over his shoulders, and his cock pressed against the fly of his trousers—trousers that were probably too expensive to be kneeling in on an old carpet. Definitely too expensive to be pressing against Cloister with sweat and come staining the pale gray fabric. Javi slid a hand over his hip and cupped the curve of his ass in one hand. He squeezed his fingers into the firm flesh and muscle. His lips brushed Cloister's cheek as he said, "*Good* boy."

Yeah. Cloister let go of the hook. No.

"You're a prick." He grabbed Javi's shoulders. "You know that?"

Javi shrugged. "I think you've mentioned it. Once or twice," he said. He flexed his fingers around the handful of Cloister's ass, and he smirked. "Yet you still want to fuck me."

Hard to argue with that. Cloister kissed him instead and tightened his fingers on Javi's shoulders as he crushed his mouth against his. He could feel Javi's sharp intake of breath stealing the air out of his throat and the hard jut of his erection against his hip.

Space in a trailer tended to be limited. It didn't bother Cloister. Five years and his life in Plenty could still fit in a couple of bags if he needed it to. And sometimes it could be useful. One step forward—a half step backward for Javi—and the edge of the bed bumped against their legs. Then all it took was a shove. Javi landed on the mattress and flexed his fingers in the crisp white sheets. Then Cloister crawled on after him. He propped himself up over Javi's sprawled body and balanced his weight on his arms.

"Any way we could fuck without talking?" he asked.

A sharp smile twisted Javi's mouth. "I don't see that happening," he said. "You?"

There was a sharp tension to the question and in the tight line of Javi's body. Not unhappiness, exactly. It was more pissiness. The same bitten-back, pissy irritation that festered behind gritted teeth in the field every time people—and once, well, twice if you counted today, Cloister—did something Javi hadn't approved ahead of time.

Cloister's cock was aching so hard he could feel the blood rushing to it. He wanted to fuck or *be* fucked. Either would do as long as it was hard, hot, and sticky enough to wear his brain out and turn it off. To cut short the guilt-inducing list of the people he *hadn't* been able to bring home. It wasn't like he didn't know the names—the list started with his brother and ended with Julie-Anne Judson, who went missing in the mountains—and his mother's tear-cracked, Midwest-flat voice narrated it. He didn't need that stomach punch tonight.

One of the advantages of screwing the sort of man who turned up for a booty call at past midnight with a bag of cheap food and a hard-on had to be that you didn't have to care about them. Except, of course, he did anyway. Cloister Witte—damned romantic and eternal goddamn doormat.

"Go on, then," he said as he dipped his head to press a stubble-rough kiss against the crease of Javi's neck. He could taste salt and the sharp, musky dryness of the cologne on Javi's skin. "Spit it out."

Javi twisted his fingers in Cloister's hair and tugged his head back until they were looking at each other.

"Did you get hit on the head?" he asked, and he lifted his knee so his thigh pressed against Cloister's cock. "You haven't come yet, idiot, and for your information, I swallow."

That mental image—bruised lips, sweat, the swipe of Javi's tongue after a drop of salty come, and Cloister's cock drained and wet—clenched lust from Cloister's knees to his shoulders and everything in between. He swallowed hard, and his breath didn't want to cooperate.

"Tell me what you want me to do to you," Cloister got out, his voice harsh as gravel in his throat. He sat back, knelt across Javi's thighs, and tried to ignore the ache in his balls. "Order me about, Special Agent. You know you want to."

Javi stared up at him as he considered that with his dark eyes hooded thoughtfully. After a moment he stretched up, the muscles in his stomach and chest slid elegantly under his pale amber skin, and he folded his arms behind his head.

"Since you don't want to talk," he said, his voice harsh and strained, "why don't you find something better to do with your mouth? Suck me off, Deputy."

It had been his idea, but Cloister still felt the brief impulse to tell Javi to fuck off. From the smirk Javi gave him, that urge showed on his face. Cloister resisted it, swallowed the words, and unbuckled Javi's belt. The leather was soft under his fingers, the metal buckle cold, and the thought skittered through his head that Javi might want to use that on him. The image of it, half-formed and tentative, was ridiculous. He was six foot one, and the one time his uncle tried to leather the attitude out of him, he'd punched him. But it was kind of hot as hell.

Not as hot as this, though. Cloister finished unfastening Javi's trousers. His cock jutted up out of the fly, and Cloister pulled them down. He bent over to press his mouth to Javi's taut stomach. The muscles clenched under his lips and clenched again—harder—when he scraped his teeth over the ridge of muscle. He shifted to the side. The mattress shifted under his weight, and he ran his hand up Javi's thigh. With his fingertips he skimmed the tight skin through the scattering of fine hair and brushed the velvet-soft skin of Javi's balls. The contact made Javi suck in a hard breath, and his cock bounced impatiently. Cloister slid his hand back and followed the hard ridge of skin back from Javi's balls toward his ass. The rough swipe of a callused finger against the nerve-rich area made Javi curse and squirm in place.

"Mouth," he ground out through clenched teeth. "Not hands."

"Recon," Cloister said. He grinned when Javi lifted his head off his arms long enough to glare at him. "What? I'm taking your advice."

It took a moment—Javi stared at him like he'd never seen him before—but then Javi snorted. "Shut up and suck me off."

Cloister ignored that pinch of rebellion again and did as he was told. He tugged Javi's thighs apart with his hands and pressed a wet, tonguing kiss against the base of his cock. Every breath he took was thick with the smell of sex and Javi, the taste of him on Cloister's tongue. He licked his way up the shaft, the pulse of blood under the skin tangible against his tongue, and wrapped his lips around the head.

The glaze of precome was sticky. He lapped at it, rolled his tongue around the hard curve of the glans, and dipped into the slit. The noise that scraped out of Javi wasn't quite a swear word, but all the guttural intensity was there.

Cloister slid his head down and rubbed his lips against the shaft and his tongue against the base. It pressed against the roof of his mouth—thick and hot as he breathed around it. He swallowed hard, and the convulsive movement of throat and tongue made Javi groan out his name. He tangled his hand in Cloister's hair, pressed his knuckles against his skull, and pulled his head back. The dark length of his cock slid wetly from between Cloister's lips, and he lifted his eyes to look up at Javi.

His crisp white shirt was wrinkled and stained, glued to Javi's shoulders and ribs with sweat. His face was set in controlled, reserved lines, but arousal flushed his cheekbones and up to his temples.

"I was right." Javi tugged Cloister's head back a notch farther. His eyes were very dark as he studied the tight line of Cloister's jaw and throat. Behind him Cloister could see the night sky through the long, narrow window that stretched across the back of the trailer. "You look good with your mouth wrapped around my cock. I think I have an idea for where you'd look even better."

He flipped Cloister onto his back and left him sprawled there while he got off the bed. Cloister reached down, cupped his hand around his cock, and idly stroked it while he watched Javi strip off his trousers. Javi retrieved a condom from his back pocket and then folded the pants neatly and set them on the narrow bedside table.

"So you were a Boy Scout?" Cloister asked.

"It you fail to plan, plan to fail," Javi said. He slid the thin, latex sheath on and added a slippery layer of lube. He squeezed roughly at his cock as he worked it from base to tip. "Maybe you should try being prepared."

Cloister stretched, touched his fingertips to the window, and extended his bare feet over the end of the bed. "I date guys who carry condoms in their pocket," he said. "That's good enough for the Scouts, right?"

For a second, Javi hesitated with his hand on his cock. Maybe he *had* been a Boy Scout and was offended at Cloister dragging them into this, or he was just disgusted at Cloister's lack of foresight—although there was a box of condoms in the bathroom. Whatever he was, he got over it after a second.

Javi grabbed Cloister's legs, graced a caress around the bump of his ankle with his thumb, and pulled him to the end of the bed. Cloister squirmed as Javi reached a lubed-up hand between his legs and probed his fingers into his ass. Cloister bit his lip and took a deep breath, enjoying the slippery intrusion and aching for more at the same time.

"Nothing to say?" Javi taunted.

Cloister swallowed. His throat was so dry it felt like his voice needed lube. "Fuck you," he cracked out.

Javi smiled. "Since you asked nicely." He took his fingers back, and Cloister's ass clenched around the absence. "Lift your legs."

Cloister raised his knees and pulled them toward his stomach. He could feel the strain in the backs of his thighs as the position drew his ass tight. It felt more vulnerable—more exposed—than fucking against Javi's window. Javi stroked the taut cheeks. The trail of his fingers sent tickles of anticipation down Cloister's nerves, and then he pushed them apart with his thumbs. The hard nudge of Javi's cock against his ass made Cloister suck in a breath and the muscles in his stomach tense. It turned into pressure and a dull, heavy burn as he stretched around the width of Javi's erection.

It felt good. The heat crawled up and followed his taint from his ass to his balls. A hot weight pressed down in his groin. He lifted his hips and pushed up into the thrust until he could feel Javi's thighs and the swing of his balls against his ass.

Javi moved his hands to Cloister's knees, and his fingers grazed over the old nightmare-proof scar tissue on one leg. Javi looked down at the join of their bodies.

"Look at that," he said. "I told you this would look even better."

Javi leaned in with his weight against Cloister's legs, and his cock managed to somehow fit an impossible half inch deeper. With a smirk tucked into the corner of that thin, FBI-smug mouth of his, he watched Cloister pant and squirm as his muscles flexed helplessly around the cock inside him.

"Sonofabitch," Cloister muttered as he pressed his head back against the bed. Heat pulsed inside him—a steady ache of pleasure that balanced just on the edge of being more. "Javi. Please, just, God, please?"

The begging struck heat in Javi's eyes and flared in the back of his pupils, and he began to move. Cloister gagged out something that was half cursing, half taking the Lord's name in vain and Javi's name mixed up in both. He clenched his fists, twisted the sheet into knots between his fingers, and rocked his hips into the thrusts.

Javi shifted forward, braced his knee against the mattress, and dropped one hand to Cloister's hip. He dug his fingers in and hooked his thumb over the ridge of Cloister's hipbone as he thrust harder. Each thrust buried his cock inside Cloister, and jolts of sharp, black sensation shot up his spine as it jostled his prostate.

He shook one hand free of the sheets and grabbed his cock. The tender skin folded and wrinkled as he tugged at it roughly, closed his eyes, and imagined Javi's hand on him instead.

"Open your eyes." Javi's voice straggled on the ragged edge of breathless. "Look at me when you come."

Cloister opened his eyes, tightened his fingers around his cock, and pumped his hand up and down in skin-chafing time to Javi's thrusts. He watched the play of muscle under sweat and Javi's skin, the clench and stretch of it, and the way Javi chewed his lower lip as he struggled to hang on to control. The orgasm wrung out of Cloister spilled white over his fingers and across his skin in a wash of almost pain. It left him sweaty and limp, with come smeared over his stomach and his brain waiting to reboot.

Javi pulled out of Cloister and stepped back from the bed. He closed his eyes as he brought himself over the edge with two harsh tugs on his cock, and come filled the tip of the condom. His chest rose and fell in slow, ragged breaths, as he visibly pulled himself back under control before he opened his eyes.

Cloister scruffed his fingers through his hair where sweat glued it to his scalp. He wondered whom Javi was thinking about when he came. Then he winced and tried not to think about it.

"You fuck like you're going to be scored at the end of it," he said instead.

Javi stripped the condom off. "You fuck like you're aiming for a C," he said.

"I was always an overachiever," Cloister said. Then he yawned hard enough to crack his jaw and bring tears to his eyes. He weighed the prospect of a couple of hours sleep against having to shower off the night in the morning. Sleep won. "Shower's in there. Wake me up if you want to leave."

"And disturb you?" Javi said. "After your considerate disappearance last night? I wouldn't dream of it."

"Up to you," Cloister said. "I mean, Bon Bon has never bitten off anyone's balls. She *could*, but she hasn't."

The bed tipped, and weight tilted it toward the wall. Cloister opened his eyes, and Javi cupped his chin in his hand and grazed his thumb over the curve of his lower lip.

"Or I could just stay," Javi said.

Cloister didn't know what his face looked like, but it made Javi smirk. Cloister cleared his throat. "If you want."

Javi leaned down and skimmed a kiss across Cloister's mouth and caught his lower lip between his teeth. He dipped his tongue into Cloister's mouth, and he tasted himself there.

"I'll think about it," he said as he sat back and ruffled Cloister's hair. "Get some sleep, Witte."

CHAPTER TWENTY-FOUR

BUCKING THE trend, Cloister did sleep.

For a few hours, anyhow. He woke up to the wind howling through the trailer park and the insistent factory-installed ringtone on Javi's work phone. His side was sweaty warm, and the seaside smell of Javi's cologne was rubbed onto his skin, but Javi was already on his phone.

Javi's voice had a rasp to it from sleep, but his words were crisp and clear—more than the grunt Cloister would have mustered at that time of the morning, even if he'd been awake.

"Special Agent Merlo," Javi snapped. "What is it?"

Cloister stretched and scratched himself. His bladder demanded attention. He rolled out of bed, left the bedroom to Javi, and ducked into the bathroom to piss and step into the shower for a brisk, cold shower.

When he came out of the bathroom, scrubbing his hair with a towel, Bon Bon gave him a reproachful look from inside her crate. He slung the damp towel around his hips, patted his thigh, and gave a sharp whistle. She bolted up to her feet, nosed the door open, and let herself out. He followed.

She clamped her tail, sidled over to him, pressed against his leg, and sighed pointedly. Most nights she slept by his legs on the floor, close enough to touch him if she wanted. She knew she had to be good if she was put in her crate or her kennel, but she didn't like it.

Cloister crouched down and fussed over her. He scratched under her jaw and play-bowled her over to rub her belly. She kicked him like a cat and grumbled happily with her tongue hanging out of the corner of her mouth like a wet pink ribbon.

She scrambled to her feet when Javi came out of the bedroom, and she pricked her ears suspiciously.

"Get dressed." Javi tossed most of a uniform at Cloister. Javi was already dressed, although last night had left him looking a lot less sharp than usual. Cloister caught the Kevlar vest and pinned it to his chest, but the trousers slid free and hit the floor. "Our friend 'Bri' just Skyped the Hartley boy. I want to be there to oversee the conversation."

"Why do I want to be there?"

"Because you sometimes have good ideas," Javi said. "Besides, the boy likes you, and his parents still haven't forgiven me. So get dressed."

Cloister dumped the armful of clothes on the table and ditched the towel. He grabbed his trousers, pulled them on over wet skin, and left the fly undone as he grabbed for a T-shirt. He was halfway through putting it on when Javi touched his ribs and walked warm fingers over the scars. It felt strange. The misaligned nerves under the knotted skin didn't always fire in the right direction, and it gave the feeling of ghost contact where Javi's fingers weren't. Not bad, just weird.

Cloister tugged his T-shirt down over the scars.

"Motorbike accident," he said. He'd had the ink for three days before it got scraped off. The remaining Rorschach mangle was more familiar than the original pattern had ever been. "I was fourteen. Still don't know what my stepdad was more pissed off about, the ink or that I'd totaled his bike."

He felt—briefly—bad about lying about the scar. But Javi didn't need any more ammunition, and besides, it wasn't even really a lie. Almost everything he said was true. He just left out the small explosive charge someone had strapped to the fuel tank. There were a lot of people who didn't like Cloister's stepdad, and to be fair, there were even more who didn't like his actual dad.

His family was fucked up.

IT TOOK fifteen minutes to get to the Hartleys' in the suburbs. They lived in a sprawling, seashell-white house just like all the other houses. There were two sports cars in the driveway. The dusty, scouring wind was doing a job on the glossy metallic paintwork, but Cloister supposed they had other things on their minds.

He parked behind the cherry-red Porsche and reached back to unhook Bourneville. She scrambled between the seats, jumped out, and shook her head as the wind tossed sand in her ears. Cloister gave her a conciliatory pat, looked around, and squinted into the low morning sun.

Javi had parked on the street. When he got out of the car, Cloister noticed that, somewhere between the trailer park and there, he'd managed to change into a fresh shirt and uncrumpled tie. He smoothed the second down over the first and held it against his chest as the wind tugged at it.

"You can tell me the truth," Cloister said when Javi joined him, squinting into the wind. "You really were a Boy Scout, right?"

It wasn't a great joke, but it wasn't that bad. Not bad enough to warrant the tight-lipped grimace Javi gave him.

"Cloister," Javi said as he touched his arm, "look, I don't want you to get the wrong idea. We're not dating. You know that, right?"

Oh. Okay.

"Did not think otherwise," Cloister said.

"It's just that I don't," Javi said. "I don't date or do relationships. I didn't want you to get the wrong idea."

"I haven't." Cloister slapped him easily on the shoulder. He smirked. "Look, if I wanted to eat with someone that didn't like me that much, I'd be heading home for Thanksgiving. We're fine. It's fun. It's sex."

Javi stared at him for a second, and with his dark eyes, he searched Cloister's face for the lie. When he didn't find it, the tight line of his mouth relaxed into a more natural-looking smile.

"And no reason it can't continue to be fun sometimes," he said. "As long as we're on the same page."

Cloister shrugged. "Maybe if I don't have a better offer."

He let Javi take the lead as they headed for the house and fell in behind him. Cloister buried his hand in the coarse hair of Bon Bon's ruff. It was weird how good he was at lying about what hurt him. Maybe it was yet another leftover from his childhood. It always made Mom sad when she realized she was unkind.

Hell, it wasn't as though he'd even had the wrong idea. He just—

Been an idiot, he cut himself off. He'd been an idiot, and that wasn't exactly new. So get over it. There was a little boy out there who needed him to do something he was actually good at—find him.

Lara opened the door before Javi had a chance to knock. Whatever relief she'd felt about her oldest son not being a killer had been worn away overnight by the realization that her youngest son was in the hands of a serial predator. Her face was drawn, her skin stained with an undertone of gray all the way down to her lips, and her hair scraped back roughly. She glanced past Cloister and searched the street with bloodshot eyes.

"The press was here all night," she said. "People are still saying that Billy did this. It's all over the internet."

"People are scared," Cloister said. "They'd rather have a face to pin the blame on, rather than have to suspect it could be any face in the street."

It wasn't much comfort. He doubted anything would be right then. She sniffed and wiped her nose.

"I hate this," she said. Her hands were raw. She was picking at her nails in the same nervous habit Billy had. "I don't want this bitch... bastard... God, I don't even know.... I don't want them talking to my son."

Javi stepped forward and put his hand on her arm. "We need to do this, Lara." He gently urged her back into the house. "It will bring Drew home, and then we'll lock this guy away. Somewhere he can never hurt anyone again."

The rug under her feet—a tapestry of ochre and blue that looked expensively handmade—bunched under her bare feet as she shuffled back. She put her hand over Javi's and squeezed her fingers around his knuckles.

"No," she said. "You don't get to touch me. We are not friends. You wasted time that you could have spent looking for this... this pervert trying to blame this on Billy. If it weren't for you, nobody would have thought it was him. He wouldn't have known we... they... thought he killed his brother. So we are not friends. You find my son, and then you will never come into my house again."

She peeled-shoved his hand back at him and wiped her hand on her leg when she was done.

"That's not fair, Lara," Javi said. "I—"

She curled her lip. "My son being missing isn't fair. So don't expect me to feel sorry for you. Just do your job." She flicked her gaze past Javi's shoulder to Cloister. "Or let him do it for you. I don't really care."

She stalked away, and her feet slapped on the glossy wood floor. Javi stared after her, his jaw clenched on his own temper.

"Families always get angry," Cloister said awkwardly. "Usually at us. The—"

"I don't need my hand held, Deputy," Javi said icily. "This isn't my first investigation. Doctor Hartley's dislike for me is why you're here, remember?"

That didn't mean that hearing her say it out loud didn't sting. Cloister knew that firsthand. He also knew that sometimes sympathy made it worse. So he shrugged and changed the subject.

"Where did you put the equipment?" he asked.

"In the kitchen," Javi said. The ice had gone from his voice, leaving it brisk and dry. "I didn't want to risk Billy being able to communicate with her without being seen. "He still thinks that it's some sort of misunderstanding. He still thinks that love is real."

Cloister winced. Right then he wasn't entirely sure whom he felt sorriest for.

A huge wooden table made of pale oak and well waxed dominated the Hartley's kitchen. It was the sort of table that made a statement about the owner's commitment to sit-down dinners and family time. That they meant well, but—based on the unmarked wood, free of dents or scuffs— they never really got around to it.

Occupying the table was a tangle of equipment, a frustrated computer tech from the sheriff's department, and Billy hunched on a kitchen chair, trying to disappear inside his own T-shirt.

"I dunno," he mumbled, presumably in response to something the tech had asked him. "Maybe. I don't see why we have to do this. Bri didn't do this. She's not like what you've said."

The staunch defense made Lara shudder. She pushed the heel of her hand against her forehead, pressed hard enough to blanch the skin, and then turned away. The job of making coffee gave her hands something to do, and she fumbled awkwardly with the coffeepot and faucets.

"Where's Ken?" Javi asked.

She gave him a dirty look but didn't have the energy to hold on to the emotion. Her shoulders slumped, and she went back to frowning at the coffee canister. "He went out," she said. Her voice was small and very precise. "He won't be long. Do you want a cup of coffee, Deputy Witte? Oh, would the dog like a drink?"

"She'd appreciate that," Cloister said. "Me too. Thank you, Doctor Hartley."

The only one she didn't offer a drink to was Javi, but Cloister had learned his lesson. He ignored the snub. While Lara opened and closed cupboards looking for something to fill with water, Cloister went to the table. He put his hand on Billy's shoulder.

"You doing okay?" he asked.

Billy shrugged. It was as much of an answer as Cloister could have expected—more of one than anyone would have gotten from Cloister at that age, probably. He'd done a lot of grunting and sullen staring.

"We need to get our suspect to log in to Skype," the tech said. He pulled his glasses down onto the tip of his nose and scratched between his eyebrows with the end of a pencil. "Once they do that, I can sniff out the VoIP ID's datagrams and use geolocation tools to find out their current location. I'll also be able to get their ISP, and we can ask for a warrant to get their internet activity. But we need them to log in and contact us first."

"I don't like lying to her," Billy said to his knees. "You don't know her. You're all wrong about her."

"Billy—"

"Tell him," Lara interrupted. She dropped a Pyrex bowl into the sink, and the crack of glass on metal made them all jump. "Tell him the truth about this person, this 'Bri.' I don't want him going anywhere near them if he doesn't know the truth. If he doesn't believe it."

"I do, Mom," Billy protested. "I've seen her pictures and her family and...."

Cloister glanced at Javi and got a slow, uncertain shrug in answer. It was up to Cloister, apparently. He'd always thought the truth was better than a lie, however comforting. At least the truth was an end.

"The girl in the pictures you have? Her name is Birdie Utkin," Cloister said. "Her father is a property developer, and she dated your uncle."

Billy's face creased with disgust. "He's, like, thirty."

"Twenty-five," Lara corrected him. She flicked the tap on with a hard twist, and water splashed noisily into the bowl. "He's twenty-five, and so is Birdie Utkin now. Not fourteen, not your girlfriend."

"No. She's…. I don't believe you."

Javi stepped forward and held out his phone. "This is Birdie Utkin," he said, "with her father. It's one of the pictures he gave the police when she went missing."

Billy shook his head. "No," he said. "They just look alike. Everyone has a double, right?"

He looked at Cloister for reassurance, and his eyes begged for them not to take this away as well. Unfortunately that was going to happen eventually.

"This isn't the first time they've done this either," Cloister said. "They've used Birdie's identity to approach other people, to get them to do what they want."

The breath that rattled out of Billy was almost a sob. He sniffed hard and folded his lips in over his teeth. "Are they…. Did she kill them?"

Maybe it was always best to know the truth, but Cloister didn't know if the details were what Billy needed right then. He was scared enough.

"That's not what they want," he said. "But the person they're pretending to be, that isn't real. They're not Bri, they're not Birdie, they're not your friend."

Billy sniffed again, wiped his nose on his sleeve, and looked at the picture again. His eyes hit on the pixels that made up Birdie's face, and then he dodged away again.

"You could be making it up," he said. His voice was tight and scratchy sounding in his throat. "I don't know this is a real picture."

Lara folded over in frustration, braced her elbows on the sink, and covered her mouth with her hand. She was scared for her son, but Cloister wasn't. The defiance was gone out of Billy's voice. Now he was trying to convince himself, not them, and it wasn't working.

"It could be," he said. "Unless we were sure she was guilty, though, why would we bother."

"I don't know," Billy muttered.

"Me either," Cloister said. He tapped Billy's knee to get his attention back. "If we're wrong, I'll take you and Bri on a ride along one night. I don't think I am, though."

The sharp bump of Billy's Adam's apple jerked in his throat as he swallowed hard. He gave a small nod, and his chin dipped an inch as he turned to the tech who slid the keyboard toward him. Billy started to type, but his fingers stalled on the keys as though they still weren't happy to betray their friend.

CHAPTER TWENTY-FIVE

BEFORE SHE went outside to take a call from "Grandma"—Ken's mother; her mother had died years ago—Lara set a bowl of water by the back door. The dog had her face buried in it, and the pink of her tongue was visible through the clouded glass as she drank.

On the tech's screen, Billy's Skype message hung in stark black and white.

Where were U the other nite? Lost my phone. Only got home to the computer. Call me. U won't believe wot happened.

The loose approach to the English language made Javi wince, but it matched the construction of the other messages in the account. Most had been composed on the phone, so short and sweet was the route Billy had taken.

Although their suspect didn't seem to find it all that sweet. "Bri" hadn't taken the bait. Not yet.

"Sometimes she—they—don't answer for a while," Billy said. "Her—their—dad doesn't like them being on social media. That's what they said, anyhow."

"Probably working," Cloister said quietly. He had a mug of coffee cradled in his hands, and he leaned back against the kitchen counter with his legs stretched out and crossed at the ankles. "We know he has a car, keeps it running, and most likely he's a farmhand or laborer. So no breaks to check his email."

Javi caught a gibe between his teeth. He still didn't know what the hell he'd been thinking last night. Not wanting to disturb the sleeping dog cop was not a good reason to spend the night in his bed. He couldn't have blamed Cloister if he thought it meant... something... and since it didn't, that would have ruined their working relationship.

Luckily no matter the kick to his pride, no strings attached seemed to be what Cloister wanted too.

Probably, Javi admitted with a jab of bitter self-awareness, because he was an unpleasant bastard. Good in bed—he would give himself that—but out of it, he wasn't much good at boyfriend stuff. It was fine. His job didn't care about his emotional availability, and neither did Cloister. So he could do both with a clear conscience.

"Have they ever called you before?" he asked Billy.

"Couple of times," Billy said. He wrinkled his nose. "It was always a bad connection, like crackly, and I could hardly hear them. She said it was the hotel they were staying in—old vents and no signal. Out in the boonies."

Javi noted that. It wasn't much of a clue, but liars often used the truth as much as they could. It was easier to remember, and for details that weren't a preplanned part of their lie, it was right in front of them.

"I can't believe I was so stupid," Billy said, and anger jerked at his mouth. He scrubbed his arm impatiently over his face and dragged at the skin. "Maybe that's why they picked on us—because I'm so stupid I'd fall for it. Only I fucked that up, and they took Drew instead."

"He fooled other people," Javi said. "He knows what he's doing."

"I still should have.... I shouldn't have lied. I shouldn't have talked to them," Billy blurted in frustration. "This is all my fault. I wish I hadn't lost my phone that night. I wish they'd taken me instead of Drew."

"That wouldn't have helped anything," Javi said.

Billy gave him a scathing look. "It would have helped Drew."

It was difficult to muster a coherent disagreement. The wrong brother being taken had helped the investigation. Without that mix-up, the police might never have realized there was a suspect other than teenage disaffection, but that wouldn't be much comfort to Drew, wherever he was.

Cloister set his mug down and pushed himself off the counter. "This won't either," he said. "You weren't taken. Drew was. What will help now is us finding who did the taking."

Billy looked unconvinced.

The computer chimed suddenly and made the tech jolt up out of his slouch. Plastic rattled as he hammered at the keys with stiff fingers.

"He's logged in," he said as he wrinkled his nose to push his glasses up. "Let me...."

He stopped abruptly, his fingers frozen in awkward poses as the computer trilled. His glasses slid back down his nose, and he looked up at Javi with wide eyes.

"They're trying to connect."

Javi grabbed his shoulder, hauled him out of the chair, and gestured for Billy to move in front of the computer. Billy hesitated and then slowly slid across and moved as though he expected the chair to give him a shock as he sat down. He reached for the mouse and then hesitated and looked at Javi for permission.

"Get them to meet with you," Javi said quickly as he hooked up the speaker-headset and passed it to Billy. He pulled on a pair himself and left one earpiece tucked behind his ear. "If they sense anything is wrong, blame it on your brother. We talked about this. You know what to say. If you get worried, just pay attention to me. Don't go to video."

While Cloister ducked outside to get Lara, Billy took a deep breath and accepted the call.

"B... Bri, is that you?" he choked out. "Did you see the news?"

Once you knew the voice belonged to a man, it was obvious. You could hear the strain on the vocal cords, the smoky hint of a lower register—although still tenor—trying to get through. If you didn't know, it could pass as a shy teenage girl keeping her voice down to avoid attracting a parent's attention.

"I saw," he said. "I can't believe it. Are you okay?"

"No," Billy said. He didn't need to be prompted. It was an obvious answer. "I'm not. We still haven't found Drew."

"I thought you were angry at me."

"No," Billy said. "Why would I be?"

2"That... that sucks. It's not fair. I really wanna see you."

"Really?"

"Yeah. I miss you."

There was something aching in his voice. It sounded almost painfully true. Despite everything, he did miss the person he thought he'd known. Javi felt a pang of sympathy but squashed it. There was no response from the other end of the link.

"Bri?"

Javi glanced away from the conversation to check in on the tech, who had dragged the keyboard toward him and was clattering away on it. He briefly freed up one hand long enough to give Javi the thumbs-up and then got back to work. The door to the backyard opened slowly, and Cloister quietly ushered Lara back inside. Her hand was clenched in his sleeve, and she twisted the black fabric into knots as she watched.

"Do you think I'm stupid?"

"W… what?" Billy stammered. He gave Javi a panicked look. Holding up his hand, Javi gestured for Billy to keep going. "Of course not. You're the smartest person I know."

The voice cracked down a register. "I'm not stupid. Just because I didn't go to a fancy school, I'm not fucking stupid."

Billy flinched back from the table, and the legs scraped over the floor. The headphone lead pulled taut, and the jack popped out of the splitter. The angry voice spilled out of the computer's speakers, sounding harsh against the domesticity of kitchen cupboards and twee tin containers.

"…spoiled rotten brat. You think you can fool me? Use my own trick on me? I'm smart. I'm smarter than you."

Lara let go of Cloister's arm, threw herself forward, and grabbed the computer with her fingers. Her knucklebones pressed tight against her skin as she clutched it.

"Where is he?!" she yelled, her voice cracking. "Where's my son? What have you done with my son, you bastard?"

Cloister caught her wrists, pulled her back into a restraining hug, and grimaced as she stamped a bare heel down on his boot. The commotion had disturbed the dog, and she barked once and moved back and forward along a short, anxious fulcrum.

"I'm sorry." It was like someone had turned off the anger in the suspect's voice. It had gone mild, almost meek. "You seem like a nice lady, but you don't understand what they did."

"My boys never did anything," Lara yelled. She struggled as Cloister tried to calm her down. "Drew's just a baby."

"Your boys get to be babies," the suspect said. "Spoilt, stupid, greedy babies. I show them."

"Show them what, Hector?" Javi asked, testing the name.

Silence. He glanced at the tech who was still typing away frantically, his glasses barely clinging to the tip of his nose.

"Hector," Javi pressed—confident that it was Birdie's ex, "we just want Drew back. If you give him back, you won't be in trouble. Not if you haven't hurt him."

There was a dry little puff of air as Hector cleared his throat. "I wouldn't hurt anyone," he said. "I just show them."

"What about Birdie?" Javi asked. "What happened to her?"

The throat clearing turned into a dry cough, and Javi heard Hector spit in the background. "I didn't hurt her. I loved her, but when I tried to show her, she couldn't see it. She stayed spoiled. She stayed rotten. That was her choice."

"I don't think she had a choice."

"I should go," Hector said abruptly. "I'm keeping the boy. I'll stop him being spoiled."

He hung up.

A low, breathless groan burst out of Lara as though someone had punched her in the stomach. She went limp in Cloister's arms, and he set her back on her feet and helped her over to a chair. The dog stopped her nervous, pacing patrol—looking for the threat she could sense from the atmosphere but not find—and went over to check on her.

"I'm sorry," Billy blurted. He shot Lara guilty, terrified look. "I tried. I'm sorry."

He bolted out of the room. The sound of his feet hammering on the stairs echoed through the still house, and then a door slammed. Lara looked up, and her nostrils flared as she breathed in.

"It's not his fault," she said. It sounded as though she were trying out the idea for size. She winced at the sound of it and tried again. "It's not his fault."

Cloister squeezed her elbow gently. "You should go and check on him."

She smiled slightly with a rueful fold of her mouth. "I know. Could you get me a bottle of water first, please?"

Javi left Cloister to calm Lara down and turned to the tech instead. The man continued to jab at the keyboard.

"Did you get a location?" he asked.

The tech looked up. "I've got his IP address and general location," he said. "Give me a couple of hours, and I'll be able to chase down the ISP and address."

"Anything to work with on the general location?"

The tech shrugged and scratched his head, and his nails slid through his short-cropped hair. "It was in Plenty." He lifted his fingers off his skull in a half-hearted approach to a shrug. "North of the city. For anything else you'll need to wait until I finish."

It was frustrating, but Javi nodded brusquely. "Fast as you can."

The tech flicked his eyes to Lara, and sympathy puckered his mouth. "Of course."

He got back to work, and Javi turned toward Lara.

"I'm going to leave an officer here," he told her. She held a bottle of water in her hand as though she'd forgotten it was there and absently picked at the plastic label with her nail. "However, I don't want Billy getting in contact with the suspect again. It's too much of a risk. So if you could make sure—"

"Who did he kill?" Lara looked to Javi. Her eyebrows pinched together over her nose. "How many did he kill?"

"He didn't say—"

"I work in the ER. Drug addicts, child abusers, victims. They all think they can lie by misdirection. 'It was my fault,' when what they mean is 'He got angry and hit me. Again.' So don't. Who did he kill?"

Javi traded a quick glance with Cloister. "Lara, it won't make this any easier if you—"

"There's nothing easy about this," she said. "I asked for the truth."

Her eyes were bloodshot and bruised with exhaustion, but they were unflinching. She looked painfully like her father in that moment. Saul had never cared much for lies—not other people's, at least.

"He doesn't mean for anyone to die," Javi said. "But some people still did."

"Who? Birdie?"

"I can't tell you that. There are people we have to inform first. People we haven't informed because we don't want to scare whoever this is into running."

For a moment he thought it was going to be too much for her. She looked brittle, as though this final blow might be the one that would make her shatter. Instead she pulled up the neck of her T-shirt, wiped her eyes on the collar, and got up to follow Billy.

"Ten years," she said as she paused in the doorway and looked back at them. "I don't want to wait ten years to bring Drew home."

Javi didn't want that either. But Hector knew they were looking for him, and if he went to ground, the investigation might be at a stalemate until he struck again. Despite being a compulsive offender, Hector had a lengthy enough refractory period between crimes that it could be another year or longer before they heard from him again.

He squelched the frustration before it could turn into anger. The chance to trap their suspect had been too good to resist, but even if it worked, the case wouldn't have been closed. There was no way Javi could justify letting a probably delusional offender kidnap a child, even if they had Billy wired, so Drew would still have been missing. In fact it could have made finding him more difficult. A drug dealer always brought a healthy dose of their own self-interest to the table. They couldn't depend on that with a kidnapper who thought he was "showing" something to spoiled children.

But they had other leads. They'd find Hector.

The tech agreed to stay at the house until the liaison officer—and Javi would be conveying his official irritation to Frome that they weren't already there—arrived. While he was doing that, Javi could chase those other leads.

Outside the house, the day was just starting for the rest of the street. Commuters lingered by their cars and pretended to be occupied with anything that gave them an excuse to stand and gawk over at the Hartleys'. The few stay-at-home parents in the street had gathered on the driveway and gossiped in pajamas and yoga gear.

"There's a homeless camp up around the Glades in north Plenty," Cloister said as he opened the door of his car to let the dog leap in. "A lot of casual and seasonal laborers live up there."

Javi's phone buzzed against his hip.

"I'll send some uniforms up to search," he said as he pulled it out. "But even if Hector is up there, Drew won't be."

The text was from Sean. "Found B. Sobering her up."

"Go back to the station," Javi told Cloister without looking up from his phone as he tapped out an answer. "See if anyone has gotten in touch with Luna or the dead boy's father. The ex-firefighter."

He waited for some dry snark, or at least for a question about what he was doing. Instead Cloister just grunted his agreement and slid into the car. "I'll do that. If I find anything out, I'll let you know."

The "Special Agent Merlo" loitered on the end of the sentence, unsaid but pointedly there. It was professional. It was even pleasant. Javi was mildly disgusted to realize he'd have preferred the drawled "fuck you" he expected.

"Cloister," he said as he grabbed the edge of the car door before it could slam, "I—"

"What?"

It was a good question. Javi just didn't have the answer. That was what he needed—polite distance and occasional fucking. It was what he had the time and inclination to cope with. Anything else would get messy, and he couldn't afford that. He just wanted to get what he needed without losing what he wanted.

That wasn't fair. It probably wouldn't have stopped him if he could work out a way to pull it off.

"Don't let them go too easy on the fireman," he said instead. "He's grieving, but he hasn't got clean hands in this. You don't need to mollycoddle him."

Cloister nodded. "I'll pass it on." After a second he quirked his mouth in a half smile. "Besides, despite what you think, I'm more of a glowering brooder than a hand holder."

CHAPTER TWENTY-SIX

THE BLACK lettering on the frosted-glass window read Stokes Investigations, Inc. It was the punch line to the joke that had been Plenty PD. What do you call a retired crooked cop? A successful private investigator.

Javi opened the door and stepped into a ripe fog of ethanol sweat and lavender air freshener. The cloud of chemical scent had been so freshly sprayed that it still hung in the air.

"Sorry," the man behind the reception desk said. He dropped the canister of air freshener into a filing cabinet and shoved it shut with his foot. "We don't take walk-in clients. Referrals only."

Javi reached into his pocket for his badge and flipped open the leather wallet to flash the shield and ID.

"My referral," he said.

The man raised a perfectly groomed eyebrow, leaned over the desk, and supported his weight on one hand as he studied the shield. After a second he nodded.

"Of course, Special Agent Merlo," he said with a perfectly empty smile. "If you could just wait here, I'll let Mr. Stokes know you're waiting."

He stepped out from behind the desk and headed down the hall. Javi sat in one of the low black leather chairs. He tapped absently against the arm as he glanced around. Unlike Sean's stripped-clean suburban house, his office looked like it had been designed. Black wood and leather hovered carefully between modernism and the gumshoe aesthetic of the movies. Framed photos on the wall chronicled Sean's qualifications—from the gold-sealed diploma from the police academy to a story cut out of the newspaper, praising Plenty PD for catching a serial rapist.

That tweaked Javi's interest enough that he got up to try to read it through the glass. He remembered the story. It was one of the last good things the papers had reported on Plenty's police department. Javi recalled that even Saul, who took the department apart in his investigation, approved of the detectives involved.

But Sean Stokes wasn't one of the names Javi's scan picked out of the text.

The mutter of voices in the other room suddenly rose.

"...you son of a bitch!"

Javi turned. One of the office doors slammed open—hard enough that the handle dug a dent into the plaster—and the receptionist stalked out. He passed Javi without a word, grabbed his coat from the rack, and shoved his arms into it aggressively.

"You know what?" he said as he turned toward Javi. "I hope you are here to arrest that prick."

He slammed the door behind him as he left. Javi glanced back at the wall. The impact had left the framed news story crooked. He put a finger under the corner and straightened it and then headed to the still-ajar door. A nudge from his toe swung it open.

"Sean?"

"Special Agent Merlo," Sean said. He was perched on the edge of his desk, hands hanging loosely between spread thighs. At least he was dressed, although the unbuttoned cuffs and yanked-loose rag of a tie made him look like he regretted it. "Sorry about that. You just can't get the staff these days."

"Your ex?" Javi asked.

"Ha, no," Sean said. He rubbed his thumb along his clean-shaven jaw where a bruise smeared under the skin like a stain. "My ex would have laid me out. That was... nothing. He'll be back. You're not here about my staff, anyhow. You're here to meet Betsy Murney."

He jerked his chin to the other side of the room, where a woman who looked like Angelina Jolie playing a wino sprawled on the black leather couch. Betsy was beautiful in a way that cheap makeup, old clothes, and the stench of hard living couldn't quite hide. Javi would lay money that she'd had occasion to wish it did. She was also snoring like an asthmatic old man and hugging a bottle of cheap whiskey in her arms as though it were a cuddly toy.

"I thought you were sobering her up," Javi said.

"I was," Sean said as he pushed himself up straight. He gave his tie another tug, and the knot gave up completely. "Unfortunately I had to step out, and it turns out she's pretty damn good at picking locks."

"Wasn't it the daughter who was an addict?"

"Yeah, well, bottle doesn't fall from the tree," Sean said. He levered himself off the desk and shoved his hands in his pockets. "Ask my brother. You want me to put the coffee on?"

"That's a myth," Javi said. He went down on one knee next to the bed and carefully pried the bottle out of Betsy's grip. "It doesn't actually help sober you up."

Besides, if Betsy had been boozing long enough and hard enough, she'd be more lucid with some in her system. He passed the bottle back and waited until Sean took the sloshing weight from his hand.

"Ms. Murney." He took her hand and patted it gently. Her palm was rough against his and cracked and hard from work and weather. "Betsy, I need to talk to you for a minute."

She stirred and moved abruptly from unconscious slumber to confused but awake and shoved herself back into the cushions. She registered Javi with dark, bloodshot eyes and then flicked them over his shoulder to check out Sean.

"Last time anyone wearing a fancy suit wanted to talk to me," she said, voice gently slurred around the edges, "I spent three weeks in a church-sponsored rehab listening to how Jesus loved teetotalers."

"I'm a federal agent," Javi said. "We're looking for your daughter."

Resistance washed visibly over Betsy's face. It set her mouth like a knife. "I don't know what you're talking about."

"She's not in trouble, Betsy," Sean said. It might have been a lie. "We—the police just need to talk to her about something."

Betsy tucked her chin in and looked down. She picked and rubbed with her thumb at a stain on her shirt. "Can't help. I ain't seen her in years."

Javi let the silence hang just long enough to get uncomfortable. "I don't suppose this is the life you planned for yourself, Ms. Murney," he said. Under a lowered shroud of still-thick lashes, she watched him suspiciously. "I assume that this is the result of some very hard choices, so I don't really want to make your life any more difficult. But I will."

She pulled a sour face. "Everyone does."

"A child has gone missing," Javi said. "If you impede this investigation—"

Betsy snapped her chin up. "Alice didn't have anything to do with that," she said. "She's not even in Plenty."

Sean snorted. "I thought you hadn't seen her in years."

Javi twisted around to level a cold look at the ex-cop. He didn't need help from a private investigator with a suspiciously nice location and a suspiciously expensive house. "Mr. Stokes, I can manage."

They traded not entirely friendly looks for a second, and then Sean shrugged and spread his hands. "Sorry. Didn't mean to tread on your toes, Special Agent Merlo."

"It was a good question, though," Javi said as he refocused on Betsy. "When was the last time you saw Alice?"

"Three, four years ago," Betsy said. "She took off with this woman she'd met, some do-gooder with a whole bunch of fancy ideas. Turned out… snotty cow actually did some good. Alice got clean. Alice got a job. Alice don't want anything to do with me. I don't blame her. She sends letters sometimes. No return address."

Javi tilted his head curiously to the side. "No offense, Ms. Murney, but I assumed you were homeless."

"I sleep in my car, up in Groves," she said. "But Tranq helps me out. He stores my old clothes, keeps letters for me. Alice sends her letters there."

"Tranq?"

It had apparently been long enough, and Sean had gotten bored behaving himself. "Tranquil Reed… at the Retreat," he said. "Betsy used to clean for him, didn't you, Betsy?"

She gave a dirty look. "Not many other jobs around here, back then," she said. "Man gave me a place to live, some money under the table…."

"You harvested and cured weed for him," Sean said. "He wasn't helping you out of the goodness of his heart."

Javi held up his hand and pointed back over his shoulder to tell Sean to be quiet. "Did Alice work at the Retreat too?"

Betsy nodded uncertainly. She scraped her hair back from her face with both hands until she could knot it behind her head. It pulled the skin tight across her temples and made the blue veins visible under the skin. Her hands trembled as she worked. "Lot of us did, back then," she said. "The hippies were nice people. Didn't ask too many questions, fed everyone. You were supposed to meditate every morning, but lots of us just napped. After they left, Tranq tidied it up. He said I could stay if I kept myself clean, and I did. For a while. It was Alice that couldn't. We got kicked out, and I didn't see any point in not drinking. Then she left, and I kept drinkin'. Like I said, she got married, and she got clean and straight, and she's never coming back here. Certainly not to snatch some kid."

She shifted on the couch, leather creaking, and itched at the back of her hands in distraction. Her attention kept slipping over Javi's shoulder, back to the bottle Sean was minding. Javi put his hand on her knee.

"Betsy, when you were living up at the Retreat, do you remember a boy called Hector? Hector Andrews? He'd have been around the same age as your daughter."

She pressed her lips together as she thought and thumped one hand at her temples as though she could jostle it out that way. It didn't budge. She shook her head hesitantly.

"There were a lot of people," she said. "My memory ain't what it was."

"He'd have been friends with your daughter. Or spent time with her."

A ghost of maternal pride and shame slid over Betsy's face. "My girl was pretty, Agent Merlo. Lots of boys wanted to spend time with her. Men too. Maybe I should have kept more of them away." Her gaze drifted again, and she licked her lips. "Can I have a drink? My mouth's dry as the wind out there."

"In a minute," Javi said. He shifted to block her view of the bottle and hold on to her attention. The gravity of the investigation was shifting. All he needed was a few more answers from Betsy. "Do you remember nearly six years ago? Alice was still in town then, wasn't she?"

Betsy nodded slowly. A confused frown creased her forehead. "Yeah," she said slowly. "I remember. She had a bad trip, took her forever to put Alice back together out of it. Voices. She said she could hear me thinking. Said I hated her."

"Why?"

"Because she was an addict?" Betsy lifted her shoulders in a tired shrug. "Because she knew I was going down with her? Because I was not a good mother?"

"Not why did you think she hated you," Javi said. "Why did she think it?"

The frown deepened. Betsy chewed her lower lip and picked at the dry skin with her teeth until it bled. "I don't know. It was all broken—sense and nonsense shaken together. She said that we knew what she'd done, that everyone knew what she'd done, but then she wouldn't tell me what it was. Whatever it was, she probably did it for a hit. Us addicts would do anything for a hit of what ails us. Can I have a drink? I'm thirsty."

Javi had more questions. He usually did. But the well had gone dry. Betsy might have the information he needed in her head, but she didn't know it was the answer to his questions.

He rocked back on his heels and onto his feet. Halfway up he stopped to brush the carpet lint and dust from his knee. "Give her a drink, Stokes," he said.

"I've got water in the fridge," Sean said. "Still and sparkling. I think it's lemon flavored."

Betsy barked out a laugh. "What the hell, Sean. You think you can still save me? Doesn't matter how many times someone cleans me up, props me up, dries me out. I'm always going to end up back down here. So I'm not even going to try anymore. The least I can do is stop hurting the people that wanna help." She held her hand out and made grabby gestures with her fingers. "Give me the bottle."

He did.

They left her to drink herself back to sleep on the couch with three quarters of a bottle of very mediocre whiskey, and Sean walked Javi back down the hall. The phone rang with no one to answer it. Sean picked it up and put it back down again.

"Did you get what you needed?" he asked.

"Yes."

Sean shoved his hand through his dark hair. Silver showed through the dark brown at the roots, and he scratched at his scalp absently. "This. Birdie. According to the press, you found a dead body you can't identify hidden on a building site. What's going on in Plenty, Agent?"

"I appreciate your help with Ms. Murney, Stokes," Javi said. "But you aren't a police officer anymore."

"This is still my city."

Javi glanced at the framed story on the wall. "Why do you have a story you're not even mentioned in on your wall?" he asked.

"Because Plenty PD weren't just scumbags," Sean said with a shrug. "Because unpopular cops don't get name checked by their superiors. Because it looks good on the wall, and most people don't bother to read past the headline. Take your pick."

To Javi, Plenty was a pit stop on the way to a better career. He imagined his prospects as a line that trended steadily upward from Plenty to Washington, DC. Sean, despite the "tarred by association" crookedness of his old boss, seemed to actually care about the place.

"We found Birdie," he said. "She'd died ten years ago."

Sean swallowed hard…. "Damn. Poor little bird. So this—"

"This is an open case," Javi said. "And I'd appreciate it if you kept the information about Birdie to yourself until we're ready to inform the press."

Sean stuck his hands into his pockets and rounded his shoulders. He nodded. "For her sake. Her family."

That made Javi glance down the hall to the closed door. He wasn't sure if he felt guilty, grateful, or just sad that Betsy had gotten to the point where she just gave up without even trying. It was something, though, enough that he asked, "Will she be okay?"

"No," Sean said. "Ship sailed on that a long time ago. I'll let her sleep it off in my office, give her money for breakfast, and pretend I don't know it's for drink."

Javi supposed that was Betsy's version of a happy ending, and it wasn't his job to fix it. Or even to care.

"I appreciate your help, Stokes," he said.

"Don't get used to it," Sean said. He straightened his shoulders and smirked. "I still don't like Feds."

"I think I'll live. Stay on the right side of the law in your new career, Stokes."

Sean curled his lip in a half-hearted sneer at the idea. "Didn't do me any good before."

WITHOUT THE Hartley family and their suspect son at the Retreat, the density of the press outside had thinned enough that Javi could get through the gates.

"It's too many coincidences," he said, his voice pitched to carry to the Bluetooth. "Drew disappeared from here, and the girl that impersonated Bri lived up here for a while."

Cloister grunted. "You shouldn't go up there without backup. If Reed is involved, even peripherally, he could react badly. If you wait, I'll be there in fifteen minutes."

"I don't need you to watch my back," Javi said. "Half the deputies working Plenty are up here with the search party."

There was a pause. Cloister didn't say anything, but Javi could hear the echoes of their earlier conversation haunting the line. He grimaced to himself, but Cloister didn't give him time to fumble over a cover-up.

"Frome sent a car to pick up Scanlon, the firefighter," he said. "He should be here soon. I'll let you know if we get anything useful."

He hung up without fanfare, but that wasn't new.

"...fire risk is high." The radio DJ's voice took over as the call cut off. Javi didn't really need the warning. You could tell. The desert wind felt like sandpaper, and the air smelled like a box of matches. All it needed was a spark, and if Drew was still up here, Hector would have another murder to his credit.

If he didn't already.

Javi parked next to the unmarked cars in the small lot. There was no one around as Javi strode to the main office. From the empty parking spaces and open doors, he guessed half the guests had left—either because their reservations ran out or because they were scared of fire or kidnappers—and the remainder, along with staff and volunteers, were out searching for Drew. He could hear the search parties in the distance, their calls of "Drew" stretched out and attenuated by the wind. The hall they'd been using as a base was closed up and padlocked. They must have moved down to the road.

The office building was also closed up when he got to it. Javi tried the door, but it was locked, and the dusty blinds were pulled down over the main windows. Some atavistic compulsion made Javi cup his hand against the glass and try to peer through the slats. It was gritty against the side of his hand, and the dust smeared where he touched it.

Wood creaked under someone's weight. Javi shifted back onto his heels and reached down. His hand wasn't on his gun, but it was close.

"You looking for someone, sir?" a low, raspy voice asked politely. "Everyone is out lookin' for that little boy."

Javi turned and saw the groundsman he'd spoken to before on the porch. Matthew. The man wiped his hands on a dirty bit of cloth and squinted into the wind.

"Reed," he said. "I need to talk to him. Is he out with the search party?"

Matthew scratched at his neck nervously and picked at a scab on his throat. "No," he said. "He's at the bank."

That made more sense. Spending all that time as a hippy could not have been easy for Tranquil Reed.

"What about our officers?"

Matthew squinted and reached up to tug on the bill of his cap to protect his eyes from the dust. The shadow shifted down his nose to cover the scruff of stubble on his upper lip. "They went with the search party. I can let you into reception," he said. "If you want to wait inside, out of the wind?"

Javi nodded his agreement and stepped back to give him room.

"Have you had any luck?" Matthew asked. He bent over the handle as he rattled the key into the lock. "With finding who took the boy?"

"We're confident that he'll be in custody soon," Javi said. "And Drew will be back home with his family."

"You've been trying real hard," Matthew said. He pushed the door open and went through ahead of Javi to kick the doorstop into place. "Try that hard, and you gotta find him."

"We try." Javi ducked in out of the wind. He straightened his tangled tie and brushed the clinging dirt off his sleeves.

"I can call Mr. Reed," Matthew said. "Let him know you're here?"

The phone Matthew pulled out of his pocket was old and battered, the screen spider-web cracked from a chip in the corner. He muttered an apology and shuffled outside to make the call. Javi watched him through the window as he talked on the phone, his body language almost aggressively subservient. He paced along the porch as he talked. He bobbed his head in a series of nods, and he scratched nervously at the back of his head. There was a scar under the hair—a stripe of uneven texture that looked like candlewax.

After a minute he came back. His face, under the tan and the dirt, was flushed with embarrassment and anger. His voice was still low and uncomfortable.

"Mr. Reed said he was coming right back. He said to make you comfortable. Do you want some coffee or tea?"

He wiped his hands on the thighs of his grubby jeans as he asked. Javi pinned a grimace between his teeth and shook his head.

"Just water will do," he said. He nodded to the cooler in the corner of the room.

"I'll get you a glass," Matthew said. He looked up and smirked a little. "Mr. Reed doesn't believe in plastic cups."

He crossed the room, circled the mat with his dirty boots, and disappeared into what Javi assumed was a small kitchen. Glasses clinked, the tap turned on and off, and Matthew came back out with a sparkling glass of ice water and clean hands.

"He won't be long," he said as he sat a glass down in front of Javi. "You'll see."

Matthew set the glass down and slipped out the propped-open door, presumably to go and do some chores.

It was the head-scratching that clicked it into place for Javi. When his father turned fifty, he'd gone away for a week and come back with a tan, a new hairline, and a scar on the back of his head. It was a lot neater than Matthew's, but then, his father had paid a very good plastic surgeon. Better than they had at Plenty General to repair a teenager whose scalp had been peeled off by a bottle.

By the time he put the pieces together, Javi had already drunk half the glass of water in an attempt to wash the dust out of his throat. He cursed, scrambled to his feet, and braced one hand on the back of the chair as he doubled over and shoved his finger down his throat.

Bile and water splattered his shoes, and his nose stung with sour-water puke.

"I don't think that will help," Matthew—or Hector—said.

Javi tried to straighten up and nearly tipped over instead. His head was thick, stuffed with wool, and it seemed to take a very long time for information to make its way along his nerves. Everything felt slow. The ground suddenly bounced up toward him, and it took far too long for him to register the crack of his knees on wood.

"What did you give me?" he asked. Or tried to. The words sounded odd.

"I think you know," Matthew said. When he wasn't pretending to be someone else, his voice was a husky tenor. He walked over—the sound of his boots on the floor was painfully loud in Javi's ears—and crouched down. "A higher dose, though, and some GHB. I didn't want anyone to get hurt."

Fuck.

Javi tried to get to his feet, but Matthew caught him under the arms. His breath, up close, was sour, and now that he'd taken his sunglasses off, Javi could see his pupils were blown.

"You wanted to know where Drew was," Matthew pointed out.

CHAPTER TWENTY-SEVEN

THE PHONE rang twice, and someone picked up. The sound that came down the line was more of a grunt than a greeting, though. Cloister leaned against the door of the bull pen and kept one eye on the main entrance as he tucked the phone against his ear.

"Bo, you still owe me?" he asked the grunt.

"You know I do. Hold on," she said.

Fabric rustled, and a woman's voice said something querulous in the background. After a minute and the click of a door shutting, Bo came back on the line.

"What do you need? Please tell me it's a wingman for another trip down to Mexico?"

Cloister snorted. Last time he went over the border with Bo was an experience he wasn't in a hurry to repeat. A busload of college students had taken the wrong turn and rolled the bus on a back road. The ones who weren't trapped or injured had decided to hike back to the road. Except it wasn't in the direction they thought it was. The two of them—along with the border patrol agent with them—had the job of tracking down the hikers. And those kids managed to go surprisingly far in entirely the wrong direction.

"No. You ever work with a firefighter called Ben Scanlon?"

"Work with him, no. I've seen him around, though. He still drinks with us. Why?"

"He might know something that can help with this missing-kid case."

"The Hartley boy." It wasn't a question.

A flint clicked and sparked, and Cloister heard the deep inhale against his ear. "In your line of work, don't you need your lungs?"

"Not since they put me on desk duty." The exhale was long and slow. It bought time for Bo to think too. "Is he a suspect? Because I won't be able to back up anything I tell you on the stand."

"He's not a suspect. We've got a request in for his personnel file, but before it arrives, I just need to know if he's a stand-up guy or—"

"Like I said, he still drinks with us," Bo said. "Scanlon is old school, hard-nosed, but fair and all that. He still has friends out here. The guys he trained back in the day always buy him a drink. He's made no bones about the fact he doesn't like women firefighters, and I keep my distance, but he's never gotten directly in my face about it."

"Do you know why he quit?"

Instead of answering, Bo took another delaying puff on the cigarette. As Cloister waited, he saw the main door open and a wiry bald man with a lot of beard walk in. He said something to Andy on the desk, who pointed him to the bench. While the man sat down, Andy glanced back at Cloister and nodded.

There he was.

Cloister pushed himself off the door and turned the phone over on his shoulder for a second. He glanced back into the bull pen and caught Tancredi's attention. "We're up."

She hopped to her feet and shuffled all the reports she'd been reading back into their file. Cloister put the phone back to his ear in time to catch Bo's irritation as she realized she'd wasted words on a dead line.

"Sorry," Cloister said. "Speak of the devil. What did you say?"

"He jumped before he was pushed," Bo said. "Never did anything that put anyone's life directly at risk. But he turned a blind eye. He did some favors. You know how it goes."

"Okay. Thanks, Bo."

She grunted and hung up. Cloister turned to Tancredi, who had just pulled the pen out of her hair. She raised an eyebrow at him expectantly.

"Looks like he was in someone's pocket." Cloister pushed himself off the door. "Not enough to be dirty, but—"

"Enough to explain why he made it onto Hector's shit list with the other families," Tancredi said. "Maybe he even got paid out of a Hartley pocket. Okay, I can work with that. Are you sure you don't want to sit in?"

He shook his head. "I'm going to try to get in touch with the other possible victims again."

Tancredi nodded and went out to talk to Scanlon. She shook the man's hand as he stood up, and she gestured toward the interview room. Cloister tried Luna McBride's number first, but it was busy. Again. He left the same message as he had the last time. It probably wasn't going to work. Leo had spent the last five years reliving his kidnapping, but from Luna's sterling record and straight-arrow testimonials, she was dedicated to ignoring it.

He could hardly throw stones.

The absence of Bourneville's heavy, warm body on his feet as he worked his way through the list was odd. The noise of her breathing was the usual background to his day, but they weren't usually in here for that long or that often. She was happier down in the kennels with her favorite toy and her lunch until they could get back to work.

It wasn't the only thing that had him on edge. He just had less justification for feeling on edge over Javi's absence.

Five calls to the possible victims. Two of them went unanswered. One of them was picked up by the guy's mother, who promised to pass on the message but said he'd moved out. Another was to a teenage girl who abashedly admitted she'd run away to Vegas with her best friend and ended up having to call their mom from a truck stop when they got scared.

"We were lucky," her mother admitted when she took the phone back. "I guess you're looking for someone who wasn't."

Cloister let her get back to probably reminding her daughter how lucky they'd been. He picked up her file and stretched over to add it to the pile of cleared cases. Just as he was about to let go of it, the phone rang. He jumped and sent the file skidding off the desk. It hit the floor and sprayed paper everywhere."

"Shit." He grabbed the phone and tucked it into his shoulder. "Deputy Witte."

"Deputy," Andy said. "There's a Doctor Galloway here? She wanted to see Special Agent Merlo, but since he isn't here...."

"I'll be right out." He hung up, gathered up the papers from the floor, stuffed them into a file on the desk, and headed out to the desk. Galloway stood in front of it with a padded computer bag hung crosswise over her chest and a wheeled Captain America suitcase at her feet.

"Doctor?"

She turned around and stuck out her hand for a brisk shake.

"I was looking for Special Agent Merlo," she said. "Apparently he's not around?"

"Not at the moment," Cloister said. "He'll be back shortly. Can I help?"

"Probably," Galloway said. A wry smile crossed her face, and she shrugged. "To be honest I could have just emailed it. I suppose I just wanted to show off a little. He asked me to find a case that matched certain parameters, and I think I have."

"You have?"

She hitched the laptop back around so she could get into it and pull out two clipped-together pieces of paper.

"I couldn't find a 'Hector' with a relevant case history. But this case comes close. A toddler died of hyperthermia in a car after her mother had been picked up for trespassing and spent the day in jail. The mother killed herself a few days later from an overdose, and there was one surviving son." She extended the paper to him. "I'm going to be away tomorrow, but if Special Agent Merlo needs to get in touch, the morgue can forward my calls."

Cloister took the pages from her. The details stripped some of the tragedy from the sad little record, but not all. He scanned down over the names, ages, and causes of death, and he stopped sharply at the location.

"Mallard Park?" he said.

Galloway pulled the handle up on her suitcase and used her elbow to swing the laptop bag around onto her back. "Yes," she said. "It was, I think, back before they stopped work on it."

She tilted her suitcase toward her. "Tell Special Agent Merlo that he owes me."

"I will. Before you go, though, who found them?"

Galloway pursed her lips and shrugged. "I believe there was a call to emergency services," she said. "So paramedics, firefighters. Why?"

"I think there's someone else here who'll remember it." He nodded to Galloway, who raised her eyebrows at him. "Thank you, Doctor. Have a good trip."

She sniffed. "My grandfather died."

"Sorry."

Her pale eyes went stony. "For him? Don't be. He was evil," she said. "It will just be a chore managing his estate, otherwise known as his last chance to hurt his nearest and dearest. Good luck with the case, Deputy. Try not to have more work for me when I come back."

He nodded. "I'll try."

Galloway turned and left, and her luggage bounced over the tiles behind her as she walked.

"MY SON isn't missing." Ben Scanlon leaned forward and stabbed his finger against the table for emphasis as Cloister let himself into the interview room. "My son is dead. So I don't see what the hell this has to do with me."

Instead of answering him, Tancredi turned to Cloister. "Deputy Witte, can I help you?" Her voice was even and pleasant, but there was annoyance in the tightness around her eyes.

"Hettie Spence." Cloister put the report down on the table in front of her. "She died of hyperthermia in Mallard Park fifteen years ago."

Tancredi's eyebrows shot up and she looked down at the page. She traced her finger over the ink as she read and stopped in the same places that had caught Cloister's attention. On his side of the table, Scanlon sat back and crossed his arms.

"What's that got to do with me?" he said.

Tancredi glanced up at him. "I think my question would have been 'What does that have to do with my son?'" She rested her fingers on the paper and turned it around so Scanlon could see it. "You were a serving firefighter at this time, weren't you, Mr. Scanlon? Do you remember this call?"

He glared at her sullenly, heavy lids hooded over brown eyes and the tendons in his neck tight under his loose, weathered skin. He worked his jaw from one side to the other, and the hinge clicked as it shifted back into place.

"It's a big city." He enunciated each word carefully and stripped them of emotion. "I don't remember every call."

"That's not what I asked you." Tancredi tapped her finger against the paper. "Do you remember this call? Do you remember Hettie Spence?"

He shrugged his wiry shoulders and looked away from the paper. There was a nerve just under his eye, and it fluttered in a steady pulse that would have been a gift to a poker player. "I was a firefighter for twenty years. I—"

Tancredi slapped the flat of her hand on the table. The hard jolt of noise made Scanlon jump, but despite the violent action, Tancredi's voice was calm as she asked, "How many times in those twenty years did you pull a cooked baby out of a car, Mr. Scanlon? I mean, I have a child myself. I'd remember that. It's the sort of thing that would stick with me."

He cleared his throat. "Maybe I did? So what? There's some cases I try not to think about. I still don't see what it's got to do with me now." He glared at Tancredi and added, "Or my kid."

Cloister pulled up a spare chair and sat down. He was too angry to pull off "approachable," no matter what Javi thought, but aggressively neutral came naturally.

"Mr. Scanlon, we found Birdie Utkin's body in Mallard Park yesterday," he said. Under the ruddy outdoor tan, Scanlon blanched. "If we're right, and we are, then Mr. Utkin is going to tell us everything we ask him. Believe me, once he sees what is left of his daughter, he'll tell us exactly what you did. By then it might be too late to rescue Drew Hartley. We'll just find him. And your old firefighting buddies aren't going to stand you a round then, are they? So answer the fucking question."

Scanlon blustered in his chair. "You can't talk to me like that. I'm not under arrest. I can leave if I want."

"You can," Tancredi said. "Like Deputy Witte says, though, when my cousin—he's an alderman—when he asks me why we didn't find Drew Hartley in time, do you really want me to name you? Especially when we're going to find out what you did anyhow." She tapped her finger pointedly against the paper and repeated her question. "Do you remember Hettie Spence?"

Suddenly he did.

CHAPTER TWENTY-EIGHT

SCANLON GULPED down a cone of water from the cooler. He crumpled it up in his hand when he was done, and then he unfolded it.

"It was an accident." He watched his hands as though they were doing something interesting while he tore a chunk off the cup. "That's the only reason I did it. The only reason I went along with it. It was an accident."

"A little girl died," Cloister pointed out. "A six-year-old boy was left with permanent damage."

"Nobody wanted that to happen." Scanlon looked up sharply. "Nobody had any reason to think that would happen. "Look, I wasn't involved. I didn't do anything. Okay? I just… moved the car in my report."

"Why?"

Scanlon wiped his nose on the heel of his hand and looked down. He folded his lower lip between his teeth and chewed on it for a second.

"I don't know the full story," he said. "I didn't need to know it to do my bit."

Tancredi leaned forward and tilted her head until he had to meet her eyes. "Tell us what you do know."

"Plenty was different back then," he said. "The place was dying. The farms were derelict, the only job with any prospects was dealing drugs, and people who could afford it were just leaving. A couple more years and the town would have just dried up and blown away, but then people started moving in, and houses started going up. So when it started to slow down, when people wouldn't sell… sometimes it got a bit nasty."

"Is that what happened with the Spence family?"

Scanlon shrugged. "Look, it's not inside knowledge or anything. Everyone in town saw it happen. The bank foreclosed on that whole block practically overnight, and the houses that didn't have mortgages got condemned. Next thing you know, the fences went up, and Town Hall was handing out a construction permit to Utkin to put up Mallard Park. Maybe the foreclosure wasn't entirely aboveboard. Maybe some people who didn't deserve to lose their houses did. But no one was asking questions because Utkin was going to give work to over a hundred people, one way or another." He stopped ripping up the cup and brushed the shreds off the table into his hand. "But yeah, the Spences were one of the families who lost their house. That was about four months before."

Scanlon jabbed his finger against the paper hard enough to make it slide over the table toward Tancredi. He waited a second, as though he expected them to say something. When they didn't he cleared his throat uncomfortably and started again.

"Anyhow, the mother had been kicking up a fuss about the foreclosure. She wrote letters, she'd turn up at Town Hall meetings with her kids in tow—the baby and the little boy—and ask questions, and she'd yell abuse at the crews on the construction site. Eventually they got sick of it. So when they found her on the site one night, they had her arrested. It was the weekend, so you know, they figured it would keep her out of their hair for a while." He stopped and swallowed hard. The self-justification of it being an accident, of it being nobody's fault, really was starting to flag. "They didn't know that she'd been sleeping in the car, you see. Her and the kids. It was parked in the parking lot, and… she had the child lock on, so they couldn't get out and wander off."

"She didn't tell anyone?" Tancredi asked. "Didn't tell the cops to get her kids?"

Scanlon shook his head. "Not at first," he said. "I guess she thought she'd get out in a couple of hours, enough time to get back to them, and she didn't want to risk having the children taken away. I guess by the time she realized that they weren't going to let her out… no one was listening."

Or if they heard her, they didn't believe her. People shoved in the cells overnight came out with a lot of reasons why they *had* to get out. Cloister had closed his ears to enough of them. If it had been his arrest, he couldn't swear he wouldn't have assumed Hettie's children were as imaginary as the drunk's Hollywood job interview. "How long?" Cloister asked.

"Saturday night. All day Sunday," Scanlon said. "The foreman parked next to the car when he came in Monday and saw the boy in the car. He called it in."

"Then you lied."

"Yeah," Scanlon said. "Look, it wasn't Utkin's fault. Who leaves their kids locked in a car in California? In the middle of Santa Ana season. They didn't know. It's not like they'd have left the little girl to die. She just did, so… they just asked me to move the car out into the street. So that when the news hit the press, the development wouldn't be blamed. I mean, it wasn't their fault. Not criminally. It was just a favor. What harm did it do?"

It was Tancredi who lunged to her feet. The chair skidded back and hit the wall. She grabbed the report, crumpled it in her hand, and shook it in his face. He cringed back from her.

"What harm?" she said. Her voice shook on the edge of a shout. "A little girl died. Her mother committed suicide because she got the blame, because she blamed herself, and what happened to that little boy?"

Scanlon looked affronted. "I got him out of that car," he yelled back at her. "I got him to the hospital. If it weren't for me, he'd have died as well."

"If it weren't for you? If—"

Cloister caught Tancredi's arm before she could finish. "Can you give me a minute, Deputy?" he asked.

She irritably jerked her elbow free but nodded.

"If you'd just give me a moment, Mr. Scanlon," she said.

He shrugged and wiped his hand over the back of his neck. There was sweat on his high forehead and drops of it caught in his receding gray hair. "I still don't see what this has to do with my son," he said.

Neither of them enlightened him before they left the room. Cloister, at least, was tempted. He closed the door behind him. Tancredi stalked down the hall with her hands clenched and her shoulders hunched. She got six paces away and turned to stalk back.

"Just kick a chair," Cloister told her.

She snorted. "Is that what you do?"

He grinned at her. "I punch walls and tell Feds to go fuck themselves," he said. "But you have ambitions and unbroken knuckles, so I'd stick to chairs."

She glared at him but still turned and lashed a foot into one of the plastic chairs lined up against the wall. It went into the air and then dropped onto the other chairs. The metal legs tangled and scraped over the floor. Tancredi huffed out a sigh.

"That asshole," she said. "That fucking asshole." She sniffed and turned her back. "Goddammit," she muttered with another sniff. "You tell anyone."

He handed her a tissue. Some people cried, some people puked, and he punched things—the ones to worry about were the guys who didn't feel anything. "Why do I know the name Spence?" he asked.

Tancredi scrubbed her eyes like she was punishing them and wiped her nose. "Fuck," she muttered as she refolded the tissue to find a clean bit to wipe again. "Other than we were just talking about them?"

"I've heard it before," he said. "I can't place it, but it's come up."

She snorted ungracefully into the tissue and frowned. "You've gone through a lot of old case files," she said. "Maybe it was in one of those? If this older boy is our 'Hector,' then maybe he got close to one of the other victims?"

Maybe. Cloister couldn't refute the theory, but the context didn't feel right. "I don't think so. It was something else. Something…."

Tancredi blanched suddenly, and her mouth dropped open slightly. "Shit."

"What?"

She tossed the tissue in the trash and took off at a jog back to her desk. Cloister followed on her heels. "He had an alibi," she said over her shoulder. "It came up in the background check, but he had an alibi, so I didn't think about it."

"What are you talking about?" Cloister asked.

Tancredi scrabbled through the paperwork on her desk and dumped handfuls of it onto her chair as she looked for one particular file.

"This," she said eventually. She shoved the file at Cloister. "He changed his name to Tranquil Reed years ago, legally and everything, but he was born a Spence. He's our killer's father. That's the link to the Retreat."

Dread caught in Cloister's stomach like a stone. It was stupid. So it had been a while since Javi called in about heading to the Retreat. That didn't mean anything. Javi could take care of himself. But the dread didn't care about any of that. It stayed lodged in his gut.

"I'll call Agent Merlo," Cloister said. "You tell Frome."

Tancredi took off at a run and Cloister grabbed his phone. The call rang through to voicemail.

It still didn't mean anything. Except neither Cloister nor the dread in his gut believed that.

TRANQUIL REED hadn't been happy to see the police turn up in force at the Retreat again. He was even less happy when he found out why they were there. The ex-hippy's usual linen-pressed charm was frayed at the edges as he hunched behind his desk and fidgeted. It was the first time Cloister had ever seen Reed sweat, and he took a certain vicious enjoyment in it.

"You're wrong."

"We're not," Tancredi said. She dealt out the photos of the confirmed victims and laid down each photo to create a perfectly straight line. "The nephew of the bank president who foreclosed on your ex-wife's house. The daughter of the property developer who pushed through the Mallard Park development. The son of the councillor who approved the construction permit. The daughter of the construction company's owner. The son of the fireman who found your daughter. He kidnapped all of these people."

"And now an FBI agent is missing," Cloister said. The words caught in his throat as though they wouldn't be true if he didn't spit them out. "Special Agent Merlo arrived here to speak to you earlier today. Now he's gone. Your son did this."

"He's not capable," Tranquil insisted as he pushed himself up out of the chair in a burst of frustration. He grabbed at his hair with tense, bony fingers, as though he needed to shake the words out. "After what happened to him and Hettie, he had PTSD and neurological deficits and all sorts of things. He struggles to do things. That's why he works here, because he can't hold down a job anywhere else."

Cloister slammed the door to the office. The crack of noise made Tranquil jerk and sit back down hard.

"Tell that to the lawyer you're going to need for your son," he said. "They'll care. We don't. Right now your son is in trouble. If anything happens to Drew Hartley or Special Agent Merlo, then it's going to be a lot worse. Where is he?"

Tranquil opened his mouth and then shut it again. He looked, all of a sudden, quite old. "I don't know," he said. Cloister made a frustrated noise of disbelief. "I don't. I'm telling you the truth. My marriage broke up because I came here, when I became this. That caused enough problems, but after what happened to his mother and sister? To my wife and daughter.

He never forgave me for that. We don't talk. He doesn't tell me about his life. I give him work when he's sober and let him sleep here if he wants. Sometimes I don't see him for weeks at a time. I don't know what he does or where he goes."

He stopped and looked at the hand of victims spread out in front of him. His face sagged with grief and the death of his denial. "Why would he do this? These children didn't hurt Hettie or Jill. They're just children."

Cloister looked down at the photos. Loved ones had picked them out, so they showed the missing teens at their best. The glossy colors captured clear skin and innocence. Cloister had grown up in a pretty shit town, and he remembered how he resented the kids who hadn't lost a sibling, whose dads weren't useless assholes, who had moms who didn't look at them with disappointment. The worst he'd ever done was start a fight with a football player out of frustration. But he still understood.

"They're just children," Cloister said. "They got to be just children because they didn't have to watch their sister die in a locked car. I guess he doesn't think that's fair."

Tranquil looked like he'd been slapped.

"Is there anything you can tell us," Tancredi asked as she swept up the photos and tapped them together.

It looked like Tranquil was going to answer. He looked up with his mouth open and his eyes desperate. Then he shrugged and shook his head.

"I don't know him." He dragged one hand down his face. The skin stretched under his fingers like it had lost all its elasticity. "I don't think I've known him for a long time."

Tancredi looked up at Cloister and gave a slight helpless shrug. They weren't going to get anything useful out of Tranquil right then. If he did know something, the revelation of the accusations against his son had driven them out of his head.

"Does he have any friends?" Cloister pressed without much hope of getting an answer that would help. "Anyone he'd talk to?"

Tranquil shook his head. He bent forward, braced his elbows on his knees, and buried his head in his hands. There wasn't time to try to coax him back. Cloister opened the door and went into the reception area. Crime-scene techs had swarmed the area to take samples and bag the splash of puke on the floor.

"Witte," Frome said. Nothing else.

Cloister stalked outside and to his car, and the wind shoved a breath of hot, dusty air up his nose. He pulled the door open and let Bourneville jump out. She flattened her ears and clamped her tail as the wind hit her. It pushed her fur the wrong way, into knotted rosettes.

"Witte." Tancredi had followed him. She held her hand up to shield her eyes. "They're going to send out helicopters from LA—with infrared. We'll find them." There was a pause, and then she added, "Him."

Cloister hooked the leash onto Bourneville's harness and gave one tightly folded ear a quick tug. He didn't know what Tancredi thought was going on between him and Javi—anything from secret marriage to unrequited crush—but it was probably better than the truth.

"Tancredi."

"You look at him like the way I looked at sushi when I was pregnant," she pointed out. "Can't miss it."

Cloister ignored her remark. "Hector—Matthew—knows that he's in the weeds." He kicked the door shut and clicked his fingers at Bourneville. She stuck to his heels as he headed for Javi's car. The fact that there'd been no attempt to move the car wasn't a good sign. The techs had already popped the doors.

"Do you even have anything with Merlo's scent on it to follow?" Tancredi asked.

"I will in a minute." Cloister told Bourneville to sit, and he opened the car. The discarded shirt would be on the passenger seat or tossed into the footwell behind the driver's seat. But Javi had folded it, bagged it, and stashed it in the glove compartment. Even better. The scent would be preserved. "If I don't find them, the helicopters will."

Even Tancredi's freckles looked disapproving, but she let him get on with it. Cloister crouched down and called Bourneville to heel with a snap of his fingers. He bent over and pressed his face in her rough, sweaty coat for a second. She smelled of dust and the Cheeto reek of sweaty dog, and her sides heaved against his face as she panted. For once it didn't make him feel better.

It was his fault. Just like last time. The guilt was an oppressive, smug stain in the back of his brain. It smothered all the justifications he tried to field. It didn't matter to the guilt that Javi didn't want to be anything to Cloister—neither his lover nor his responsibility. It still knew he'd let Javi down and lost him. Just like last time.

"Good girl, Bourneville," he said as he leaned back. The plastic bag was folded instead of sealed, hot and stretchy under Cloister's fingers. He pulled it apart and presented it to Bourneville. She eagerly pushed her nose into the ball of cotton, sneezed, and rooted around at it until she found a rich fold of sweat and skin cells. Her tail came up and wagged enthusiastically against the wind as she caught the scent. "Find Javi. Suuch."

Bourneville barked sharply and lowered her nose to the ground. She leaned into the leash as she followed the scent from one tuft of grass to the other where the scent was caught in the dirt. The track led in a straight line from the car to the reception desk.

Her nails clicked on the wood as she padded through the door and worked her way around the room. Cloister wound up the slack of the lead and balled the strap around his fist like a gauntlet to keep her out of the marked-off evidence areas.

"Witte," Frome said. He put enough snap in his voice that Cloister couldn't ignore it without being obvious.

"Sir?" He braced himself to argue that Bourneville would give them a head start—that any advantage was better than nothing.

"Take Tancredi. I don't want to end up with another officer missing."

One strand of the tension that was tangled through Cloister's shoulders relaxed. He nodded to Frome and turned his attention back to Bourneville. She had her feet up on the couch—there were dusty paw prints all over the pale cushions—as she stuck her nose under the cushions. The puke got an interested sniff, but Cloister pulled her back before her black nose could knock over one of the yellow tags.

"Pfui," he snapped. "Back to work, Bourneville. Suuch."

She grunted at the insult, shook her head to make her ears flap, and got back to work. The scent trail took her back out of the reception area and down the porch steps. She dragged him between a storage shed and the laundry and through the short alley, which was a wind tunnel as the gust whistled through it. A sharp right took them behind the big hall where the ATVs were parked up, and then she course corrected back onto the narrow, foot-worn path.

This time she was sure of where she was going. Her tongue flapped out of the corner of her mouth as she made a beeline down a hill toward a scrubby stand of trees that bent in the wind. As Cloister got closer, he picked out a flatter sheet of green flapping between the branches. It was a loose tarp, tangled up in ropes.

"What is it?" Tancredi asked as she slid to a stop next to him. Her hair was twisted into dusty knots, and she had to stop to bat a wad of leaves—freshly torn from the tree—away from her face. "Or what was it?"

Cloister crouched down and grabbed the edge of the tarp. He flapped it up and peered underneath. There were heavy-duty tire tracks in the dirt and oily, irregular stains. The tarp had the sweet, sickly smell of gas.

"Matthew had an ATV hidden out here," he said.

Tancredi puffed out her cheeks in a frustrated sigh. "By now he could have gone thirty miles? Forty."

"More, maybe," Cloister said. "I don't think he cares too much about safety right now."

He clenched his fist around the tarp and felt his stomach sink with dismay. If the foot trail was interrupted, their chances of tracking—

Bourneville suddenly barked and threw herself against the leash. She paced back and forth at the end of the two meters of braided nylon. There was something there. Cloister loped over to her, and she took advantage of the sudden slack against her collar to dart forward a few inches. Then she stopped, dropped her nose, and huffed at the patch of ground.

"What's that?" Cloister asked as he reached her. "Good girl. What have you found?"

He bent down and saw the irregular puddle of blood dried into the dirt. Fear—that old, whistling shadow in the back of his brain—was his first reaction. His second was almost heady relief.

"Maybe Merlo was able to injure his kidnapper," Tancredi suggested hopefully. But she didn't sound convinced.

"Whoever it is, I hope they keep bleeding," Cloister said. He caught Bourneville's collar and tugged her over to his side so he could unhook it. Eagerness trembled through her muscles as she waited. "She can track this."

"You hope," Tancredi said.

Cloister snorted and let go of Bourneville. She took off toward the trees, her body stretched out like an arrow and her ears pinned to her skull with speed.

"Hope is for lottery tickets, Tancredi." He broke into a run and tossed the words back over his shoulder. "I know my dog."

CHAPTER TWENTY-NINE

THE NOISE scattered Javi's wits. He was conscious and could move again—although his body felt like it was filled with clay—but every creak or breath around him rattled around his head in a distorted, atonal echo. It made it hard to concentrate.

He was folded up uncomfortably in a small space with his thighs cramped and an ache slowly building from the small of his back to his shoulders. It was hot. The air parched his mouth on the way in and didn't seem to fill his lungs. When he shifted position, his shoulder and feet hit hot metal.

Javi closed his eyes and kept his breathing steady. It wasn't a "small space." It was the trunk of a car. That was a fact, and he could deal with it. When he brought his hands up to wipe his face, the plastic cuffs around his wrists scraped against his chin. He worked his way onto his back, but his knees didn't fit, and his eyes stung as he blinked into the dark.

He could hear himself blinking.

Panic tried to crack its way out of his chest. He closed his eyes—not that it made a difference—and dissected the experience. The GHB had caused the dizziness and heaviness in his body and the spray of vomit he could feel cooking sourly under his head. Bath Salts were making him panic with increased heartbeat, a flood of endorphins, and paranoia. The needle scratch on repeat in his head, like a horror-movie soundtrack, was an auditory hallucination caused by the drugs. He wasn't losing control. There was nothing to control. It was just chemistry.

"Matthew," he said. His voice felt raw, as though he'd been screaming, and it sounded like nails on a chalkboard against the inside of his skull. Javi pressed his hands flat against the metal over his head. The pain of the metal branding his hands gave him something to focus on. "Matthew, we want to help you."

Something smacked against the trunk. It left a dent in the metal, and the harmonics of it rumbled through his chest until he felt like he wanted to puke again.

"You're lying. No one wanted to help me or my sister or my mom. You blamed us. We should have done this. We should have done that," Matthew said. He hit the trunk again and again and made it groan like a cracked bell. "All you care about are them. Rich kids. Spoiled kids."

"Like Birdie?" Javi managed to ask. He was bathed in sweat, soaked with it, and it was getting warmer.

"Yes. No. I loved her," Matthew said, his voice doubtful. The car creaked and shifted as a weight lifted off it. "But she was going to leave me. She thought she could just go away and that was it. Like it didn't matter? I couldn't let her do that, so I showed her, and then... I didn't want to hurt her. That was an accident. Death by misadventure. Nobody's fault."

"You didn't mean to hurt her," Javi repeated agreeably. If he kept his eyes closed, it was better. He felt his way around the trunk in an absent effort to map each rivet and solder mark. "I see that now. You haven't hurt anyone else."

"No," Matthew said. There was something odd in his voice. "That was what was wrong. Nobody got hurt, not really. They didn't see what I've seen."

Javi was getting used to the sound in his head. He pressed his fingers against the trunk until his nails dug into the rust. Flakes of it dropped onto his face.

"What did you see, Matthew?" he asked.

No answer.

"Matthew?"

No answer, and the sound of his own voice had a Doppler effect on the hallucination. He squeezed his eyes shut and banged his skull back against the broken plastic under his head.

Javi took a deep breath of sour, hot air and squirmed around onto his other side. He could see a thin bar of dim light where the trunk closed, and he could make out the shape of the taillights.

He felt his way around the lock and traced the open areas of metal with his fingers. Strange thoughts clawed at the back of his head. He tried to ignore the pulse-racing notion that it was Matthew out there, crouched by the side of the car as he listened to Javi try to escape. He finally bumped

into the stacked rounds of the lock mechanism. The metal was bubbled with
rust and disuse, and the lock rod extended to the left. It was clotted with old
grease, and he yanked on it. Nothing happened, and for a second, he could
actually see the scarred, glitter-eyed kidnapper with his face pressed against
the side of the car. Javi's breath was ragged despite his best efforts, and he
could feel panic like a ball of static under his skin. It would have been easy
to accept defeat, but he tried again instead.

This time the trunk lid popped open. Javi clumsily dragged himself
up. His body was still tranq heavy and his muscles cramped, but he
hauled himself over the lip. It wasn't much cooler out of the trunk. He
landed hard on a packed-dirt floor, rolled onto his back, and sucked in
fresh air. Overhead he could see the high, slatted ceiling of a barn and the
harsh red glow of heat lamps.

Grow barn, he realized. They were in the old Retreat grow barn.
Matthew had parked his car in the middle of it, where the rows of plants
would have been bathed in heat. There was no time to dwell on that. He
rolled onto his side and pushed himself up on his knees. Nausea roiled in
his stomach like slurry, as though it had an actual weight. He wiped his
mouth on his sleeve and looked around to take stock. Matthew wouldn't
be gone long.

Javi got his feet under him—they were bare, he noticed, although
thankfully the rest of him wasn't—and levered himself awkwardly to
his feet. The zip cuffs would have been worse if Matthew had cuffed
his hands behind his back, but they still threw his balance off. He dealt
with that next. The cuffs were already tight, but he was able to grab the
end between his teeth and work the lock around until it was between his
thumbs. Little curls of torn skin came with it, and the effort left him dizzy
and breathless. He shook his head, tried to make the lingering dizziness
go away, and brought his hands in hard toward his stomach. A sharp
pinch of pain and the cuffs snapped.

He peeled them off and tossed them aside. The itch of blood seeping
back into his swollen fingers made him curse under his breath. He rubbed
the feeling back into his hands roughly as he looked around the barn.
Other than the car and the grow lamps, there was nothing much to see.
The rusted framework of a disused irrigation system sagged overhead,
and there was a small desk and an old laptop set up in the corner. No sign
of Drew Hartley.

The humming from the heat lamps and the sound of the wind outside drilled into Javi's ears. He just wanted to lie down and wait for it to go away, but there wasn't time for that. He spat to get the taste of old puke out of his mouth and limped toward the front of the barn.

The door was made of old, weathered white wood, dry as a bone, and creaked open with a nudge. Outside he could see a rusted-out pickup sitting on its rims. Weeds grew up through it in fat green bunches. A shiny red ATV that Matthew was struggling to cover with a tattered old canvas tarp. The wind snatched at the corners of it and whipped his legs with the cords, raising welts where it hit bare skin.

Javi's Glock was stuck into the back of Matthew's jeans, black and bulky. The visual reminder that he'd let himself be taken unawares, drugged, and disarmed made Javi cringe, but the fact it wasn't in Matthew's hand was an opportunity. He tracked his eyes past him to the gap in the trees and the heavy, "too new to belong to the farm" gate. A quick glance up to the sun affirmed that, unless he'd been out a lot longer than he thought, it was more or less the right direction to go if he got out.

Javi took a deep breath, shoved the door open, and braced his arm against it as the wind tried to slam it shut again. He staggered into a run. The hard-rutted dirt dug into his bare feet, and he tackled Matthew from behind. It was graceless and undignified, but if Matthew got his hands on the gun, Javi would end up back in the trunk again.

The impact of his body against the Matthew's slammed them both into the side of the ATV. He grabbed the gun, the grip hot against his palm, but before he could pull it, Matthew threw his scarred head back. His skull cracked against Javi's cheekbone. The black flash of pain made Javi lose his grip. The gun hit the dirt, and Matthew lunged after him. He clawed his fingers as he tried to reach it. Before he could, Javi tackled him again.

The scuffle ended with them both on the ground, where they punched and gouged at each other with brutal enthusiasm.

Javi caught a punch to the ribs that shocked the breath out of him, but he managed to get on top of Matthew. The bony, stooped posture that Matthew adopted was deceiving—he was all wiry muscle, and he fought dirty. He grabbed Javi's face and tried to dig his thumbs into his eyes. Javi tilted his head back enough so the dirty thumbnails gouged at his cheekbones. Then he got his fingers around Matthew's throat and squeezed.

The sharp jut of the Adam's apple under his palms gave, and the tendons strained under his grip. Desperate, whooped breaths hitched Matthew's body as he gave up on Javi's eyes and clawed at his hands instead. Broken nails tore the skin in welted, bloody lines.

Javi squeezed harder and smacked Matthew's head on the ground. Matthew went limp under him, and Javi slowly loosened his grip and sat back.

"Stay down," he rasped.

Instead Matthew whipped him across the face with the knotted end of a rope pulled out of the tarp. It caught the corner of Javi's eye, and he lurched away with one hand clapped to his face as blood filled his vision.

He rolled over, and dirt scraped his bare shoulder as he tried to scramble back to his feet. Matthew got up quicker. Seen through Javi's one good eye, he was a blurry figure as he staggered over and kicked Javi in the stomach. There was nothing left in his stomach to come up, but he retched painfully anyhow.

"I knew you didn't care," he yelled. His boot caught Javi on the hip with a sharp jolt of bone pain, and his voice screeched eerily around the inside of Javi's head. "I knew it. All you care about is them. They killed my family, and all you care about is them. The rich. The greedy. The—"

There were a lot of things that went through your head when there was a strong possibility you might die. It had happened to Javi before, once or twice, and the general outline was always the same. Family, regrets, the wish that you'd told that one person that you really hated them. This time the thought that he should have kissed Cloister again slid through quickly.

Javi thought that was why he heard Cloister's voice—it was an auditory hallucination caused by regret. He realized he was wrong when Matthew staggered backward, and his face sagged with desperation. He brought his hands up, and there was blood on his forearms. Then he decided to make a run for the barn.

He didn't have a hope. Bourneville shot across the clearing like she'd been shot out of a catapult, all black fur and bared teeth. She hit Matthew square in the back and bowled him over. He hit the ground, rolled, and managed to come up on all fours. Bourneville knocked him back down, stood on his chest, and snapped and snarled into his face. Drool dripped on Matthew's face as he writhed like a broken-backed snake.

"Stay still, and I'll call her off," Cloister snapped, his voice pitched to carry. He loped into view, coated in dust and breathing hard. "Stay. Still."

Matthew tried to punch her instead. It was a flailing, ineffective swipe. Bourneville ducked, twisted like a cat, and sank her teeth into his arm. She snarled around the mouthful of flesh and shook her head from one side to the other.

"Stay still," Cloister repeated, "or she'll chew your fucking hand off."

That time Matthew did as he was told. He went as limp as he could between the obvious shock and pain. His body trembled as he sobbed, but Bourneville was still attached to his arm, and a low, muffled growl escaped her clenched teeth.

Instead of calling Bourneville off, Cloister dropped to his knees next to Javi. He cupped Javi's shoulders gingerly and then checked his body from chest to ribs.

"Jesus," he muttered. "Javi, you okay? You with us?"

Javi propped himself up on his elbow. He gripped Cloister's bicep in his free hand and thought about kissing him, but before he could get carried away, he saw Tancredi stagger up to join them.

"Help me up," he said instead.

Cloister helped haul him to his feet. He grasped the back of Javi's neck, his broad palm rough and his fingers gentle. "You look like shit," he said.

"I think I have puke in my hair," Javi said.

Cloister showed him his hand. "It's blood."

"Oh. Good," Javi said. He grabbed the edge of the ATV and sat down on the cracked vinyl seat. Nothing really hurt yet. The pain was somewhere under the pulse of energy behind his eyes. It would hurt later. He doubled over, rested his elbows on his knees, and decided to let Cloister get away with rubbing his shoulder. "I haven't seen Drew."

"We'll find him," Cloister said.

Tancredi came over with a bottle of water, and Javi took it with a grunt of thanks and poured it down his throat. It didn't do anything to quench his thirst. The liquid just seemed to soak into his body and disappear. So did Cloister. When he looked back up, Cloister was pulling Bourneville off the sobbing Matthew.

"Good girl," he praised the dog effusively as he pulled Matthew up onto his feet and cuffed him. Blood dripped down Matthew's arm. "You did a good job, girl."

Bourneville sat at Cloister's feet and listened attentively to the praise. She tilted her head from one side to the other every time she heard the word "good," and her ears flapped in the wind.

"We'll find Drew," Tancredi told him. She leaned against the ATV next to him and ducked her chin down to the radio to call in their location. "He's going to be home with his family soon."

Or he wouldn't be, Javi thought bleakly. Him screwing up and walking in on Matthew without having a plan could cause a ten-year-old's death.

CHAPTER THIRTY

BOURNEVILLE GAVE two piercing barks and raked at the door to the shed. It was old, and the dry-rotted wood crumbled under Bourneville's nails, but the padlock screwed into it was brand new.

"We've found something," Cloister yelled. He loped through the scrub of half-grown saplings and hopped over a foot-wide groove in the ground that, in wetter years, probably held water. Bourneville barked at him again. She backed away from the door and circled the structure with her tail wagging eagerly as she sniffed, barked, and raked each wall.

By the time Cloister reached the shed, she was back at the door. She pressed her nose against the crack and whined fretfully as she waited for him to open it. He grabbed the padlock and wrenched as hard as he could. Half the screws tore out of the wood and dropped splinters and sawdust on Bourneville. She shook her head and sneezed but didn't move. Another wrench, and the lock came away in his hand.

He dropped it, and Bourneville pushed the door open with her nose before he had a chance. She wriggled through the gap and barked again. Her tail thumped against the walls. Cloister pushed the door open the rest of the way and ducked inside.

Drew Hartley lay on the floor. He was flushed, his hair sweat spiky and his eyes sunken, and he wasn't moving. Not even with Bourneville barking in his ear. There was a big bottle of water next to him, but it was empty.

"*Ruhig*," Cloister told Bourneville. "Shut up, girl."

She obediently stopped barking, and he absently praised her as he crouched down. People ran around outside, yelling orders and commands through the trees. It felt very distant as Cloister leaned over and tucked his fingers under Drew's chin to take his pulse.

It was slow, but it was there.

Relief made Cloister sag. He slid his hand back to cup Drew's skull for a second. "You're going home, Drew," he said.

"IT WAS the Santa Anas that set him off," Cloister said. He sat on the bench of the ambulance as it bumped and shuddered its way along the backroads. "They were bad that year when his family died."

Javi lay on the thin white sheet, his jaw clenched and an IV plugged into the crook of his arm. There was gauze over his eye, and bruises had started to bloom on his ribs and jaw.

"I knew it," Javi said. "The car?"

"Same one," Cloister said. He paused and corrected himself. "Same make and model, anyhow."

"And the boy?" Javi opened his good eye enough to squint at Cloister. "How's he?"

"Alive."

Javi closed his eye again. "There's a lot of leeway there."

The ambulance hit a bump, and Cloister reached over to steady Javi on the bed. He pressed down on Javi's shoulder as the driver yelled an apology back to them.

"Sorry," Cloister said after a second. He took his hand back. "Drew was drugged and dehydrated, but he didn't seem hurt otherwise. The paramedics seemed optimistic, but until he wakes up…."

He shrugged his helplessness.

"And you?" Javi asked. "You found the missing boy. You're going to be the hero of the moment."

There was a faint, resentful edge to Javi's voice that made Cloister feel awkward. He didn't have any ambition. He was a man of simple tastes—he liked dogs, finding people, and the occasional beer. But people who did have ambition never believed that.

It wasn't as though it even made him feel any better, finding Drew. It never did. He was glad Drew was unhurt and was going to get to see his family, but it didn't lift any weight off Cloister. Tonight he wouldn't sleep any better.

There was probably a way to explain that, but it seemed hard. Cloister reached down and petted Bourneville instead, and she curled up around his feet. "She did the heavy lifting. Maybe she'll get the key to the city."

Javi snorted. He lifted the hand that wasn't tethered to the IV and ground his knuckles into his forehead hard enough to leave dents in his skin. It took him a minute to breathe through whatever drug-cocktail peak he'd just reached. Once he did he let his arm go slack over his forehead.

"At least Mr. Utkin will know he was right about his daughter's boyfriend."

The bumps and sharp corners of the back roads turned into the stop-and-start progress of the center of town. Cloister stood up as much as he could with the low roof and checked out the back window.

"Nearly at the hospital," he said.

Another grunt.

Cloister turned back and studied the long sprawl of Javi's battered body, the scrapes and bruises. He hardly knew him, and Javi had made it clear he didn't *want* Cloister to get to know him, but he would have liked to.

The ambulance pulled into the hospital and stopped outside the ER. The driver and his partner opened the back and helped Javi out into a wheelchair. It made him sneer, but he slouched down into it anyhow.

Cloister stopped them before they pushed Javi through the grubby, sliding glass doors.

"Special Agent Merlo," he said as he put a hand on Javi's shoulder. The muscles tensed under his fingers, taut as cords under the bruised skin. "You're not as much of an asshole as I thought."

Javi gave him a dry, unamused look. "But I am still an asshole, Witte?"

"Well, yeah. Have you met you?" Cloister stepped back and lifted his hand in a lazy farewell. "Take care of yourself, Merlo. See you around."

He waited until they pushed Javi into the hospital, and then he went to cadge a lift back to the station with one of the other deputies.

TWO DAYS later there was a bottle of wine in a classy black gift bag on Cloister's desk when he came in to drop off his paperwork. Lara Hartley sat on the other side of it. Her eyes were still bloodshot, and her nails were bitten down to ragged nubs, but her smile when she saw him was free of shadows.

"Deputy Witte." She stood up and held her hand out to him. Her handshake was firm. "I just wanted to let you know how grateful I was for everything you did."

"I'm glad we could help bring Drew home," he said with a crooked smile. "But it was mostly Bourneville, and she can't hold her wine, Doctor Hartley."

She sniffed at him. "I've already donated to the K-9 retirement program in her name, Deputy," she said. "But Billy told me what you did for him, and I wanted you to know I appreciated it too. I think I could have forgiven him, that I would have trusted that he hadn't hurt Drew... eventually. I don't think he could have forgiven himself if he hadn't talked to us. You helped both my sons, Deputy."

Cloister shook his head and gestured for Lara to sit down opposite him. When she did he took a seat as well.

"That's my job," he said. "Expecting thanks on top of my wages is why Plenty doesn't have a separate police department anymore. I appreciate the thought, but that's all I need."

Lara folded her lower lip between her teeth and studied him for a second. "Billy told me what you said about your brother." She paused for a second and then pushed the bag toward him. "It's a onetime gift, Deputy. No strings."

The bottle sat between them on the table.

"I don't even like wine," Cloister protested, although he left the bag where it was. He could donate it for the Halloween raffle, he supposed.

Lara stood up and absently smoothed her skirt down over her thighs. "Javi does." She reached out and touched her fingertip to the top of the bottle. "It's his favorite vintage."

That caught Cloister off guard. He spluttered for a second while Lara watched with amusement.

"We were friends," she said. Her mouth twisted around the unsaid fact that they weren't anymore. Maybe she could have forgiven her son, but Javi didn't get the same familial pass. "Take the bottle, Deputy Witte, and I hope that one day you find your—"

"Thank you, Doctor Hartley," he said. "You should get home, enjoy your family."

Something complicated crossed her face, but she nodded. "I should," she said. "Don't take this the wrong way, Deputy, but I hope I don't see you again."

"Same, Doctor," Cloister said.

They shook again, and Lara squeezed his hand tightly enough to remind him of her recent desperation. And then she left. Cloister sank back down and stared uncertainly at the gift in its fancy bag until Tancredi stopped on her way through and asked, "Penny for them?"

"I'd need to give you change," he shot back.

Cloister still didn't know what to do about the wine, but he had a shift to get through before he could do anything. He picked it up and shoved it into a drawer. Maybe once he'd finished for the day, he'd have a clearer mind... or be too tired to worry about it.

Besides, just because they'd found Drew didn't mean there weren't other missing kids out there waiting to come home.

EPILOGUE

JAVI LAY on the couch in his apartment with his arm slung over the back and watched the news. Drew Hartley's disappearance and rescue were already old stories. A college football player accused of misconduct ahead of a big match had taken its place.

"This is a transparent attempt by the opposing team to blacken his name," the red-faced coach, Barney Jenks, insisted. "Patterson will still be playing, and I have every confidence his name will be clear—"

Javi turned it off.

The hospital had signed him off for the rest of the week, against his wishes. He had to wait for his eye—currently puffy and bruised, with the white full of blood—to mend, and a meeting with the LA office's psychiatrist to go back to active duty.

It was too much time, and when he had too much time on his hands, he made bad decisions—like almost calling Cloister too many times in the last two days, with the number on the phone and Javi's thumb hovering over Call. It was a terrible idea, and he didn't want to hurt Cloister. He would, but he didn't want to.

The rap of knuckles on the door jarred him out of his introspection. He wasn't expecting anyone. His bruises hurt as he got up, a cracked rib ached with each breath, but he had whiskey and painkillers for that later.

"Hold on."

He padded over to the door in his bare feet and checked the security camera. Cloister leaned against the door with a brown paper bag in the crook of his arm. He was all in black, from his boots to the old leather jacket that made his shoulders look even broader. Apparently you could look at some bad ideas and just know they would be worth it.

Javi opened the door. "What are you doing here?" he asked.

Cloister held up the bag. "I owed you dinner," he said. "And this is the best fried chicken in town."

"I don't date," Javi said.

"If it were a date, I'd have brought wine," Cloister said. "You get fried chicken… if you want it."

Javi did. He wanted Cloister too, and it wasn't as though Javi had promised him anything to get him there. So his conscience was clear.

He grabbed the collar of Cloister's jacket—the leather butter soft under his fingers—and pulled him in for a kiss. The dog came in too, but Javi supposed he had to get used to that. Besides, Bourneville had saved his life.

"Chicken will get cold," Cloister said as he squirmed out of his jacket.

"Shut up," Javi told him. "And take your clothes off."

Later that night Javi had to admit that, even cold, it was good fried chicken.

TA MOORE genuinely believed that she was a Cabbage Patch Kid when she was a small child. This was the start of a lifelong attachment to the weird and fantastic. These days she lives in a market town on the Northern Irish coast and her friends have a rule that she can only send them three weird and disturbing links a month (although she still holds that a DIY penis bifurcation guide is interesting, not disturbing). She believes that adding 'in space!' to anything makes it at least 40% cooler, will try to pet pretty much any animal she meets (this includes snakes, excludes bugs), and once lied to her friend that she had climbed all the way up to Tintagel Castle in Cornwall, when actually she'd only gotten to the beach, realized it was really high, and chickened out.

She aspires to being a cynical misanthrope, but is unfortunately held back by a sunny disposition and an inability to be mean to strangers. If TA Moore is mean to you, that means you're friends now.

Website: www.nevertobetold.co.uk

Facebook: www.facebook.com/TA.Moores

Twitter: @tammy_moore

TA MOORE

DOG DAYS

The world ends not with a bang, but with a downpour. Tornadoes spin through the heart of London, New York cooks in a heat wave that melts tarmac, and Russia freezes under an ever-thickening layer of permafrost. People rally at first—organizing aid drops and evacuating populations—but the weather is only getting worse.

In Durham, mild-mannered academic Danny Fennick has battened down to sit out the storm. He grew up in the Scottish Highlands, so he's seen harsh winters before. Besides, he has an advantage. He's a werewolf. Or, to be precise, a weredog. Less impressive, but still useful.

Except the other werewolves don't believe this is any ordinary winter, and they're coming down over the Wall to mark their new territory. Including Danny's ex, Jack—the Crown Prince Pup of the Numitor's pack—and the prince's brother, who wants to kill him.

A wolf winter isn't white. It's red as blood.

LIAR, LIAR

TA MOORE

Just another day at the office.

For some people that means spreadsheets, and for others it's stitching endless hems. For Jacob Archer a day at the office is stealing proprietary information from a bioengineering firm for a paranoid software billionaire. He's a liar and a thief, parlaying a glib tongue and a facile conscience into a lucrative career. He just has one rule—never get involved with a mark.

Well, had one rule. To be fair, though, Simon Ramsey is dark, dangerous, and has shoulders like a Greek statue. Besides, it's not as though Jacob's even really stealing from Simon... just his boss and his brother-in-law. Simon didn't buy that excuse either after he caught Jacob breaking into the company's computer network.

That would have been that—one messy breakup, one ticket to Bali booked—but it turns out that the stolen information is worth more than Jacob thought. With his life—and his ribs—threatened, Jacob needs Simon to help him out. Or maybe he just needs Simon.

www.dreamspinnerpress.com

Also from Dreamspinner Press

DREAMSPUN DESIRES

ALL IN
Ava Drake

Wild Cards, Inc.

In crime, like in love, there can be no half measures....

Lightning Source UK Ltd.
Milton Keynes UK
UKOW05f1041020817
306443UK00008B/257/P